Readers love
EM LYNLEY

Bound for Trouble

"There is nothing, more enlightening and enjoyable, than to read a story where all of your attention is consumed by the words on a page. EM Lynley has done that with this story…"

—MM Good Book Reviews

"With this intriguing cast of characters, Lynley has developed a great plot that keeps readers on the edge of their seats."

—Smoocher's Voice

"*Bound For Trouble* is the complete package, with ingredients for everyone: mystery/thriller/romance/BDSM/action lovers alike will all enjoy this book."

—The Novel Approach

Out of the Gate

"Once again, EM Lynley's written a winner… I love this author's way with creating a fully formed setting that's nearly a character in itself, and making it absolutely real."

—Cryselle's Bookshelf

Spaghetti Western

"…for me this book is the best in the series so far, I found it very interesting, funny in places, I even needed a couple of tissues for my tears."

—Rainbow Gold Reviews

"It was a great, funny romance with some hot sex thrown in for good measure—enough to keep this reader up too late for her own good!"

—It's About The Book

By EM LYNLEY

Bound for Trouble
Dirty Dining
Disguises
Hostile Takeover
Out of the Gate

THE DELECTABLE SERIES
Brand New Flavor
Gingerbread Palace
An Intoxicating Crush
With Shira Anthony: Lighting the Way Home
Spaghetti Western

PRECIOUS GEMS SERIES
Rarer Than Rubies
Italian Ice
Jaded

Published by DREAMSPINNER PRESS
http://www.dreamspinnerpress.com

D!RTY **Dining**
EM LYNLEY

Dreamspinner Press

Published by
DREAMSPINNER PRESS

5032 Capital Circle SW, Suite 2, PMB# 279, Tallahassee, FL 32305-7886 USA
http://www.dreamspinnerpress.com/

This is a work of fiction. Names, characters, places, and incidents either are the product of author imagination or are used fictitiously, and any resemblance to actual persons, living or dead, business establishments, events, or locales is entirely coincidental.

Dirty Dining
© 2015 EM Lynley.

Cover Art
© 2015 Ronaldo Gutierrez, Photographer
Cover Design
© 22015 Paul Richmond
www.paulrichmondstudio.com
Cover content is for illustrative purposes only and any person depicted on the cover is a model.

ISBN: 978-1-63216-625-8
Digital ISBN: 978-1-63216-626-5
Library of Congress Control Number: 2014951648
First Edition January 2015

Printed in the United States of America
∞
This paper meets the requirements of
ANSI/NISO Z39.48-1992 (Permanence of Paper).

To the memory of Bill Gay. You never knew how much you brightened many of my days, and I thank you for sharing your light. I know you'd love this story.

With thanks to the researchers working in the field of HIV/AIDS. Someday we will have a vaccine and a cure. We're closer every day.

Acknowledgments

As always, there are plenty of people who contribute to a book, some of whom may not even realize it. This time around special mentions go to Jennifer Walter, a reader and biology PhD who helped me understand the concepts and fixed things when I didn't; to my editor Andi Byassee, whose expertise with university technology research helped make this story more accurate; and to first reader KT Hicks, who isn't afraid to cut out the boring stuff. Additional thanks to betas T.H., E.R., and P.T.

Chapter ONE

"YOU EVER do any modeling?" The guy came up to Jeremy Linden in the gym locker room while Jeremy was drying off after his shower. Jeremy had noticed him checking out a few other men in the weight room and even at the pool while Jeremy was taking a breather from laps.

"I'm not interested in whatever it is you're offering." Jeremy had heard these kinds of offers before. Friends had taken the bait, and it never ended well. No way he'd fall for the scam. It was never just "modeling."

"You could make some easy dough."

"I don't need easy dough." Jeremy opened his locker, but he didn't want to take the towel off in front of this guy.

"Sure you do. I've seen your car. Someone smashed into the side of it and you haven't fixed it yet."

"Too busy," Jeremy lied. Truth was he used the insurance money for bills, but he'd never admit as much to this guy.

"Don't you want to know what the job is?"

"No." Jeremy didn't have time to waste. He grabbed his boxers from the locker, turned away from the guy, and bent down to step into them.

"That's all you'd have to do. Just take off your clothes and let people look at you."

"I don't strip. No thanks. Emphasis on the '*no*.'"

"Three hundred bucks for about two hours' work, just to take off your clothes. Not stripping. You just remove one piece at a time. Five hundred if you let someone else take your clothes off for you. No other touching or funny business, unless you want. And that would pay extra."

"Get out of here before I call the front desk."

The guy held up his hands and backed out of Jeremy's personal space. "Sure thing. Sorry." He slid a hand into his jacket, and Jeremy braced for him to pull out some kind of weapon. All he had was a business card. "I'll leave this, and if you change your mind, call me. The job's on Friday night." He put the card on the bench and left.

Jeremy finished dressing quickly before the guy came back or followed someone else in from the gym. He was slinging his backpack over his shoulder when he glanced down at the card. More out of curiosity than anything else, he picked it up.

THOMAS JERROLD
THE DINNER CLUB
415-555-1087

He flipped it over, but the back was blank. Just a simple white card with raised black printing. For some reason the simplicity intrigued Jeremy more than anything the guy had said to him, so instead of tossing it, he jammed it into his pocket and headed out. He tossed the pack into the passenger side of his car, then walked around to look at the damage: the whole right side of the car was scraped and dented from someone opening their door as he drove by. He sure would like to get the damage repaired. He could already see a tiny telltale spot of oxidation, and even though the brutal Northern California rainy season was at least a month or so away, the exposed metal under the scraped paint would certainly begin to rust before he could afford to fix it.

Maybe he could get more hours at the tutoring center. He'd ask about it tonight when he went to work.

BUT THE center didn't have any more students for him. They had plenty of kids who needed math or writing tutors, but he only did biology and chemistry. He met with his one scheduled pupil, then went home to the apartment he shared with Doug, another grad student at Cal.

Jeremy was starting the fifth year of a PhD in molecular biology, with a specialization in immunology. While other students in his department had a free ride thanks to government and NIH grants, Jeremy's cutting edge research had won him a coveted fellowship from PharmaTek, a Silicon Valley biotech start-up working on an HIV vaccine. Jeremy's work on VLP—virus-like particles—was potentially revolutionary and would help to bring their product to the testing phase and then to market more quickly than other approaches.

He was proud to be part of such an important project. While the funding covered his fees and a generous research budget, his personal stipend barely covered the basics in the expensive Bay Area. There wasn't a spare dollar for the unexpected, like a car accident.

Well, he could just ignore the car. As he stared at it before going inside his apartment building, he thought he could see the rust spot growing before his eyes. Maybe he should just sell the damn thing and use his bike to get around. He'd long passed the point where he could ask his family for money. At twenty-seven he was supposed to be self-sufficient. He could try to get a loan from the university, or... he dug his hand into the front pocket of his jeans and pulled out the little white business card.

Three hundred bucks just to take his clothes off? A couple of hours of being naked didn't really seem so bad. He was in good shape. He cycled and swam. He'd even done a triathlon before his research ate into his training time. Nothing wrong in just checking out this Dinner Club. He was staring at the card when Doug, his roommate, came through the front door with a pizza.

"Leftovers, want some?"

Doug worked at one of the best pizza places in town, and even their leftovers were better than fresh pizza from almost anywhere else.

"Sure." For the next thirty minutes, Jeremy forgot about Thomas from the Dinner Club and concentrated on double-crust pizza with chicken, tangy tomato sauce, and marinated artichoke hearts. And they shared a few beers. By then Jeremy had already started working on his reading for class the following day and didn't have time to google the Dinner Club. He'd research it tomorrow.

Chapter TWO

"EVERYONE, THIS is Jeremy." Thomas introduced him to the other guys who would be working as serving boys at the Dinner Club that night, including one Jeremy recognized from the gym.

"Hi, Jeremy," they said in chorus.

One slim blond guy with long bangs came up and gave him a not-very-subtle once-over and, before Jeremy could stop him, pulled his shirt out of his jeans far enough to get a good look at Jeremy's abs. "Very nice."

"Just chill, Kit." Another guy shook his head and tugged Kit away. "You'll scare him off before dinner even starts."

Jeremy wasn't thrilled with the grabby hands and hoped his client—whoever it might be—wouldn't take liberties the way his fellow serving boys did.

"Let me give you tonight's assignments." Thomas spoke up to get their attention over the ensuing chatter. Jeremy was glad since he noticed some of it was speculation about him.

"Please let me have Mr. Gray." Kit sashayed up to Thomas and tried to pull the clipboard out of his hand. The same law-abiding guy pulled him back.

"Sorry, Kit. You've got Mr. Yellow."

"Oh, not so bad. I didn't know he was coming tonight." Kit grinned. "Or at least he will be," he added in a singsong that had the others laughing.

"We've one new client, Mr. Green."

"Let me have him!" It was another guy.

"Sorry, Rand, I think you're a bit too much for him. I can't have any of you scaring him off either. I think Jeremy will serve Mr. Green." Thomas nodded at Jeremy. "He seems a little shy, so maybe you two will be a good match."

"Okay." Jeremy wasn't sure if he'd been insulted or given an easy task. So far no one here seemed shy. But he needed to learn the ropes and figure out precisely what was expected of him as a serving boy.

Thomas gave out the rest of the assignments. Each client had a color-coded name, reminding Jeremy of the Tarantino film *Reservoir Dogs*. He hoped like hell tonight wouldn't end up the same way, with everyone dead or wishing they were.

Once Thomas left, one of the guys came up to Jeremy. "I'm Rand. Been here the longest, so I'll walk you through your duties. And if you're not sure what to do, just ask me."

"Okay."

"First here's your costume." Rand handed Jeremy a box. "Open it up."

Jeremy opened up the flaps and pulled out the flimsy pieces. Some thin filmy fabric, gold cord and not much else. "This is a costume?"

"Yeah. Every dinner has a theme. We're Greek slave boys tonight. Tonight's dinner has six courses, and there are six items in each costume. You take one off after you serve each course."

Jeremy swallowed. Well, Thomas had told him he'd be taking his clothes off. He hadn't realized quite how this would work, but it seemed easy enough. "That's it?"

"You let your gentleman choose which piece you remove."

"Then I take it off, right?"

"Yeah. Or if you let the gentleman do it, you get paid more."

"Just taking clothes off? No one's going to put their hands on me or request a lap dance or expect me to suck them off?"

Kit giggled in the background. "Only if you want to, pecan pie. And you may want to."

Rand shook his head. "You only do what you want. If your guy asks for something, you can say no. You aren't allowed to offer anything, or we can get in trouble for soliciting sex. There's a menu—coded of course— and the gentlemen can 'order' something extra. You just let yours know which menu items are available."

"What if I don't want to do any 'menu items'?"

"No worries. That's why Thomas put you with a new guy. The new guys don't often feel comfortable enough for anything besides the basic dinner service: just serving, sitting with them, cutting their steak, whatever. Some want you to sit on their lap. It's up to you. Thomas can usually tell what guys are going to want. They all have interviews to join, and he can figure out a lot based on what kind of questions they ask. Mr. Green is a guest of a member, but he's been advised of the rules."

"Okay." Jeremy wondered what Kit and Rand did on a normal night. He didn't think he'd want to do anything to his "gentleman." He could get through this one night and then see if he could stomach another dinner.

"Don't forget to tell him about nightcaps."

"Right," Rand continued. "That's spending the night with the guy. There's a basic fee for the hotel room upstairs. You get half. And then whatever you decide to do in the room is entirely up to you. Even if you just hold hands. You negotiate activities directly with the gentleman."

"It's optional?"

"Yes. My God, you are a nervous Nelly, aren't you? What do you think is going to happen? The guy's going to tie you down and rape you in the dining room, then carry you upstairs for round two?"

"Ooh, I hope so!" Kit trilled.

"Knock it off," another of them said and shrugged. "Don't worry. It's really easy, and it can be fun if you're in the right mood. I'm Barry." The guy held his hand out to Jeremy and they shook.

"Thanks, Barry."

"Better get dressed." Rand tapped the box and then headed over to a chair at a mirror across the room.

Jeremy put the box down on the spot in front of his assigned mirror and pulled out the costume. It wasn't much. He'd probably catch cold in it. But he could use three hundred bucks. It wouldn't cover the car repairs, but if he did this four or five times, he'd have enough.

He took his street clothes off, acutely aware of the stares of the other guys in the room, and reminded himself the job was letting other guys look at him. He slipped on the sleeveless tunic, a sheer piece of fabric that left his arms completely free. Then he put on the bottom garment, which was nothing more than two thin pieces of white fabric attached to a gold mesh belt. The back panel barely covered his ass while the front left his dick and balls swinging free.

He glanced in the mirror and moved around, realizing with every step or slight brush of air, just about everything was visible. The front barely reached past the end of his cock. He glanced around and realized the other guys were wearing equally revealing costumes, all of a similar theme. They were in slightly different cuts and colors, but all had gold or silver braid and mesh.

The rest of his costume consisted of gladiator sandals, thin leather soles with thick gold braids that wound their way up his ankles and calves, and gold wristbands. He hardly considered wristbands and shoes as items of clothing and realized the goal was to get the serving boys naked as quickly as possible.

"Forgot your headpiece." Rand came by and settle a ring of gold leaves on his hair. "Do you want some shine or color?"

"Makeup?" Jeremy glanced around to see the other boys with makeup brushes and eyeliner pencils. One guy was painting another guy's nipples with something glittery.

"It's optional, but you can decorate yourself a little. It's mostly food-grade stuff they use for cake decorating. Edible." He grinned.

"Makes your nipples nice and sweet." Barry laughed and handed a brush and pot of pink glittery powder to Jeremy.

"Just in case you let someone lick them." Rand grinned, and Jeremy moved the edge of his tunic so Rand could paint pink sugar on his nipples. The brush tickled and he squirmed at the strange sensation. He watched the others getting ready and realized a couple of them had tubes of lube and butt plugs or dildos.

Kit bent over, and another guy moved close, lubed up a few fingers, and slid one inside of Kit. *What the hell?* Jeremy stared. Several of the guys were lubing themselves or others up, sliding fingers and toys inside, stretching each other out.

"Wait a minute. Rand? I thought this was serving dinner, not fucking."

"Their gentlemen like more than dinner service. Some clients want to play with you or feel your ass is ready, even if they don't intend to fuck you. Marketing." Rand nodded. "I've seen guys slip their hand up someone's skirt, feel that slippery hole, and go for everything on the menu." He laughed. "It's optional. But I don't recommend you slick up unless you're interested in more than the basic service."

"Uh, maybe next time." At this rate, there wouldn't be a next time.

"Sure. Just have some fun with it. The guys really just want to be pampered and turned on."

Jeremy couldn't help staring. These guys seemed excited about the idea of their colorful gentleman fucking them. And Jeremy found watching them get ready was enough to get his cock a little bit hard. He glanced down and realized his little skirt-like thing lifted up, making his slight arousal completely obvious.

"Looks like someone might be on the menu after all." Barry winked and turned so he could slide a slim dildo into the guy at the mirror on his other side. "Let me know if you want some prep."

"No. Not tonight." Jeremy kept watching, wondering whether he'd ever want some stranger to fuck him. Of course he would. He'd gone home—or not home—with guys he'd hooked up with at clubs. You didn't need dinner and a movie if the attraction was mutual. Mr. Green might be exactly his type. But fooling around for money? That changed everything, didn't it?

A dinner gong sounded, and the other boys—as they liked to call themselves—put the finishing touches on their costumes and makeup and lined up to parade out in front of tonight's gentlemen. Each boy had a colored snap-on armband that would match a ribbon on one gentleman's lapel. Butterflies fluttered in his gut and soon turned to huge bats flapping their wings when the door opened and he heard the men's voices, their laughter as the boys walked into the dining room.

Rand had told Jeremy to go last, so he could see how the other boys greeted their gentlemen, and he stood in the doorway observing. Boys' bodies blocked his view at first, and he was halfway into the room, glimpsing heavyset men with gray temples and jowls, before he spotted the bright green ribbon on his client's lapel.

Oh dear. Oh fucking fuck, he thought and moved around the perimeter of the room, feeling the breeze under his loincloth as his cock and balls swung free with each step. He felt the sheer fabric flutter around his dick and tried not to be self-conscious as he exposed himself to everyone in the room.

Mr. Green was fucking gorgeous.

BRICE MARTIN hadn't known quite what to expect when he'd been invited by a colleague to the Dinner Club. He'd heard of the place—mentioned in hushed tones by his wealthier gay friends—and he'd checked the website. But outside of a few vague descriptions and tame photos, it wasn't clear precisely what went on during the dinner parties. The overly generic name only added to the mystique.

He'd been at Christie, Parker, and Lane for six months before anyone but an old friend of his realized he was gay, and then within a week he'd been invited to dinner here by one of the junior partners. He hoped it was a good sign, but he didn't know quite how to act. He'd watch Watkins and take cues from him, but the idea of paying for sex of any sort wasn't on his wish list.

They'd come here straight from work, still wearing the suits and ties they'd put on for a meeting with someone from the Securities and Exchange Commission. They'd taken a cab from the office to the posh Pacific Heights Victorian and sipped expertly mixed drinks while they waited for dinner.

Brice didn't know how to interact with the other diners. They were here for what promised to be a pretty licentious evening, but he didn't go in for either exhibitionism or voyeurism. Was he supposed to chat with these guys? He had enough to worry about with what Watkins would do or expect. Best to remain quiet and see if anyone spoke to him.

Finally, they were ushered into the dining room. In the center stood a long, wide table. It was made of sturdy wood with a dark green runner and six place settings, three to a side. The dishes, glassware, and silver were of top quality, as elegant as any San Francisco restaurant he'd eaten at. Before each place setting was a wide padded bench rather than a chair, with plenty of room between each bench.

"Sit where you like, gentlemen." The man at the door greeted them and waved them toward the table.

Watkins took a seat at one end and pointed to the opposite bench. "Sit there. Best view."

Brice complied, then wished he'd seated himself next to Watkins. With this configuration they could see each other. He didn't want Watkins observing him, nor did he want to watch Watkins with his own serving boy.

Boy. The word jarred every time Watkins said it. "Of course, they're all legal. But they're called boys."

Brice sipped his dirty martini—extra dirty, just to dilute the booze. He'd been nursing the same one since they'd arrived. He didn't drink much and definitely wanted to stay in control tonight. Watkins was on his second neat Scotch.

"Welcome to the Dinner Club. I'm Thomas, and I'll be your host tonight." Brice recognized the man who had given him a quick, but incisive chat before he was admitted. "Please ask me if you need anything you're not getting." He gave a crooked leer of a grin and some of the other men laughed. "We have a few new faces at the table tonight, so I'd like to cover the ground rules before the boys come out."

The men glanced around the table at each other, and Brice hoped no one spotted he was the newbie. He was uncomfortable enough. There was a palpable tension in the room, the others looking out of the corner of their eyes at each other, as if this was some sort of competition. Thomas opened an ornate carved chest and pulled out a shoebox-sized container. He stood behind Watkins. "Good to have you back, Mr. Orange," Thomas stated before he pinned a bright orange ribbon to Watkins' lapel. "Nice to meet your friend, too."

Thomas came around the table to Brice. "You'll be Green tonight. Enjoy yourself," he added as he pinned the ribbon to Brice's lapel and squeezed his shoulder collegially.

He moved to each man, selecting a ribbon from the box and pinning one on each guest. As he made his way around the table, he continued his explanation.

"Your serving boy will be wearing a ribbon matching your lapel ribbon. You will be served only by your boy. Rule number one is you will refrain from touching him in what we call the bikini zone, unless you have his permission. That means you ask. Not all boys are on the menu for touching tonight."

A low murmur of disapproval emanated from the table, but Brice couldn't tell who had made the sound.

"Rule number two is you will refrain from touching anyone else's boy at all, unless invited by the boy *and* his gentleman."

"Rule number three, no sex in the dining room. And by sex, I mean fucking. No fucking the boys *in the dining room*. Save that for nightcaps in your rooms if it happens at all."

Brice sucked in a breath. That was good. He hoped he wasn't going to be expected to do anything in public with this boy assigned to him.

"So, what can we do to the boys in here?" A man with a Texan drawl asked.

"If it's on their menu, hands and mouths on the boys only. Gentlemen, keep your dicks in your pants in the dining room. If you can't wait till dinner's over, leave the dining room." He glanced around and seemed to be gauging the men's moods. "But boy-on-boy, anything goes. With permission from both parties. No means no. No exceptions. My assistants will enforce that, and they're here to protect the boys. Be respectful of them. We can all have fun without anyone getting hurt." At Thomas's final remark, two heavily muscled men in tight black T-shirts and black pants straining over tree-trunk thighs entered the room. They looked like a cross between ninjas and bouncers. One moved to each end of the table and took up a post against the wall.

Thomas looked at the men again. "Now, who's ready for dinner?"

A loud chorus of whoops and affirmative noises erupted.

Brice glanced at Watkins, who was grinning back at him, nodding, with an odd glint in his eye.

"This, my friend, is going to be fun."

"Can't wait." Brice took a gulp of martini and nearly choked, then turned his attention toward the door.

He felt more than heard or saw a commotion in the hallway, and then Thomas nodded and a gong sounded. The door opened, and the first boy came through, wearing a very short gold-edged toga and a bright blue ribbon tied around one upper arm. *Not mine*, Brice thought. The boy was blond, smooth, and very good-looking in that go-go boy twink way he saw too much of at some of the local clubs.

The other men let out oohs and aahs and a few disappointed groans as they spotted attractive boys wearing someone else's color. Each boy made one round of the table before settling next to his gentleman on the wide bench seats. All were model good-looking, and none wore much. What little they had on emphasized smooth, lithe bodies, focusing attention on nipples painted with glitter, visible through the transparent shirts and tiny tunics that left little to the imagination about the size and shape of their cocks.

Despite his initial distaste for the general setup, Brice couldn't help feeling a little animal thrill at the sight of all these gorgeous bodies on display, even knowing as the night progressed, they'd be reduced to sexual objects, if they weren't already. So far four boys had entered the room, and Brice still hadn't seen his.

Then a boy with an orange ribbon flounced into the room, and just behind him Brice glimpsed a flash of bright green. As the orange boy moved out of his line of sight, he saw the one assigned to him for the night: he wore a sheer sleeveless tunic and a tiny gold-edged loincloth, fluttering with each step, enticing Brice to glance under it.

This boy was no boy in reality. He wasn't quite as smooth as the others, with a sprinkling of pale hair on his chest and the muscular upper body of someone who played sports regularly, not one who sculpted muscles in the gym. As he came around the table, Brice noticed the gold braid laced up around shapely calves and thick thighs, and he forced himself to move his gaze from the barely-there loincloth to the green boy's face.

"Hi, I'm J—Remy. Call me Remy."

"Hi, Remy, I'm—"

"Mr. Green," Thomas said from behind. Apparently the boys weren't supposed to know the gentlemen's names.

"Hi, Mr. Green." Remy sat down next to Brice, close but not so their thighs touched. He turned and smiled. He looked like he was in his twenties, with clear skin, smooth and just-shaven. He had silky hair the color of wheat and even, white teeth. He looked sober and healthy. Brice wasn't sure what he'd imagined, but it wasn't this farm-boy look. Was this better or worse?

Both, he decided. He certainly wouldn't mind touching this guy, but the downside was how much he might want to by the end of the evening.

"Another drink, sir?" Remy motioned toward Brice's martini glass.

"No thanks."

"Do you want wine with dinner?" Thomas addressed Brice.

"Just a glass, not a bottle."

"Come on, *Green*," Watkins shouted from across the table, smirking as he emphasized the pseudonym. "Look, it's on my expense account, so let's have a bottle of something good." Watkins leaned down, and before he could grab the wine list, his boy had handed it to him and opened it up. Watkins snaked his arm around the boy and they murmured, cheeks together, as he made his choice of wine. Thomas nodded.

"Boys, the first course is ready!" Thomas announced, and Remy hopped off the bench and lined up to leave the room. He moved gracefully but swiftly, as if he couldn't wait to leave. Brice wondered if he should have done or said something differently.

A few moments later the boys paraded back in, each holding a plate, again circling the table and most of them doing their best to show off their physiques. Remy came around toward Brice and bowed low, then placed the plate—a salad—in front of him.

Around him Brice noticed the other men, including Watkins, were removing clothing items from their servers. Watkins had pulled his boy's tunic off so the young man sat shirtless, dark nipples budding in the chilly room.

"What should I remove, Mr. Green?" Remy asked.

"Uh, your armband?"

"Do you w—"

Suddenly it seemed creepy to want to watch this guy peel off his clothes for Brice—even worse to do it for him.

"No, you do it." Brice watched Remy's face, saw his eyes flaring as he took in Brice's choice. The armband had to come off at some point.

Remy couldn't unsnap the green band on his own, and Brice had to help him. His fingertips brushed against the firm, smooth bicep muscles, and he felt the warmth of Remy's skin. The jolt of sensation traveling from his fingers into his core surprised him. He took his time at the task and noticed Remy's eyes flutter as he looked away. How did he manage to look so innocent and naïve?

Remy sat down next to Brice and poured him wine and another glass of water, clearly waiting for Brice to ask him to perform a task. The other men seemed to enjoy having their serving boys feed them or sit on their laps, the gentlemen stroking a thigh or pinching a nipple in between bites of salad. One man had removed his boy's shorts and was stroking the boy's firm cock while being fed. Brice wondered what would be left for later if the guy started off there.

Across from him, Watkins' boy sat on his lap, with Watkins' hand under the filmy cloth. It was hardly subtle, but somehow preferable to what the other guy was doing.

JEREMY WASN'T at all sure what to expect from Mr. Green. He was good-looking in a polished, Richard Gere way, a few strands of silver sprinkled at his temples. It looked good on him. He was somewhere in his thirties, no older, despite the gray strands. His eyes were the color of chestnuts and opened wide as Green looked at Jeremy.

At first, he glanced at Jeremy's body, but then he seemed to make a special effort to focus on Jeremy's eyes. Maybe he was embarrassed to ogle him, which made a nice change from the way some of the other gentlemen leered at him, clearly wanting to touch what they weren't supposed to. Jeremy glanced at the two guards and felt marginally safer.

The salad course was awkward. Jeremy wasn't sure if Green wanted to be fed. Jeremy reached for the fork in his hand, but Green jerked his hand away and fed himself. With nothing to do, Jeremy watched the other boys feeding their gentlemen, being fed by them, or sitting in laps and playing with the gentleman's buttons or collars. And they were all chatting. Mr. Green kept stuffing salad in his mouth, leaving Jeremy no opportunity for discussion.

"Is there anything I can help you with?" Jeremy asked, hoping Green didn't hear the tremor in his voice.

"Uh, no." Green didn't look at him. He leaned forward and his leg pressed against Jeremy's, firm and warm.

"I don't bite, you know."

"Unless I want you to?" Green actually smiled this time.

He had a beautiful smile. Even, white teeth like a model in a toothpaste ad. There was a tiny dimple in his right cheek, and his eyes crinkled up a little now he was actually smiling.

"Do you want me to bite you?" Jeremy tried to put a touch of sex in his voice as he asked. He sucked at flirting. He was more of a buy a guy a drink and leave, without much talking. But Mr. Green was a challenge Jeremy suddenly wanted to overcome.

"I suppose it depends where." Green put the fork down and turned more toward Jeremy.

Jeremy licked his lips. "Hmmm. Maybe I'd start with your… earlobe?" He reached up and caressed Green's ear before tugging the lobe. Jeremy seemed to have no control over his hand and just watched, as fascinated as Green.

"That's a fine place, to start." He turned a much warmer gaze on Jeremy, making Jeremy's pulse race.

Now he really wanted to touch this man, to be touched by him. It would feel good. It would be fun.

"More salad, sir?" Jeremy picked up a piece of cucumber and brought it to Green's mouth, letting his fingers brush Green's lower lip. His skin tingled from the touch. He breathed in Green's scent, and a wave of arousal washed over him. The tiny loincloth lifted a little, and Green noticed, glancing down. He seemed surprised; then a little smile told Jeremy he liked having that effect.

"Would you like some wine?" Green asked. He let his hand linger on Jeremy's as he passed him the cup and Jeremy took a sip. Green's hand stayed on his the entire time, burning into his skin. Jeremy's breath quickened, and the loincloth fluttered.

Green's fingers wrapped around Jeremy's wrist, loosely at first and then more firmly. He licked his lips and felt himself getting hard enough for the damn loincloth to flap like a flag in a hurricane.

A gong announced the end of the course.

Jeremy stood, Green's hand still on his wrist, as if he didn't want to break their sudden powerful connection. Then Jeremy reached for the plate, and Green let go.

BACK IN the hall between the kitchen and the dining room, Kit and Rand came up to Jeremy.

"Looks like you're having some fun." Kit lifted the loincloth and examined Jeremy's half-mast cock.

"I'm so glad," Rand said. "I could see it was a little awkward at first. But by the end of the next course, you two should be more relaxed."

They were. Even more after the third, where Jeremy was wearing just the gold leaf thing in his hair, the tunic, and the bottom piece. He sat pressed up against Mr. Green, and they fed pieces of some beef dish to each other. The banter continued as Jeremy found himself ever more turned on not only by polite but sexy Green but by the whole scene.

By now some of the boys wore only shoes. One had a shirt but no loincloth. Jeremy wore the most of the whole group. Green was still wearing his jacket. At least Jeremy had loosened his tie.

"Would you like me to help you with your jacket?" Jeremy asked in a low whisper against Green's ear. He fought the urge to take that bite he'd mentioned during the salad.

"Help me?"

"Why don't you take your jacket off?"

Green looked around as if seeking permission, and Jeremy found himself making the decision for him. He slid the jacket off Green—who pulled away at first when Jeremy took hold of it—and hung it up on the conveniently provided racks near the wall. It would have been fine, but when Jeremy stood up, his state of arousal was obvious to everyone in the room. He might as well not even be wearing the tiny squares of sheer fabric. His cock jutted out, balls bouncing slightly with each step, reminding him that everything was pretty much on full display already.

"Go on, Green, give the boy a hand," one of the men shouted. A few others offered suggestions.

Jeremy's face heated up, and Green wouldn't look at him until the course was over.

At the fifth course, dessert, Green had to choose the tunic or the loincloth. He went for the top.

"Would you mind helping me?" Jeremy wanted Green's hands on him in the worst way. In any way. He was beginning to wonder if the man was even gay. He had a nice bulge in his pants, but he hadn't yet done anything overtly sexual.

Green's hands skimmed up Jeremy's sides as he pulled the shirt off. Jeremy arched his back as the tunic fluttered from his fingertips. Now Green stared at sparkly pink nipples and Jeremy's sculpted torso. A few of the men applauded; they'd probably been waiting to get the last boy—Jeremy—out of his kit.

"Would you like me to sit on your lap, sir?"

Green just nodded, and Jeremy perched himself on one thigh. An arm circled his waist, and he pressed closer to Mr. Green. He could feel firm, warm flesh just the other side of the cotton button-down shirt.

Around them, the other men had their hands on boys' cocks or asses, and half the gentlemen's shirts were unbuttoned, boys playing with their nipples. Why didn't Mr. Green want to play with him? Clearly there were very few rules and even fewer inhibitions here.

Throwing caution to the wind, Jeremy opened the top two buttons of Green's shirt. The guy almost stood up and dropped him on the floor. Jeremy got to his feet, leaving his nipples at approximately eye level for Green, and his gaze lingered there.

"It's cake decorating sugar," Jeremy said. "One of the other guys did it for me. Too much?"

"They're… pretty."

The way Mr. Green's lips formed a circle when he voiced the *p* got Jeremy's loincloth fluttering. God, did Jeremy want that man's hands and mouth all over him.

The moment of truth came during after-dinner drinks, course number six. All eyes were on them as Mr. Green moved to unfasten the thin gold cord on Jeremy's loincloth. His fingers trembled against Jeremy's flesh, heating Jeremy from head to toe.

"Kind of like Christmas," Green said as he fumbled with the knot.

"Except you've already seen what's inside."

A shy, genuine smile flashed across Green's face, lighting up his eyes, and he laughed.

"Is it what you wanted?" Why had he asked that? God, he was being such a slut tonight.

Green stared at Jeremy's cock, then met his gaze. "It's just about perfect."

Just then, Rand grabbed Jeremy's hand and pulled him a few steps from Green.

"Go on, give everyone a good look." Then speaking to the others, he asked, "Isn't that a nice view?"

So Jeremy stood there while fourteen people stared at his hard-on.

Well, Thomas had said the job was to take his clothes off and let people look at him. Six gentlemen, five boys, two guards, and Thomas, who hovered at the doorway to the inner hall.

Jeremy wouldn't have described himself as particularly big, but he'd never gotten teased or laughed at in the locker room, and he had gotten plenty of compliments from previous lovers. But until today, he'd never gotten a round of applause.

He expected it to wither and embarrass him, but here, in this place, it only got him harder. Deep down, that reaction shamed him, but his body put his brain on hold.

He turned back to Green and straddled one leg, the way Kit had advised him. Now his cock pointed right up at Mr. Green's face. They both looked down at it. Jeremy desperately wanted Green to take hold and not let go. So far several of the boys had already gotten hand jobs or blowjobs from their gentlemen.

But Jeremy had told Thomas he wasn't interested in doing anything tonight. He couldn't ask Green, because that would be solicitation. And though Green looked at Jeremy's cock, glistening with drops of precome, with true longing, Jeremy knew he wouldn't ask.

So, the seven-or-maybe-eight-inch gorilla stood between them. Jeremy pressed himself against Green's firm abs, and Green pulled Jeremy closer with an arm around his waist.

It wasn't enough for either of them, but they stayed like that, sharing a glass of cognac that served to speed up the sensations zinging around inside, while they listened to moans and heavy breathing around them.

Jeremy just had to break the silence.

"So, how about those Giants?"

Green laughed, and it sent shock waves up Jeremy's cock and made his balls ache even more fiercely.

Then the gong sounded.

Dinner was over.

Chapter THREE

AFTER DINNER, the boys filed back out of the dining room, waving and blowing kisses. Remy had only given a shy smile when he slid off Brice's lap and followed the others to the door. Brice didn't want him to go, but he needed a break from the unbearable heat and desire zinging between them.

No one stopped to collect their discarded costumes.

"Would anyone like a nightcap?" Thomas asked as the men sipped at their after-dinner drinks.

Brice didn't need any more alcohol. A few men nodded, and Thomas bent for a whispered conversation with each one. Watkins gave Brice a thumbs-up signal, and he responded with a shrug. He'd nurse this cognac until he could make a move that wouldn't insult Watkins. Thomas, however, didn't seem to be serving any of whatever the men had ordered. Finally, he came to hover at Brice's shoulder.

"I'm fine. Nothing more to drink for me."

"Mr. Watkins has already arranged your nightcap with Remy. Anything else is between you and the boy, but the room is yours until 10 a.m."

"What?" Brice realized he'd spoken loudly when several others turned toward him.

Thomas leaned so his mouth was an inch from Brice's ear. "A nightcap here means spending the night with one of the boys—as long as it's mutually agreed upon. We provide the room and no questions asked."

"But I—" Brice stopped as he noticed Watkins looking at him. Apparently, he better accept the offer and then figure out what to do with Remy later. The whole situation was uncomfortable. What had he been thinking coming here with Watkins? He liked to keep his private life private. Was this preferable to being dragged to a strip club with women dancers and being expected to ogle and jeer and make derogatory comments? It was more honest, but Brice still felt like he was exploiting the boy who'd served him, no matter how turned on Remy was or how hot he got Brice.

But Remy had agreed to spend the night with Brice. Maybe the boy was a lot less innocent than he appeared.

"How would you like him? Please point to your preference." Thomas opened a menu—Brice was getting used to these tonight—with options: dressed, undressed, hard, prepped, in bed.

Fuck. Not very subtle, was this process? He pointed to "dressed." Thomas nodded and straightened up.

Thomas left the room, and two of the guests followed him. When he returned he placed a key in front of each of the remaining men. Brice received a key marked only with the numeral 4. It was an old brass skeleton key, gleaming on the table, with the numeral painted in gold on a leather tag.

"In order, please, gentlemen," Thomas said from the doorway. The man who presumably held key number 1 stood, and Thomas escorted him from the room.

"You got yourself a shy one there, Brice. But cute and one hell of a boner." Watkins' voice boomed through the quiet room. "You know, I just assumed you'd want *him*. Did you want one of the others? Or two?"

One of the other men joined in with Watkins' laughter.

"No. He's fine. Perfect." Brice smiled and acted like he was used to ordering boys for the night the same way he ordered a pizza.

Watkins left the room next, and then a third man followed. Brice was the last to leave.

"Third floor, sir." Thomas pointed to an old-fashioned elevator with a black wrought-iron grill. He opened the door and ushered Brice in, then closed it. The elevator rose slowly through the floors, and at the top Brice had to unlatch and open the door, then close it behind him. The key felt heavy in his hand as he made his way to Room 4. He stood outside the door for a moment, planning what he'd say when he entered. He imagined the other men opening the door to hard, naked boys, lubed up and ready to go, or whatever they'd ordered off the nightcap menu.

He took a deep breath and opened the door. The room was dim, lit by low lamps giving off a warm glow with the ambiance of a Victorian brothel, if his impression of a brothel were accurate. He noticed a leather armchair—big enough for two, just like the dining benches—a couch, and a four-poster bed. A door off the left led to a bathroom. Brice took in the furnishings as he scanned the room and came to rest on Remy, leaning against a polished wood dresser. The boy was fully dressed in a pair of jeans and a dark blue long-sleeved T-shirt. At his feet sat a blue-and-yellow gym bag with the familiar "Cal" logo and the image of a bear—the UC Berkeley mascot.

"Hi, Remy."

"Hi, Mr. Green." Remy's mouth curved in a half-smile, but he didn't meet Brice's gaze. In fact, he looked as uncomfortable as Brice felt. Brice went and sat on the couch, a frilly Victorian number. Remy moved away from the dresser and sat next to him. It was more of a love seat, and their thighs pressed together. Here they were, alone in a room, both fully dressed, when half an hour earlier Remy had been naked and aroused as he perched on Brice's lap, feeding him morsels of beef and delicious tiny squares of cheesecake.

Brice shifted as he felt his own arousal begin again. He did not want to be attracted to this man. He didn't want to use another person this way. He'd never paid for sex in his life, and he wasn't about to start. He noticed Remy glancing at his crotch, and he shifted his weight again.

"Remy, I have to be honest. I don't want to sleep with you."

Remy glanced at the telltale bulge again before returning his gaze to Brice's face. "You don't?" The tone sounded as if he were insulted. Could he possibly be disappointed? Then it dawned on Brice.

"I'll pay whatever you'd make if I did. I just won't pay you for sex. I won't do that."

"You won't pay for sex, but you'll pay me *not* to have sex?" Remy stared, eyes wide.

"Doesn't make a lot of sense, does it?" Brice laughed, and Remy joined in.

"Then what are you doing here?"

"I'm here because of my coworker. I'm new to the firm, and he thought it would be a treat to take me here. But it's just not my kind of place. He ordered you and the nightcap, and I can't just be seen to refuse."

"You're not into guys?"

Brice laughed again. "I am into guys. I'm just not into putting my private life on display."

"So you want your coworker to think you fucked me? That's better than just telling him you're not into this kind of thing?"

Brice shook his head. "Yeah, you're right. It's ridiculous. I should tell him the truth."

"That you're not into this?'"

"Right. Just tell me what I owe you, then you can go home."

"They have rules here about nightcaps. Since I'm new I don't know what happens if you break them. But I can't take your money. They pay me in the morning when I leave. Just for the night. Less if you only stay part of the night."

"You're kidding?"

Remy shook his head.

"So, if you leave early or leave before I do, then you don't get paid?"

"I don't think so. Like I said, I'm new, but that's how Thomas explained it to me."

"Then I can stay the night. I'll sleep on the couch. You take the bed."

Remy glanced down at the frilly love seat. "No, I can't take the bed. I'll sleep here. Can I use the bathroom first?"

"Sure."

Remy took his bag and walked into the bathroom, flipped on the light, and shut the door. Brice noticed the bathroom had modern fixtures, even if the color scheme echoed the bedroom. He listened to running water, and a few minutes later, Remy came out wearing heather gray boxer briefs and smelling of toothpaste. The hair framing his face was damp. He sat on the sofa next to Brice, and Brice hoisted himself up and went into the bathroom.

It was clean, with a Jacuzzi tub and a large separate shower stall, everything in elegant dark green and brown tones. Big fluffy red towels hung on racks. The modern room broke the old-fashioned image set by the dining room and the bedroom, but Brice could see the attraction to the large tub and imagined what the other couples might be doing in the shower at that very moment. He washed up at the sink, then brushed his teeth. The Dinner Club provided toothbrushes—still in the package—and a variety of soaps and creams. Everything was top quality from Armani.

Should he disrobe in here the way Remy had? He wanted to hang his suit up, so it made more sense to undress in the room by the armoire. He opened the door and walked out. Remy silently watched as Brice removed his jacket and hung it up, then did the same with his trousers. He unbuttoned the shirt and added it to the armoire before turning back toward Remy, who still sat on the love seat.

"I'll take that, Remy. You take the bed."

"I don't feel right letting you sleep here. You're the gentleman." He grinned at the term and so did Brice. "I should be helping you hang your clothes up, too. I'm sorry."

"I only expected you to serve me dinner, and to be honest you went far beyond anything I expected." Brice glanced away. It was awkward discussing this now, especially after they'd been so much more intimate earlier in the evening, each aware of the other's arousal. Had he met Remy in a different place and time, he'd gladly have spent the night with him and not in separate beds.

"I liked serving you. Really." It was Remy's turn to look uncomfortable and break his glance away. "I wasn't sure what to expect from this job. But it was fun. Serving *you* was fun. Thanks."

"Thank you."

Remy blinked, his long lashes brushing his cheeks. Brice stood in his briefs, staring at him. The room was cool, and Remy's nipples stood up darker than they'd seemed earlier and no longer sparkly. "No glitter now?" The words were out before Brice could stop himself.

Remy ran a hand across his chest, fingers brushing one nipple and making it stiffen further. He gave a shy grin again. "It's this special food coloring for making cake icing. Would you believe that? The guys paint themselves in all sorts of places. And it's all edible." Remy chuckled.

Brice licked his lower lip, trying not to think of how it would have tasted to lick the sweet glitter from Remy's pretty pink nipples. He'd wanted to. But not in front of five other men. Even now he imagined how they'd feel plump and hard in his mouth, and he felt warmth and heaviness at his crotch. Remy's gaze moved lower, and Brice recalled he was wearing boxer briefs that revealed his thoughts and urges. He'd better stop these thoughts or he'd wish he felt differently about the decision he'd made regarding Remy.

"I'm glad you didn't expect anything from me," Remy said. "I saw what the other boys did in the dining room, and what they said in the dressing room. They have lots of options on their menus, but I don't think it's the right thing for me. I never understood why guys would pay for sex when they know the other person is only saying and doing those things for money."

"Yeah. I know." Brice shook his head, moved toward the bed, then got under the covers before his ache turned to a full hard-on. Why the hell was he suddenly so much more attracted to Remy? But the truth was he'd been attracted to him the whole evening, and he kind of hated himself for falling under the spell of this place and this boy. It went against so many things he'd believed about himself, but maybe underneath he was just like those men who paid pretty boys or girls to treat them nicely.

Remy stretched out and dangled his legs over one arm of the love seat, settling his head against one of the cushions. The thing was too short for him, and he'd probably wake with a sore neck and aching back. If the poor guy even fell asleep in the first place.

"Look, Remy, this bed's huge. There's room for both of us. I promise to keep my hands to myself." Brice shifted over to one side of the bed and patted the other.

"Well, if you're sure." Remy didn't make a move yet, as if weighing the options. "Okay. Thanks." He got up and moved toward the bed. Even in the low light, Brice could see the outline of his cock against the thin cotton of his shorts. Remy lifted the comforter and slid under, then turned so he faced away from Brice.

This was going to be one hell of a long night, Brice realized.

JEREMY SLID into bed and turned away from Mr. Green—hell, he still didn't know the man's real name. Was that part of the rules, too? He hid his disappointment Green wasn't more attracted to him. He wasn't sure he wanted to let Green fuck him or suck him or get him off or get himself off, but maybe Jeremy's pride was a little wounded. He'd wanted Green to at least ask him for something, tell him how hot Jeremy was and how he made Green crazy and *please*? But instead, Green seemed like a nice, honest guy. On the other hand, Jeremy was in bed with him. And Green had the makings of another nice hard-on when he'd gotten undressed and headed for bed.

Jeremy would be happy to fuck or be fucked by Mr. Green. For free. If they'd met in a club or a bar, he'd pass all of Jeremy's tests for a casual fuck mate. All the activity at dinner had Jeremy far more turned on than he'd ever expected to be. He liked sitting on Green's lap and feeding him. He liked watching the boys playing and sucking each other off, and he even wished he'd been brave enough to let Green know it was okay to play with him during the meal. And now, Jeremy had just agreed to spend the night with Green, hands off, despite the fact that Mr. Green was apparently as attracted to Jeremy as Jeremy was to him.

Well, it was a long night, and maybe somewhere in the middle, they'd both come to their senses and give in to the urges they both pretended to ignore.

AT SOME point during the night, at least part of Jeremy's wish came true. He woke up to discover he'd rolled over and was pressed tightly against Mr. Green's back, enjoying the contours of Mr. Green's shapely, firm ass.

"Uh, sorry," Jeremy whispered and pulled away. He needed to pee and moved carefully toward the bathroom in the near darkness. He hoped Green hadn't woken. When he got back to bed, he discovered he was wrong. Green was lying on his side, eyes open and glinting.

"It's cold without you," Green whispered. Jeremy felt a little warmer at the words and slid in under the quilt.

Green moved close and took Jeremy into his arms. He'd taken his shorts off, so his erection pressed against Jeremy's hip and he radiated body heat. They were skin to skin above the waist, so Jeremy slid his own shorts off. Nothing in between them now but the self-control they'd both ignored.

Jeremy rolled onto his back, and Green lay on top, mouth quickly finding a nipple even in the near dark.

A loud pleasurable groan escaped from Jeremy's lips, and Green sucked harder. Jeremy was rock-hard now. He bucked up against Green's firm muscles and soon felt a strong, but gentle, hand wrap around his cock.

"Is this okay?" Green said, lips slippery against Jeremy's chest.

"You have to ask?" Jeremy panted the reply.

"I need to ask. Is that a yes?"

The man must be a lawyer, Jeremy thought with the last shred of clear thought. "God, yes."

Mr. Green slid down and tongued Jeremy's cock into complete submission. Finally, he took Jeremy deep into his mouth. The heat and pressure was too good. It didn't take long before Jeremy lost control.

"Merry Christmas," he said as he came down Mr. Green's throat.

Chapter FOUR

JEREMY LEFT just after 8:00 a.m., in line with the morning rule—stay past eight and the gentleman paid the room charge. He wanted to leave before Green woke up again. Why hadn't he asked his real name? Of course, real names were against another of the strict rules. The gentlemen stayed anonymous for many reasons. Some weren't out, some were married, others might be embarrassed if their Dinner Club activities were discovered. And the club had the practical purpose of keeping the boys from meeting the gentlemen elsewhere, thus depriving the club of its reason to exist. They thrived on repeat customers who wanted to see their favorite boy, or so it seemed from what Jeremy had heard from the others in the short time he'd been at the house.

He took BART across the San Francisco Bay to Berkeley, then cycled home from the station and tossed his bag into his room once he got into the apartment. He lay on his bed staring up at the ceiling trying to process the night before. He needed to get to the Life Sciences Building and check on some lab work that would finish around eleven, but he was in no hurry. He was reluctant to wash away his memories of the night with Mr. Green. He wanted to keep Green's scent close, think about how his body had felt against Jeremy's. His hands and mouth—God, that mouth!—on Jeremy's body.... No, he had to stop thinking about this. Too late. His cock thickened and tension hummed through his body, the familiar ache tightening his balls and quickening his breath.

Why not? He slid one hand into his jeans and grasped his cock, imagining Mr. Green's hands on him, Green's mouth sucking at a nipple. The ache grew, and Jeremy slid his pants and shorts down, not bothering to remove shoes or socks. He started with long smooth slow strokes, eyes closed to heighten the fantasy of Green pleasuring him. He heard himself groan, quickened his strokes, and let go as the first wave of pleasure shook him. He shot thick spurts onto his torso and gave in to the overwhelming sensation of physical bliss.

Afterward he lay panting, remembering fantasies weren't really bliss, just a quick respite from the reality of his lonely life.

Serving Mr. Green had been another pleasant detour. He'd enjoyed taking care of his gentleman, knowing he got the man so worked up and surprised by his own arousal in the overtly sexualized environment of the Dinner Club. He'd gone only for the chance to earn some money, expecting the worst, assuming he'd feel used and degraded in the process. But Kit and the others clearly had a good time, enjoyed getting each other off for their own pleasure as much as for the amusement of the gentlemen. Was there really anything wrong with it, if everyone consented every step of the way?

Even the nightcap had been no pressure. Jeremy had wanted to do far more than he'd originally agreed to, and it had been awkward. But what was wrong with any of it?

Nothing.

Jeremy decided then and there if Thomas would have him back, he'd work again at the Dinner Club. And he'd loosen up and have some fun. Not all the gentlemen had been as handsome as Mr. Green, but Green had said he wanted to come back too. A win-win, right?

Jeremy spent another twenty minutes fantasizing about having Mr. Green's hands on him at the dinner table and letting the other boys watch Jeremy's gentleman ordering from the menu. God, how ridiculous their code phrases were, but Jeremy wanted to be on Mr. Green's menu and wanted to perform whatever the man might ask.

Let's just hope he asks.

LATER THAT day Thomas called to let Jeremy know he'd performed well enough to become a regular. He needed to let Thomas know his availability. Which days could he work, and how many nights a week did he want? Jeremy agreed to one night a week and told Thomas which days were best and how far in advance he needed to schedule around his academic commitments. Now all he had to do was wait.

Chapter FIVE

BRICE WOKE up alone in the room. Sunlight flickered through the edges of the heavy drapes, but there was a chill anyway. Remy's pillow bore an indentation, but it was cold. He'd gotten up and left long ago. He glanced toward the bathroom, but it was wishful thinking. Remy was gone. His sports bag wasn't in front of the armoire, where it had been the night before.

Brice checked the clock on the night table—an old-fashioned one with a second hand that clicked its way around the face. It was after 9:00 a.m. Remy only had to stay till eight to get his payment. Was the money all he cared about? Despite both their comments to the contrary, Brice thought they'd connected on more than just a physical level, though the physical had been satisfying. He sat up in bed, craving coffee. It was Saturday, and he wouldn't need to go into the office. He'd just check e-mail. Reluctantly he crawled out of bed, visited the bathroom, and grabbed his phone out of his jacket pocket as he made his way back to the bed.

He sat there for a few moments, then crossed the room to the armoire and began dressing. He checked his reflection to make sure he looked presentable and then slipped into the hallway. The elevator was on his floor already, and he rode it down slowly, then got out at the ground floor. He didn't know if he was supposed to check out. He left the key on a table near the door, then slipped out of the Dinner Club and into the bright, clear sunshine of a San Francisco autumn morning.

He'd taken a cab with Watkins the night before, and he walked toward the next main street—Mission—stopping along the way at a tiny grocery store for their largest cup of coffee. The Starbucks across the street would be packed, and he didn't fancy standing in line wearing yesterday's suit, his dress shirt unbuttoned, and his tie rolled up in a pocket. He didn't like announcing he hadn't been home the night before. Coffee in hand—and after ignoring the judgmental stare of the turbaned man behind the counter—he hailed a cab and headed for home.

BY MONDAY Brice realized he couldn't get the thought of Remy out of his brain. He found himself far too obsessed with the young man. Ten times during the weekend he'd considered calling the Dinner Club for another reservation, and ten times he stopped himself. Thankfully, the number was unlisted, or he might not have had the necessary willpower. He certainly couldn't call Watkins on the weekend to ask for the number. He'd never live it down.

Brice had been in his office less than an hour Monday morning when Watkins slipped in, carrying a large Starbucks cup with half a dozen instructions penned on one side. Figured this guy would be high maintenance, even when it came to his coffee.

"So, Martin, how'd you like the club?" Watkins oozed into one of the leather chairs opposite Brice's desk, wearing an improper sneer.

Brice had steeled himself for this conversation. He smiled and nodded, hoping he looked knowing and suitably debauched from the activities. It wasn't how he felt, but he had to keep up appearances.

"Loved it. Thanks for taking me."

"Loved it? That's all you're gonna say?" Watkins leaned forward, one hand on the edge of Brice's desk.

"Yes."

"Well, you'll need to loosen up a little next time. Maybe we can...." Watkins' voice trailed off as he must have realized Brice wasn't into anything involving the pronoun "we" and naked serving boys. Watkins nodded and grinned again. "Kit's a pistol. Took me most of Saturday and part of Sunday to catch up on my sleep."

"I think he'd be a little too much for me." Brice made sure to sound like he envied Watkins' sexual prowess and might save the knowledge for future use.

"That Remy, he's nice and fresh. Kind of like the boy-next-door quarterback of the high school team. Nice change from the pretty boys. Should I give him a run next time?" Watkins paused but not long enough for Brice to answer. "I usually like 'em squirming a little more in my lap, you know? Like to get a real feel for a boy during dinner. Remy's new and maybe he's a little shy—or maybe he's just uptight—otherwise you two could have had some real fun at dinner and treated the rest of us to a little show. Well, he won't last long if he's a prude. Thomas likes the boys to be a little more *active* during the meal service. But maybe he saves his energy for the nightcaps." Watkins gave Brice another lecherous grin.

Brice felt a heaviness in his chest. He hated the thought of Watkins with Remy. At least based on what Brice thought Remy was really like. Maybe the guy had only acted shy for Brice's benefit, and the following night he'd gone down on every other boy in the room? The idea of Remy sucking off the other boys both repulsed and slightly aroused Brice, and he felt a little sick over his reaction. Whatever Remy was really like, Brice wouldn't wish a night with Watkins on him.

A low buzz sounded, and Watkins grabbed his chest pocket, then pulled out a cell phone. He glanced at the screen and replaced it without answering. "Gotta run. Need to get some signatures on a contract. I'll be back later to have you check that everything's A-OK on the paperwork. What time you here till?"

"Till at least five. Buzz me when you're on the way back if you'll be later."

"Gotcha!" Watkins rose and gave Brice a salute and a conspiratorial leer before heading out of the office.

He'd left his ginormous coffee on Brice's desk, and Brice waited a few minutes to see if Watkins would return. When he didn't, Brice dumped the contents out in the kitchen sink and tossed the cup in the compost bin.

The rest of Monday and most of the week passed without incident. Unless one counted that Brice wanted to see Remy again so badly he was ready to get the number of the club from Watkins. He managed to make it through Friday night by heading to a favorite bar just off Castro with some friends and getting drunker than he usually did. He stuck to beer to minimize the aftereffects the following day, then went for a long run in Golden Gate Park on Saturday morning.

By Sunday night he fell into bed exhausted, and he thought he was over the pull of the Dinner Club. As much as he would like to see Remy, he hated he had to do so through the repressive system of paying for favors. He didn't want Remy to feel exploited, and as long as they interacted at the club, Brice would never know for sure whether Remy was with him for money or because he actually liked spending time with Brice.

Brice's well-laid plans and hard-won victory over his baser desires blew up in his face Monday morning. Ron Templeton, an old college friend and now Brice's boss at the venture capital investment firm of

Christie, Parker, and Lane, rolled into his office, not bothering to knock on the half-shut door, and deposited himself in the same chair Watkins had used a week earlier.

"Hope you're not busy tomorrow night. And if you are, cancel your plans."

"Okay. Why?"

"Got an investor who's looking to plant about fifty mil. I need your help to land him."

"What can I do?"

"Cathcart runs a private equity fund in Missouri, and he's pretty excited about visiting San Fran again. We lost out to Valley Ventures last time he was looking to invest. I need you to take him around and show him a good time."

Brice sat back in his chair. This was Ron's code that the prospect was gay, most likely closeted back in his red-state home life, and wanted to blow off more than steam while he was in town. The added implication was that if Brice showed him the right kind of fun, he'd toss them fifty million to invest.

"Cathcart? Did I sit in on meeting with him a while back?"

Ron nodded, a smile just starting to play around the edges of his mouth.

"So, what did you have in mind?" Brice asked, dreading the answer.

"Somehow he heard about the Dinner Club. Can't wait to go. Make some reservations for tomorrow night, and you've got Wednesday off. Let him do or have whatever he wants. Money is no object here."

Brice shook his head. The last thing he wanted was to see Remy again while a client watched. He'd been able to stay away from the place only by pushing his willpower to the limit. Now his boss had asked him to go back.

"Sorry, Ron, I can't make it." Best not to explain why.

"I don't care what it is, cancel it or postpone it."

"It's not that…. Why not send Watkins? He loves the place."

"What is it, then?" Ron paused. Brice could almost hear his brain whirring, trying to decide whether to mention outright Brice being gay or say anything remotely sexual, even though they'd known each other for years and Brice had never been in the closet. California and federal laws could be tricky on the issue of what might be considered inappropriate.

And Brice was the firm's attorney. "Cathcart doesn't like Watkins. He likes you."

"Do you mean 'like' as in the high-school-girl usage of the word, or just that he doesn't care for Watkins' personality."

Ron chuckled. "Definitely the latter. I'm not sure about the former. But he won't hit on you if you're someplace with willing participants." He paused and smiled mischievously. "Look, I don't think he's got the hots for you. But if he did, couldn't you just smile at him? For fifty mil?"

"I can't believe you just suggested that." But Brice was more amused than annoyed. He could hold his own, but sometimes a little extra smile—from the right guy or woman—could grease the wheels on a business deal, even when nothing was expected to come of the flirtation. "I could sue your ass."

"Well, I suppose that's better than the alternative," Ron said. It was only because they were friends Brice let him get away with the comment.

"You don't know what you're missing." Brice gave as good as he got. He leaned back in his chair and considered his options. He really wanted to see Remy. And Brice admitted the blatant sexuality of the club was a lure. He didn't feel entirely comfortable with being on display, but who was even looking at him? Watkins had had his mind—and his hands—on his own serving boy and hadn't cared what Brice was doing. "Okay. I'll do it this one time, for you. And the knowledge of how much of the fifty mil I'll get." As a junior partner, he got a tiny share of profits.

Ron stood up and leaned across the desk so he could slap Brice on the shoulder. "There you go. Take one for the team." He straightened up and looked at Brice. "I'm not sure what's not to like about the place. They have another club with women servers, and I'd love to go there. Marilyn wouldn't like it, though. But you're single, or so you've been saying. Is there someone who might be getting jealous?"

Brice shook his head. "Quite the opposite."

"Hang in there. And thanks. I owe you one."

"Yeah, one *million* dollars." Brice delivered the line like Dr. Evil in an Austin Powers movie, and Ron laughed his way back down the hall to his own office.

Brice got up and shut his door. He needed to think about this. Did he really want to see Remy? He admitted he was physically attracted to the young man. Could his politeness and charm be just an act? Some of these pros got their clients hooked on their company, as long as they were spending money, but the affection and attraction wasn't reciprocal. Remy had said he was new, but it could have been a lie too.

The best way to handle this would be to assume the attraction to Remy was nothing more than the normal sexual tension and desire the Dinner Club existed to provide. When Brice looked at it that way, he'd been the naïve one. No wonder they'd called him Mr. Green. Greenhorn, newbie, easily influenced. An evening with any of the other boys would be just as enjoyable. In fact, he *shouldn't* have Remy again, to guard against the misplaced emotion.

He hadn't walked into a real-life version of *Pretty Woman.* He wasn't going to ride off with the hooker for a twisted fairy-tale happy ending. That wasn't the kind of "happy ending" Remy represented.

Brice picked up the phone and buzzed Watkins. "Can you give me the reservation number at the Dinner Club? I need to bring a client." Brice kept his request short and businesslike, with no room for Watkins to wrangle an invitation to come along.

"Sure. Let me find it." He paused, and Brice expected to hear him tapping at keys, but there was silence. Watkins told him the number—apparently he had it memorized. "Have fun, Brice." Watkins chuckled lasciviously, and Brice hung up without thanking him.

He picked up the phone again and took a deep breath before calling.

"Men's Dinner Club," a pleasant-sounding woman announced on the other end. Brice had expected a breathy-sounding man to be taking reservations, getting the clients worked up on the phone before they ever set foot in the place. "How can I serve you?"

Brice tried not to imagine how the phrase would sound uttered in a husky male voice. "Can I book two seats for tomorrow night?" He half hoped they were booked up.

"Your color, please?"

"Green."

"Just green? Not forest green or Kelly green?"

"I don't know. I've only been there once, and I was the only Green that night." He gave the date. He'd wondered how he'd gotten such a common color.

"Oh, yes, sir. Green is a first visit basic color. Here you are in the database under a corporate account. From now on you'll be Hunter Green for reservations. I'll need to get some additional information and assign your personal membership number."

He spent five minutes providing the details, and she verified his authorization to use the business account.

"Do you have a preferred serving boy?" she asked as if she were inquiring about whether he wanted sugar for his coffee. "You had Remy last time."

"No, but…" He certainly *had* had Remy. He paused, not sure he was making the correct decision. "No preference. But I'd rather not have the same boy."

"Weren't you pleased with his service?"

He didn't want to get Remy in trouble. Damn, he shouldn't have said anything. "Oh, I was. Very pleased." Fuck, that sounded perverted. "J-just I'd like to try someone different."

"No problem, sir." She tapped away at a keyboard. "Just as well, since Remy isn't working tomorrow. I'll put you down for two seats. Your companion will be Mr. Mauve. If he joins, he'll get a permanent color."

"Thank you."

"Dinner is at eight. Would you mind having your guest arrive thirty minutes early for a new-visitor discussion?"

"Thanks." He hung up. Good, Remy wouldn't be there. No guilt over passing him up and no temptation to see him again. He'd get a completely different boy, one who he would avoid forming any connection with. Maybe he'd even go for something on the special menu. Why not?

Chapter SIX

JEREMY'S WEEK was full of disappointments. Suddenly, finding instrument time was impossible, potentially putting his research behind schedule, and he didn't get any tutoring appointments. His research was now stalled, mainly because he found going to the lab frustrating. He didn't have the hours to do all the experiments he needed for his dissertation, which meant he might need to stay an extra semester or two. He needed to discuss these problems with his adviser, but Dr. Morrell had been scarce around the department, and he wasn't returning e-mails or calls. He was probably speaking at a conference; he was one of the world's foremost authorities on VLPs.

To make matters worse, Jeremy found himself thinking of Mr. Green. He was sexy in a sort of shy way, like he wasn't aware of how hot he was and didn't want anyone else to pay attention to his looks. But Jeremy could also tell he was smart. Smart enough to find the artifice of the Dinner Club a little overwhelming. The other boys poured on the sex appeal and compliments, and their gentlemen ate it up like it was foie gras.

Jeremy sensed Mr. Green wouldn't want that kind of treatment, and it wasn't Jeremy's personality to lavish unearned praise on anyone. Even for money. Though it would certainly work better for tips at the Dinner Club than it did with PharmaTek—the biotech start-up was rumored to be planning to further cut funding to the grant covering Jeremy's research. They blamed their venture capital investors. Too bad he couldn't just fawn all over the start-up and VC guys and get his grant back.

Early Sunday Jeremy headed back to the lab. Plenty of other doctoral students were there, checking on experiments or prepping others. The faculty rarely came in on weekends, so the atmosphere was relaxed and fun. Someone had the radio on so they could listen to the Giants play in Atlanta.

Jeremy put on his protective gear and set his materials up at his workstation. He carefully rinsed the cells in the petri dish; he needed to change the cell media before adding the latest sets of antigens that he wanted to test. It wasn't hard, just time consuming and somewhat tedious. Most grad students got their undergrad assistants to do this work for them, but Jeremy enjoyed the chance to let his mind wander. Once the new media was on the cells, he started adding the tiny amounts of antigen to each well of cells. They would need to incubate for several hours before he could analyze them on the flow cytometer.

He spent the rest of the day at the lab and finished two experiments. The results looked pretty good, and he was eager to analyze the data further and show them to his adviser. Another month of this kind of progress would mean he might get additional funding and have enough data to publish in one of the top journals. In this haze of semicelebration, Jeremy raced down the steps—all six floors, because the elevators were a little untrustworthy and the last thing he needed was to get stuck in one on a weekend—and out the front door of the lab building, realizing it had gotten dark while he was working.

He turned right and headed for the bike rack. There had been four other bikes when he'd arrived hours ago, and now there were two. But neither of the two were Jeremy's.

"Fucking bike thieves!" He kicked at the metal rack and pain shot up his leg and continued to radiate through his foot. Stolen bikes were one of the major issues on campus. Last thing he needed right now. He dug in his pocket for his cell phone to open the app for campus shuttles. The last one had come by five minutes earlier, and the next wasn't due for an hour. He'd just walk back home. He could use the fresh air and exercise after being cooped up in the lab all day.

He'd have to spend hours the next day with police reports, and he didn't relish the waste of time. Especially because it was his morning at the tutoring center. With the probability he'd need to buy a new bike looming over him, he wondered if a police report was worth the time. Stolen bikes were rarely recovered, and it hadn't been insured.

He wound his way through campus rather than walking along the perimeter. The paved paths were deserted, and the scent of pine trees and grass calmed his frazzled nerves. His stomach growled; he couldn't remember the last meal he'd eaten. Breakfast probably. He'd make something when he got home rather than stop at one of the tempting restaurants. Ramen or pasta or salad. That's what was in the kitchen. Not very appetizing.

By the time he arrived at his apartment—located on a quiet tree-lined street just three blocks off the northern perimeter of campus—he'd formulated a plan to get a new bike and at least one decent meal this week. He wanted to sleep on the idea before he committed himself.

By the next morning he'd decided. He called Thomas at the Dinner Club and asked if there were any open slots this week.

"Glad to hear from you, Jeremy," Thomas said as if he meant it. "I have one on Sunday and… oh, hang on. Steve can't do his shift tomorrow. Do you want to fill in for him?"

"Sure. I can make it tomorrow." He hesitated for a second, wondering if he should ask whether Mr. Green might be there, then decided against it. "Thanks, Thomas."

"No problem. Let me know if you want the Sunday shift too."

"Yeah, I'll take Sunday also. See you tomorrow." He put the phone down.

It was done. He wouldn't second-guess himself or his motives beyond needing cash. He wouldn't spend the next twenty-four hours wondering if he'd see Mr. Green again or not. But if he did… well, best not to contemplate what he'd do—or how far he'd go—if Mr. Green was dining again the following night.

Chapter SEVEN

JEREMY HAD to set out earlier to get to the city Wednesday night. Without a bike he was forced to use the campus shuttle to BART and arrived at the club's staff dressing room with barely enough time for a quick shower. Three guys from his previous shift were here: Kit, Rand, and a slim Asian guy named Law—short for Lawrence.

"Hiya, my tasty macaron, nice to see you back again." Kit gave Jeremy a European-style double kiss, though the second one landed on his mouth and not on his cheek. "Have fun last time?" he asked with innuendo dripping from each word.

"Fun enough." Jeremy grinned and gave the other boys a wave. "What's with Kit and the bakery talk?"

"Oh, he's on a diet and can't eat any of that. It's the only way he can handle the deprivation." Rand shook his head. "Anyway, glad you're back," Rand said and introduced Jeremy to the two boys he didn't already know.

"Tonight's costume theme is sailor boys." Thomas handed out costumes. They were all variations of blue and white, with caps and blue or white shorts. He had a handful of sailor scarves in different colors, but he held onto those. "Need to get the assignments first. You'll get a scarf to match your gentleman."

Jeremy went to one of the stations and slipped into his: tiny white shorts, a sleeveless white shirt with buttons down the front, and a little white cloth cap. He practiced sitting in the tight white shorts so he could find the most comfortable way and not risk pain and damage to his balls. Kit noticed and came over.

"You can let your cock hang down below the shorts, or...." He paused and cupped Jeremy's dick through the tight, thin fabric. "Or you can arrange it so it points up and over the waistband when you're hard. You're big enough for that. The little guys look better hanging down." He gave Jeremy another wholly unnecessary squeeze. "To get you started." He winked and went back to fixing his own costume.

Like last time some of the guys lubed up or played with dildoes or butt plugs before getting dressed. Jeremy again passed. He hadn't decided what would be on the menu tonight.

"Remy!" Kit came back over. "Your Mr. Green's here again tonight. He was delicious. Probably tasted as good as he looked, huh?"

Jeremy felt his cheeks warming. He shrugged. He hadn't tasted much of Mr. Green, but he'd certainly like to. "Am I serving him again?"

"Can't see the assignments yet. But usually you'll get the same gentleman unless they didn't like you. But if that happens, they generally don't schedule you at their table again. Avoids any uncomfortable situations."

Rand came in. "Thomas needs to know if you're on the menu tonight, Remy? Any extras at the dinner table this time? Kissing, hand job, blowjob, boy-on-boy play?"

Jeremy hesitated. He looked to Kit. Kit was no role model. He seemed to enjoy anything and everything. But he did enjoy working here and playing with the gentlemen and the other boys. "Yeah, okay."

Rand handed him the signup sheet. There was a list of activities and how much he would be paid for each one. He could easily get a new bike if he signed up for two or three. He checked off a few boxes and signed his name at the bottom of the sheet. He wouldn't mind kissing any of the other boys or hand jobs. And he'd certainly enjoy a hand job from Mr. Green or another toe-curling blowjob. Green might not want to play in the dining room, but if he did, it would be a win-win-win situation. Getting paid was just icing on the cake.

Thomas came in and took the scarves from Rand. "We had to switch a few boys around. Here's your assignment." He handed out the first four scarves, still holding a sky blue one and the green one as he approached Jeremy. He gave Jeremy the blue scarf.

"Hang on. I thought I'd be getting Mr. Green again."

Thomas looked at Jeremy head-on. "Sorry, Mr. Green asked for someone else tonight. I double-checked because I thought you two worked out well last time." He spoke softly, but the others could see which scarf he had been given. It was obvious what had happened. Kit looked away.

Jeremy's stomach felt like it sank through the floor and kept going. "Didn't he like me?" He whispered the question, ashamed to have his rejection so public, despite Thomas's obvious attempt to spare his feelings.

"Yes, he did. But he wanted variety. We can discuss this in private later if you want."

Jeremy blinked. Why did he take this so personally? This was supposed to just be a job for quick easy cash, not a matchmaking service. He wondered if he'd like some other man putting his hands on him. "Shit, I signed up for extras. I don't know now...."

"Mr. Sky Blue is a regular. He's nice, and he keeps his boys happy." Thomas winked.

"I like him a lot," Kit said. He came over and put a consoling arm around Jeremy. "You'll like him too." Kit cocked his head. "Despite what you may think, I *don't* like everyone."

"Jeremy, if you work here, you don't get to choose. The gentlemen choose who they want," Thomas said. "You need to understand this. But we have strict rules, and the men are all approved. Sky Blue's a regular, and if he likes you, he'll be a good client." Code for he'll tip a lot.

Jeremy nodded, reminding himself he was only here for the money. When he scheduled the job tonight, he didn't even know Mr. Green was coming. It had been a nice surprise, but now he felt the pain of a rejection he hadn't expected. "I understand. I'm sorry. I'll get used to this."

"If you don't like the system, that's understandable and you don't have to come back. Not everyone is suited to this job," Rand said, and Thomas nodded.

"We start serving in five minutes, so get yourselves ready to go," Thomas said and left the dressing room.

"I feel like an idiot," Jeremy said as he tried to tie his scarf. His hands shook. Law came over and helped him knot it.

"I'm sorry. If we could switch, I would." Law rubbed Jeremy's upper arm. He pulled at his own scarf—the green one. "But that's against the rules. Only Thomas can change assignments."

So damn many rules! But Jeremy nodded. He shouldn't take this out on Law or any of the others. He'd do this one night and then decide if he could keep coming back here and taking the luck of the draw.

Kit sprinkled a little glitter over Jeremy and gave him a peck on the cheek. "You look great. We'll have fun tonight. Don't worry."

"Servers, line up!" Thomas called, and they filed out of the dressing room. The dinner gong sounded, and they were on.

THE PROSPECT from Missouri, Red Cathcart, was excited about the dinner from the moment Brice collected him from his hotel in a taxi.

"You been here before, right?" he'd asked before he'd even shut the taxi door.

"Yes. Just once."

"What do the boys do?"

"Serve dinner and they take off a piece of clothing—"

"Yeah, I know that. What *else* do they do?"

Brice tried to hide his frown. "It depends on the boy. You'll get a menu of activities, and you choose what you want to do."

"Can you fuck 'em at dinner?" His tone was half-shocked and half-excited.

"No."

Cathcart's face showed disappointment. "No fucking?"

"Not at dinner. After dinner, if you want." Brice sighed. "You do whatever you want after dinner. I've arranged an overnight room for you." He put on a brighter smile than he felt. "Have fun. That's what tonight's all about."

"I will. I'm gonna have a great time." He clapped Brice on the shoulder and started whistling.

The taxi dropped them off, and they entered the club, where a young man wearing a white bow tie and apparently nothing else greeted them from behind a podium. "Good evening, gentlemen. I'm Paris. Welcome to the Dinner Club. Your colors?"

Brice told him. Cathcart rubbed his hands together in a disconcerting manner. "I like this color-code name thing. Mysterious. Fun."

Paris—who was in fact wearing microscopic white shorts revealing more of his impressive anatomy than they concealed—escorted them to an office off the entry hall. Brice had been here his first time for a short discussion before dinner. Thomas, the dining-room host, greeted them. He welcomed them into his office and explained the ground rules to Cathcart, then turned to Brice.

"Just wanted to double-check with you about the boys. You didn't want to have Remy serve you? Is that correct?"

Mention of the name stirred something in Brice's chest and something far lower. A bad sign. "No. Just want some variety."

"Fine. I'll keep that in mind with the seating arrangements tonight. Sometimes it can get awkward."

"Awkward? How?"

"I'll put his gentleman at the other end of the table to minimize any contact. Don't worry."

"Remy's working tonight?" Brice felt a stirring settle somewhere in the middle, in his gut. He hadn't expected Remy here tonight.

"Yes. I've got it under control." Thomas handed each of them a colored lapel pin with ribbon: a hunter green one for Brice and mauve for Cathcart.

As Brice attached his pin, he turned over his options in his mind. He could still ask for Remy after all. Should he? Before he had a chance to say anything, Paris entered and asked them to follow him to the dining room. Brice paused in the doorway, but Thomas was gone—he'd apparently left out of a back door to the office.

Brice and Cathcart sat at the table as the gong sounded. This time Brice arranged to sit next to Cathcart, with the boys in between, so he wouldn't have to watch or be watched.

As they waited, Brice wondered whether he'd made the right choice. He remembered how Remy felt sitting in his lap, feeding him, the warmth of his body through the fabric of Brice's pants. Whose lap would he be in tonight? Who would be touching him the way Brice wanted to touch him but hadn't? Was it out of prudishness or some misplaced respect for Remy?

He glanced around the table at the other men's faces. Which one of them might share his bed with Remy that night? Brice remembered how he smelled and how he'd felt cuddled up during the night. And the way he'd tasted when he'd finally decided to let Remy know what he wanted. Why did he have these thoughts about a guy who took his clothes off—and probably more—for money?

Next to him, Cathcart sipped a single-malt Scotch and grinned like he'd won the Powerball jackpot. Brice felt like a different kind of whore, bringing a client here so he could close a big deal for his firm.

The gong sounded, and Cathcart put his glass down with a *thunk*, sloshing some of the amber liquid onto the table. The men turned their attention to the door at the far end of the room.

Cathcart grabbed Brice's knee. "Oh, the boys are coming now!"

The first one entered, wearing a blue-and-white sailor suit and a dark blue scarf. Cathcart sucked in his breath. "Which one's mine?"

"He'll be wearing a scarf the color of your lapel pin."

"Oh, right."

So far Remy hadn't entered the room. He'd been last when he came in with the green armband destined for Brice. Who here would have Jeremy tonight? He didn't think it would be Cathcart, since he was Brice's guest. Thomas understood that wouldn't be very acceptable to a new member. The second boy out the door, a lithe blond, wore a mauve tie. He brushed a hand along Cathcart's shoulders as he filed past on their circuit of the room before they would sit down with their gentlemen.

"Oh, he's pretty, Brice. I like him."

Four boys had entered. So far Brice hadn't seen either his green boy or Remy. Then a slender Asian boy entered wearing green. Brice couldn't recall if he'd been there the previous week. He was as attractive as all the others, and his exotic looks made a few of the gentlemen let out a soft gasp. Last was Remy, wearing sky blue. Brice couldn't take his eyes off him, and not just because the tight sleeveless shirt or the tighter white shorts showed his anatomy to its best advantage.

Brice's gaze followed Remy around the room. As Remy was opposite him, their gazes met for a flicker of a second. Brice had to look away, but he hadn't missed the hurt he saw there. Could it be real? Or just another ploy these boys used on their clients? Brice broke the eye contact first but wished he hadn't. He watched the boys move around the room, smiling and showing off their costumes. Then the green boy sat down, and Brice couldn't keep watching Remy.

"Hi, Mr. Green. I'm Law," the Asian boy said with a sweet smile.

"Law?"

"Short for Lawrence." He grimaced, clearly not enamored with his given name.

"Hi."

Law sidled up to Brice so their thighs were pressed together. "Here's my menu." He leaned forward, picked the small leather folder from the table and handed it to Brice. "And nightcaps." He whispered the last into Brice's ear with a warm breath and a soft brush of lips against the lobe of Brice's ear. It was a sexy touch. Before Brice's brain could process the physical stimulation, Law was gone.

Cathcart's boy had gone too, to bring in the first course, and he grabbed at Brice's elbow. "Jee-sus, we don't have anything like this back home. Nothin'! My boy's called Kit." Cathcart held Kit's menu out. "Look at what he'll do. Damn, I don't think I'm gonna have time to eat."

Brice laughed. He couldn't help it, despite finding Cathcart's prurient interests somewhat disconcerting. But down at the other end of the table, Brice wondered what the man with the sky blue lapel pin was reading in Remy's menu. Last time he didn't have one, but tonight, apparently, he was prepared to do more than serve dinner. Trying to ignore those thoughts, Brice opened Law's menu.

It wasn't extensive. Hand job, blowjob, and some boy-on-boy action: kissing, hand job, blowjob, and toys. Brice hadn't planned on ordering anything during dinner, but he wouldn't completely rule it out.

As the first few courses were served, Cathcart got into the swing, removing his boy's clothes between courses. Brice left him to his own devices and chatted when the boys weren't in the room. If Cathcart's enjoyment had any correlation to his interest in investing with Brice's firm, they were set for at least the fifty million and possibly more.

Brice kept his attention on Law, who straddled his lap and fed him seafood—in keeping with the nautical theme. He avoided watching Remy, but couldn't completely ignore him since the boys made a circuit of the room with each course, slightly surprised when Cathcart asked his boy if he would go and kiss the pretty sky blue boy. Remy clearly made an impression on everyone.

REMY NEARLY stopped in his tracks when he spotted Mr. Green at one end of the table. He wore another well-tailored dark suit with a brightly colored, expensive-looking silk tie. Versace? That was probably the only designer whose work Jeremy could recognize. But it contrasted pleasantly with the somber look of the suit. Jeremy made sure not to look directly at him. He couldn't bear that. Instead he looked for his gentleman.

The man with the sky blue lapel pin had well-cut salt-and-pepper hair and a wide smile. His eyes crinkled in the corners as he gazed at Jeremy. He wore a navy suit and a tie with green and blue dots. As he moved around the room, Jeremy found Green watching him. Their gazes met for a split-second before Green glanced away. Jeremy pretended it never happened and tried to act interested as he sat down and introduced himself to Mr. Sky Blue.

Sky Blue shook his hand, then brought it up to his mouth and planted a soft kiss on the back of Jeremy's fingers. Then he turned the hand over and placed another kiss on the palm as he looked up into Jeremy's eyes. It was a look full of pleasure and lustful promises. The caresses sent pleasant tremors up his arm, and Jeremy couldn't pretend he wasn't intrigued by what this man might do next. He sat down, and Sky Blue smiled and traced a line up Jeremy's thigh from knee to crotch with gentle fingertips.

Despite the possessiveness of the gesture, Jeremy felt a thrill travel to the base of his spine, and his cock thickened and felt heavy. *Oh, damn.* If the man could do this to him with a single touch, what else would happen at dinner?

As Sky Blue traced his way back down Jeremy's thigh, he couldn't wait to find out.

At the first course, Jeremy's gentleman had him remove his shoes. At the second course, he pulled off the socks. The cap came off at the third course.

In between, Jeremy sat on Sky Blue's lap, letting the man touch him through the thin fabric of his shirt and shorts. The caresses were firm, but gentle. He unbuttoned the top button of the little shorts but didn't move to grab at Jeremy's cock. Across the way, Mr. Brown had his hand down Rand's shorts while he sucked at Rand's nipples, his shirt long ago discarded. Kit wore only his scarf and cap and socks. His gentleman was Green's guest, and he'd gone directly for the shorts and barely let go of Kit's cock since the first course.

Then it happened. An order off Jeremy's menu. Mauve wanted Jeremy and Kit to play. Sky Blue gave Jeremy permission, and the whole table watched as Kit and Jeremy moved together at Jeremy's end of the table and started kissing.

"Don't worry, I'll be gentle with you." Kit winked and gave Jeremy a very sweet, sensual kiss. The kiss deepened, and he put his arms around Kit's waist and slid one down along Kit's ass the way Kit had instructed him if he got invited to kiss. Then Sky Blue told Kit to unbutton Jeremy's shirt, and Mauve wanted Jeremy to play with Kit's cock.

Jeremy was embarrassed at first to enjoy having his new friend touch him—and more embarrassed to be stroking Kit's dick. But he soon released his inhibitions and got into the play. The gentlemen cheered and commented as they played, and Jeremy was almost impossibly hard by the time the bell sounded for the next course. Kit winked and tweaked a nipple as they pulled apart.

Sky Blue grabbed Jeremy's hand as he moved toward the door. "Don't worry. I won't make you wait too long." He slid a hand up Jeremy's thigh and stroked his balls, exposed beneath the minuscule shorts. The small touch sent additional stimulation Jeremy hardly needed, but it felt good. Too good. The tiny shorts felt like they'd shrunk another two sizes as he noticed his cock stuck out a good inch over the waistband.

Jeremy wasn't sure what Sky Blue's comment meant as he made his way back to the kitchen.

"Good job, Remy." Rand came up to him as he grabbed the plate for the next course, coconut shrimp with a spicy dipping sauce. "You and Kit were great. You feeling okay, then?"

"Yeah." Jeremy glanced at Kit, who was smiling slyly. "It was fun."

"It's supposed to be fun," Kit said and gave Jeremy's scarf a little yank. "You're a good kisser. Thanks." He winked again. Kit's cock was still hard, standing nearly straight up and bouncing with each step. He gave himself a few tugs before he reached the dining room.

Jeremy glanced over at Law, who was wearing shorts, his scarf and cap. He had dark brown nipples that looked even bigger because he had small areoles. He was only half-hard. The little white shorts didn't hide anything. Clearly Mr. Green hadn't been pawing at him.

Law rubbed himself and let out a soft sigh. "I don't think my gentleman's really into me. Remy, he's been watching you."

"He has?" Jeremy glanced down at his erection straining to escape his shorts and felt a twinge of embarrassment. Well, Mr. Green could have had him.

"Ready, boys?" Thomas called them to attention and opened the door.

Back in the dining room, Jeremy slid into Sky Blue's lap and fed him shrimp, letting the gentleman feed him a few pieces. The food at the club was unexpectedly delicious. Sky Blue tugged on the scarf and pulled Jeremy in for kiss. It was spicy and not sloppy or aggressive. He opened his mouth and enjoyed the kiss as Sky Blue pinched a nipple. His cock swelled even more, and he let out a little moan.

"Those shorts are just too small for you, aren't they?" Sky Blue asked playfully. "Time to remedy the situation. Stand up."

Jeremy backed off his lap and stood in front of him, breath catching in his throat as Sky Blue slowly popped open the buttons on his shorts and finally freed his aching cock. He yanked the shorts, and they slid down Jeremy's legs. A little cheer echoed around the room as Sky Blue moved Jeremy around so he faced the others The gentlemen always cheered or clapped when someone's shorts came off, admiring the boys' cocks, with extra cheers for impressive hard-ons.

Jeremy felt Sky Blue pulling him onto his lap, his back to Sky Blue's chest with Jeremy's legs straddling his.

Oh shit. Now what? Jeremy wondered as Sky Blue slid his hand under the shirt and across his back, then around the front and started moving down his abs. With a hand on each hip, Sky Blue pulled Jeremy tight against his body.

Chapter EIGHT

BRICE TRIED to look away, but it was impossible. Remy was the center of everyone's attention, even before his gentleman pulled his shorts off. He'd been aroused from the first course, and Brice couldn't suppress the jealousy coiling through him as Sky Blue slid his hands along Remy's skin. Brice remembered how soft that skin was.

Not that Law wasn't attractive or very touchable. He had smooth, nearly hairless skin, and the hair at his crotch was so dark it was visible even though the shorts. Brice had kissed him and stroked his chest and nipples, though it hadn't done much for either Law or Brice. But watching Remy with Kit and then with Sky Blue had Brice squirming as his pants got increasingly tight around his swelling cock.

Now he watched Remy settle back against Sky Blue's chest, legs straddling the man's thighs. Sky Blue moved his knees apart, opening Remy's legs even wider, showing his cock and balls to everyone. And everyone was watching. At least Brice wasn't the only voyeur. Law shifted on his lap, no doubt keenly aware of Brice's sudden hard-on. He slid a hand up Law's thigh so the boy wouldn't feel ignored, and Law pushed another bite of seafood into Brice's mouth. He chewed without tasting the morsel.

Remy's eyes were shut. Sky Blue wrapped one hand around Remy's thick shaft and stroked a few times, then whispered to the boy to his right who splashed some olive oil onto his palm. He returned to smooth, slow strokes. With the other hand, he cupped and squeezed Remy's sac, rolling it around, and even at the other end of the table, Brice could hear Remy's soft sighs. The sight of the pale hand sliding up and down the hard swollen flesh made Brice's breaths shorten. Then Sky Blue let go of Remy's balls and played with his nipples, causing Remy to arch into the touch. Brice remembered how they felt between his fingertips, and in his mouth, and his own nipples hardened and ached at the sight.

Then Sky Blue grabbed an ice cube and slid it up Remy's thigh, just grazing his balls and up his abs, leaving a shining wet trail before circling each nipple. Already tight and hard, Remy's nipples reacted, and his entire body shuddered at the obvious pleasure Sky Blue lavished on his body. His chest heaved, and his eyes fluttered. His sighs became gasps and precome trickled from his cockslit.

Brice licked his lips. He glanced around and saw everyone else's gaze still glued to Sky Blue and Remy. As Sky Blue stroked, Remy's balls swung back and forth, low and heavy. He sped up, then slowed down the movements, and Brice could see him whispering against Remy's ear and Remy smiling and nodding, ecstasy plain on his face even with eyes closed.

Any remnant of jealousy had long since passed, and Brice was overcome with growing desire and pleasure at the sight of Remy's enjoyment. He'd also given up any sense of shame or modesty at becoming completely aroused at the scene playing out a few feet away. Video porn had never done much for him, but watching live was completely different.

Sky Blue's strokes sped up, and Remy's balls tightened. He trembled and shuddered, and nearly everyone else sucked in their breath with anticipation. A few more slow strokes and Remy gasped before he squeezed his eyes tightly shut and the fireworks started. His lids fluttered open for a split second, and Brice realized Remy was staring at him, a glimmer of something darker than passion—shame or regret?—flickering before he shut them again and his body's reactions overpowered him.

Sky Blue watched intently as the first thick splashes hit Remy's chest—one nipple—and his chin. Then he grabbed his empty Champagne flute and angled Remy's cock so the rest of the pearly strands went into the glass.

He squeezed Remy dry, which took at least another dozen strokes. Brice wondered if he would come in his pants watching. Law wriggled again, providing friction, but Brice didn't want to cross that line in the dining room. He'd booked a room purely for show again, but now he considered the possibilities with Law. *Later*. He turned his attention back to Remy.

Remy lay limp and spent in Sky Blue's lap, leaning against his chest. He sucked in gulps of air. Another boy poured Champagne into Sky Blue's glass, mixing it with Remy's semen, and handed the glass to Sky Blue. He took a few sips, then held the glass to Remy's lips and helped him drink.

Brice wasn't sure if that was the hottest thing he'd seen tonight—or the most depraved. The consensus around the room seemed to be the former. Once the action was over and they'd gotten their fill of watching Remy, the men turned their attention back to their own boys, pinching and stroking and playing. But Brice kept watching as Remy recovered.

"YOU WANT a lap dance next course, Mr. Green?" Law offered, grinding his ass against Brice's erection. "Or we can go upstairs now if you want me to suck you off. I'd love to, but we're not supposed to do *that* in the dining room." Law slid his hands under Brice's shirt and played with his already-sensitive nipples. Law let out a little moan and leaned to suck one through the fabric of Brice's shirt.

"You are evil. Evil." Brice nearly grunted out the words and forced his overheated body back under control. He threw a quick glance at Cathcart, who only had eyes and hands for Kit. Brice pulled Law onto his lap to straddle him chest-to-chest and enjoyed the curve of Law's ass. But over Law's shoulder, he still watched Remy, whose legs gave out at the knees when he tried to stand. Sky Blue pulled him back into his lap.

When the bell sounded for the next course, Law slid sinuously down Brice's body and shook his ass at Brice before parading out of the room. Sky Blue kept Remy on his lap, fingertips caressing him and whispering into his ear. Remy's eyes remained shut. Brice wondered what the man was saying. Planning their night upstairs? Offering more pleasure or listing what he wanted when they were alone? Brice shook his head to rid his brain of the thoughts. Remy didn't belong to him, no matter how much Brice wanted him and regretted not asking for him. He wanted to be the one giving Remy such pleasure, but not in front of a room full of other men. Remy deserved more respect.

Another boy brought in Sky Blue's last course, and it was time for the fifth article of clothing to be removed. Law had returned with all the buttons already undone on his shorts, his cock harder and partially visible. It was the shorts or the hat.

What the hell, Brice decided and pulled the shorts off. Law grinned and did a little pirouette that made his cock bob and bounce. Brice reached out and wrapped his hand around it, feeling the hot flesh harden in his hand. He wasn't as long or thick as Remy, but playing with him was fun, and Brice had long since shed his inhibitions.

Across the table, Sky Blue pulled off Remy's shirt, leaving him wearing just the pale blue sailor scarf tied around his neck. Flaky white streaks covered Remy's chest, and the tails of the scarf were still damp from Remy's ejaculation. There was something possessive about Sky Blue leaving Remy wearing the colored scarf, proclaiming that this serving boy belonged to him. Remy now sat across his gentleman's lap, back facing Brice as he reached down to the table and up to feed Sky Blue.

During the last course—dessert—Remy kept his gaze down, not looking up at anyone, even his own gentleman. He did the circuit of the room but without his former charm and bright smile. Brice didn't have trouble imagining what Remy might be feeling or thinking. Even when the other boys had their final clothing removed and were completely nude for dessert service, Sky Blue kept that damn scarf on Remy.

Cathcart and Kit had left the dining room before dessert was served, and two of the other men made their boys come as part of the last course. Then the boys left as the gentlemen gave Thomas orders for nightcaps.

Even though the room's atmosphere had cooled off, remembering Remy's body responding to Sky Blue's skillful hands kept Brice hard and aching until he got his key for the night.

Room 4. Again.

Chapter NINE

WITH THE metal from the key hot in his hand, Brice left the dining room and headed for the stairs. He didn't want to wait for the damn elevator this time. He was unbearably horny, and he saw nothing wrong with taking care of it with Law. He adjusted his trousers, but his erection still made an obvious tent as he climbed the first steps.

He glanced down as he heard footsteps in the entry hall. It was Remy. He was in jeans and carrying his Cal sports bag. He was chatting to another serving boy, who only wore underwear.

"See you on Sunday, Remy!" the other boy called out and waved as Remy headed for the front door.

So he wasn't staying the night with Sky Blue? Brice moved to the next step, and it creaked, causing Remy to look up. Their gazes met, and this time it was Brice who had to look away in shame as Remy took in his arousal as he went upstairs to meet Law. Brice sped up his steps, and it was only as he put the key into the door of Room 4 that he let himself analyze Remy's expression, a mixture of disappointment and surprise.

The hypocrisy of that didn't dawn on Brice. He felt as if he'd somehow let Remy down. Even though Remy let Sky Blue jack him off for an audience, Brice spending the night with Law was somehow worse. A heavy sense of shame washed over Brice as he opened the door.

And then he saw Law, wearing the green scarf and the tiny white shorts—unbuttoned so Brice could see his cock springing out of a nest of silky black hair.

"Hey, sailor," Law said with a wink and put his cap on Brice before slamming the door shut. He wrapped himself around Brice, arms and legs twined around him so their bodies made contact in a thousand different places.

"Hey, back."

Law kissed Brice and let go, tugging him toward the full-length mirror. He slid Brice's jacket off and hung it up in the armoire. Then he came up behind Brice and reached around under his arms and slid his hands up along his chest and down his abs, just palming Brice's aching cock through the fabric of his trousers. Law started again with Brice's hands, skimming his own hands up Brice's arms, with firm pressure along his forearms, then biceps and up his shoulders. He left a path of tingling heat as he moved down Brice's neck. He pulled Brice's tie off and tossed it onto the chair.

With the same heat and contact, he shifted his attentions to Brice's back and over the shoulders, pushing Brice's arousal level to its limit. He undid the first button of Brice's shirt, then slid his palm along Brice's chest, friction across his nipples and then back to the next button. Fire burned through Brice's core, under his balls, and his ass tightened with each touch. It took Law five minutes to get Brice's shirt off, massaging and tormenting his chest and abs. All the while, Brice watched Law's hands in the mirror and saw how his cock reacted.

With the shirt off, Law reached around again and applied his magical touch to Brice's bare nipples. If he could do this with his fingers, how would his lips and tongue feel? Brice wasn't sure he could handle any more stimulation. Behind him, Law pressed his cock against Brice's ass or hip or thigh.

"Take my pants off already," he practically growled, and Law grinned behind him as their gazes met in the mirror.

"All you need to do is ask." Law winked and slid his palms down toward Brice's belt. Once Brice's pants were down, he could feel Law's erection sliding along the cleft of his ass. The front of Brice's boxer briefs had an embarrassingly large wet spot. He'd probably been dripping precome since before Remy's shorts came off.

Unable to wait, Brice yanked his own underwear off, and behind him Law continued to rub and press against Brice's naked skin, the fabric and buttons of Law's shorts scraping pleasantly as he reached around and grasped Brice's cock with both hands.

"Mmm, Mr. Green, very nice." Law slid his hands loosely up and down the length. Brice liked how Law made him feel he was huge, even though he thought his cock was pretty average, at least compared to his previous sex partners. "Please let me suck it."

How could Brice say no to that? He didn't. He just nodded, and Law slid around and onto his knees in nothing flat. He smiled and looked up from under thick, dark lashes, took Brice's cock with both hands, and brought the tip to his lips. Damn, but this boy was a tease. Just a little tongue flick into the slit, and then he pulled back. A little lick on the underside. A few more teasing tastes before a lick to the sensitive spot just under the head, and Brice's entire body shuddered.

Law positioned himself between Brice and the mirror so Brice could watch his cock slipping between Law's lips and still get a gorgeous view of Law's ass as the little shorts slid down his hips, revealing most of his bottom, probably the sexiest ass-crack ever. In front, Law's erection jutted out of the open shorts and bobbed as Law sucked away at Brice's cock.

With one hand Law pulled Brice's hand onto his head and squeezed his fingers through Law's hair. It didn't take Brice long to catch on. He gripped Law's head by the hair, firmly but gently, and took more control of the speed and depth. Law glanced up with obvious pleasure and made encouraging noises around Brice's cock. He also did some incredible things with his hands and tongue to Brice's cock, balls, and ass, keeping Brice just this side of the edge. Every time he thought he'd come, Law would ease off and prolong the pleasure. Brice watched Law's cock, planning to return the pleasure at some point later.

Before Brice even realized it had started, orgasm ripped through his entire body, starting from his balls and core and thundering up his cock till he pumped his release down Law's throat. He hadn't even asked if that was okay. But the smile on Law's face as he swallowed was all the answer Brice needed. Law kept sucking and massaging his cock.

Finally Brice pulled himself free. His dick was too sensitive for any more contact. Law was still on his knees. Brice needed a moment to recover; then he'd get to work on Law. He stepped back into a warm puddle on the carpet.

Law blinked and looked up through those silky lashes again with a sly smile. He'd already shot his load without any more stimulation than Brice's cock down his throat. That was certainly flattering.

"You took away my fun," Brice teased as he pulled Law up from his knees. He reached down and tugged at Law's cock a few times. It was half-hard and still looked very attractive hanging out of the shorts.

"You want me to keep these on?" Law put a finger through a belt loop.

How did he keep reading Brice's mind? It was spooky. But the boy was good at his job.

"Shower or bath?"

Brice would fall asleep in a tub. "Shower."

Despite Law's best efforts to turn the shower into another pleasure overload, Brice kept it short and productive. He slid under the sheets warm and dry, and Law eased in beside him. Brice curled up on his side and felt Law spoon him from behind.

The next thing Brice knew it was morning. Sun peeked through the drapes, and the clock showed eight thirty. Brice shifted his weight, and Law slid an arm around him and went straight for his cock.

"Good morning, Mr. Green." A warm squeeze emphasized the sentiments. "Do you want some *breakfast* in bed before breakfast in bed?" The question was inviting, and so was Law's warm flesh pressed against Brice's back.

"I don't—"

"Would you fuck me, please?"

No one had ever asked so politely. "What?"

"Not for a tip. I don't want the tip. But I really want your cock in me. It's just so perfect." Law slid across Brice's body and started playing with him. It didn't take long for every inch of Brice to wake up and agree with Law's plans.

Brice lay back to consider the possibility. Law shifted to give him a nice view of his ass. "Please? You can do it on the little couch, and we can both watch in the mirror." He blinked slowly, and the lush eyelashes started to work their magic along with the view of Law's ass and his active hands.

Then Brice glanced over to the little couch and he remembered Remy offering to sleep there and not fitting. Remy. Why had his face popped into Brice's mind at this particular moment? The effect was immediate—Brice's cock thickened and throbbed. Law noticed and moaned before returning his full attention to Brice's morning wood.

But Law's touch somehow backfired, and Brice felt himself softening. Law's hands did nothing for him now. Brice's brain had short-circuited his body into craving Remy and not Law.

"I knew that wasn't such a good idea. I have to get to work for a meeting. But uh—" *What am I supposed to say to him? Maybe next time? I'll call you?* Brice was such a neophyte at this stuff. "Thanks for serving me last night." God, he sounded so lame. But this wasn't a date. He didn't have to impress Law to have him again—if Brice wanted. And if he didn't, no one's feelings would get hurt.

If he wanted Law. But Brice wouldn't request him again, even though he'd provided pleasure and distraction the night before. Distraction was the key word. Brice hadn't wanted Law. He'd wanted Remy, and Law took the edge off that desire, but didn't satisfy him. Brice had hoped playing with someone else would get Remy out of his mind, but he admitted to himself no one would.

Not until he could make Remy his.

Brice hopped out of bed, used the bathroom, cleaned up, and got dressed. Law watched from the bed, lazily stroking himself as Brice dressed and left the room. As he rode home in the taxi, he thought again about Remy.

Brice had never been this obsessed about anyone before. It was ludicrous to contemplate anything beyond the physical, and Brice wouldn't have kept thinking about Remy if he hadn't seen the flash of remorse and shame in Remy's eyes when he'd looked at Brice in the dining room, sitting on Sky Blue's lap and on the verge of coming. And then there was Remy's obvious disappointment at seeing Brice heading upstairs afterward. The only reason for Remy to display those emotions would be if he had some interest in Brice beyond simply playing at dinner. At least that's how Brice rationalized what he'd seen.

Chapter TEN

JEREMY RAN toward the BART station, hoping he wouldn't miss the last train to the East Bay. Without his bike he'd be stuck in SF until the first train at around five in the morning. He could probably go back to the club and crash in the dining room or an unoccupied bedroom, but Jeremy couldn't stand the idea of walking back in there tonight.

Or possibly ever again.

He felt his cheeks flaming at the recollection he'd been the evening's main entertainment—for the gentlemen and the other boys. He wished he hadn't glanced over at Mr. Green right at that moment, right when he started coming. God, how humiliating. Jeremy wasn't sure which was worse, that he'd actually enjoyed what Sky Blue was doing to him or that Mr. Green had seen him enjoying it. For some crazy reason, Jeremy wanted Green to see him as more than a plaything for a few hours or a night.

Any chance of that was gone. Green hadn't wanted Remy to serve him, but he'd kept his gaze on Jeremy for a good part of the evening, not just as he was getting jerked off. Well, Green had requested someone else. Why did it bother Jeremy so much to think of Law with Green, touching him, pleasuring him in an upstairs room after dinner? Green had been pretty aroused watching Jeremy, and he still had an impressive hard-on as he climbed the stairs to Law.

Stop thinking about him! Jeremy practically shouted the words. He must have said something out loud because an old homeless woman ahead on the sidewalk turned around and scuttled out of his way. If he'd scared her, then he'd been acting really crazy.

Back home in his apartment, with the bedroom door locked, he finally summoned the courage to look at his tip folder. A thick wad of cash lay inside, and he pulled it out. His dinner fee would be direct deposited—the club wanted to look legit for taxes—but the tips for extras at dinner were paid in cash by the gentlemen. Jeremy pulled out a pile of crisp new twenties and his heart raced as he counted.

"…twenty-five, twenty-six… forty-nine, fifty!" He stared at the money. A thousand-dollar tip on top of the regular dinner fee. There was another envelope in there with some crumpled twenties—extra tips from the other gentlemen, two with Post-its giving their "colors" and an invitation to serve them in the future. Rand and Thomas had told him he'd done well and could expect requests from now on. Jeremy wanted to talk to Kit about handling requests, but he'd run off with Mr. Green's friend before dessert. Kit was probably getting a tip that very moment—one way or another, but probably every way and everywhere possible.

Jeremy laughed and lay back on the bed, tossing the cash into the air and watching the bills flutter down around him. He could afford a new bike now—a very nice bike—and still have money for rent. When he added in what he'd earned the first night, he was okay for at least another month even if he didn't get any tutoring work. If he worked once a week at the club, he'd never need to worry about cash while he finished his degree.

A knock at the door startled him. The doorknob turned, ineffectually. "Dude, whatcha doin' in there with the door locked?"

"I wouldn't have to lock it if you didn't try to come in!" Jeremy hopped off the bed to let his roommate in, forgetting about the cash bonanza all over the bed and floor until he turned back around.

"Jesus, Mary, and a baked potato!" Doug crashed onto the bed and handed Jeremy a beer. "What the hell did you do to get this much money? How much is it?" Doug stared at the bills as Jeremy rushed to collect them.

"About thirteen hundred." Jeremy shrugged as he stuffed them into his backpack.

"Fuck. You earned that much in a week, for serving at two dinners?"

Jeremy sucked in a breath. "No, just for tonight."

"What did you have to do for this much cash?" Doug shook his head and put his hands over his ears. "Don't tell me. I don't think I can handle the truth."

Jeremy pulled one hand away. "The guy took my clothes off, like usual. This time I kissed another serving guy and just touched him some."

"That seems like a lot of money for playing with a guy's cock." Doug stared Jeremy down.

Jeremy didn't reply, debating how much to reveal. "Then, my gentleman, uh, jerked me off while everyone else watched." He stared back at Doug, waiting for the inevitable disgust.

"Okay, then. It's still a lot of green for a hand job. Nothin' that hasn't happened before, just maybe not in public." Doug glanced up at Jeremy. "Has it? In public, I mean? Oh, sorry, none of my business."

"No. Not in public for someone else's entertainment." Jeremy paused. "It was kind of embarrassing, actually."

"Then you *earned* the money. But what was so embarrassing? Having an audience? Couldn't you get it up?" Doug grinned.

"Yeah, they liked the goods just fine, thank you. But I don't think I want to do it again."

"Really? Even for this much money?"

"Yeah. Especially for this much money. It makes it feel really wrong."

Doug settled onto the bed, and Jeremy felt grateful. He needed to talk about this, and he trusted Doug.

"Did you enjoy what he did, Jer?"

"Yeah, that's part of it. It felt good. In some ways, it's fun going there and playing with the other guys, just throwing away the usual inhibitions. No one forces you to do anything, and the gentlemen want to get you off. They seem to get their own satisfaction out of it."

"So what's the problem?"

"It kind of scares me because I liked most of it. Just seems wrong. I wouldn't tell my mother what I'm doing, and for me, that's the test."

"Do you tell your mom sometimes guys suck your dick or you put your dick up another guy's ass?" Actually, he was more of a bottom, but he wasn't having that discussion with Doug, ever.

Jeremy sat up straight and shook his head. "Of course not."

"I rest my case. You don't tell your mom everything and you shouldn't."

"I guess."

"Okay, clearly there's more to your dilemma. Just get it out." He tipped his bottle. "I need a refill. You too? Then we'll get to the meat of the problem." Doug left, then returned with two more bottles and settled back down. "Spill the beans, dude."

"Yeah, there is something else."

"Some*thing*?" Doug winked.

"Someone. Mr. Green, remember him?"

"How can I forget? You talked about him continuously for two days after the first night."

Jeremy blinked a couple of times. Had he talked about Green that much? "Well, he was there last night."

"Oh, nice. Was he the one?" Doug made a jerking-off motion and raised his eyebrows.

"No."

"And that's your problem?"

"Yeah, I felt kind of weird with him watching."

"Jer, dude, he was *watching*. If he didn't like it, he wouldn't have come back, right? I still don't get why you aren't just laughing all the way to the bank."

"He told the host he didn't want me tonight. He wanted someone else."

"You're feeling rejected? Would *he* have paid you this much?"

"No, I don't think so. But he wouldn't have jerked me off in front of everyone."

"You said he didn't do much even when you spent the night together. I'm really confused, Jeremy. I'm not sure if I need more beer, or you do." Doug broke out laughing but stopped when Jeremy didn't join in.

"I'm confused too. I felt some kind of... thing with him. Like he was above all the sex play stuff."

"Jeremy, I'm not sure what advantage there is to a guy who doesn't want to have sex with you. Did we wake up in a Victorian romance novel or something?"

Jeremy shrugged again. He was a scientist, not an English major. Words weren't his forte. "I can't explain it. Like sex is more than these games to him. I know it doesn't make sense. I-I.... Hell, I don't know." Jeremy took a few long pulls at his beer and held the bottle to his chest as he leaned back against the wall. "I'm supposed to work again on Sunday. What should I do?"

"You're asking me?" Doug shifted his position so he was sitting next to Jeremy. "Give it one more chance. If you don't enjoy it, then give up. You've gotten some money, and you had some fun. Forget about the Green guy. Decide in here—" He touched Jeremy's head. "—not here." He touched his chest. "Well, maybe there too." Doug pointed to Jeremy's dick. "Two out of three."

"Okay, two out of three." Jeremy held up his bottle, and Doug clinked his against it. Then they both drained their bottles.

Chapter ELEVEN

THE NEXT morning Brice made it to the office just before eleven. He hadn't been at his desk five minutes before Ron came in and sat down. He leaned toward the desk and peered at Brice, making him very uncomfortable. He'd checked his appearance twice before he left home, to make sure he didn't show any signs of his evening activities.

"Well, how'd it go? Or should I ask, how'd it come?" Ron let out a loud bark of a laugh and sat back in the chair. "Seriously, though, news?"

"Cathcart left dinner early, and I haven't heard from him."

"Left early? He wasn't having fun?"

"On the contrary. He was having plenty of fun. He and his server left before dessert. I imagine he'll call when he gets back to his hotel."

Ron wiped a hand across his brow dramatically. "Thank God. That club almost always works when the client asks specifically for one of the partners to take him."

"You've taken others there? To the Dinner Club?" Brice raised his eyebrows. He didn't know Ron swung both ways.

"Well, not the men-only club. They run another one with women servers, also for male clients. I take people there if they ask."

"Ah. I see. Where do you take the female clients?"

"That shit doesn't work with them. They're all business. Look, why don't you just take the rest of the day off? You look beat."

Brice sat up straight. "I do?"

"Yeah. Go home early. Unless you hear from Cathcart and he wants to go out again. I'll need you fighting fit if he does."

"Oh, please no. Don't make me take him to go-go bars in the Castro or—"

"Gay go-go bars? You have those?" Ron grinned. "He might have mentioned something about leather...."

Brice got a sinking feeling in his gut. He was *not* taking a client to a leather bar. He'd quit first.

Ron winked.

"You fuckwad." Brice picked up a Nerf ball and tossed it at Ron's head.

"Am I missing all the fun?" Watkins stepped into the doorway, the ubiquitous giant coffee cup in his hand. "What's up? Did Cathcart sign yet?"

"Not yet. He wants to visit a leather bar first. Got any suggestions?" Brice asked, giving Ron a sideways glance.

"Oh, sure. There's 440, or if he wants to go a step down—" Watkins stopped and glared at Brice, who tried not to laugh. "Fuck you, Martin. And the fucking horse you rode in on!" He spun on his heel and stomped down the hallway.

Ron was shaking his head and wiping tears out of his eyes. "Well, if Cathcart really does want leather, we know who to ask."

Brice's cell phone buzzed, indicating a new text message. He glanced at Ron, then picked up the phone. "From Cathcart."

"Go on, read it." Ron drummed his fingertips on the armrest of his chair.

"Start chillin' the champagne, boys," Brice read. "Be there by two."

"Yowsa. All right!" Ron leapt to his feet and high-fived Brice.

"Not so fast, Ron." Brice sat back down. "It could just mean he and Kit are engaged or something."

"Probably not. Cathcart is married. I thought you knew."

Brice shook his head. He felt a little sick over the whole concept of sex sealing the deal. And he didn't condone cheating, especially what he'd seen Cathcart get up to, not even considering what might have gone on in the privacy of his room.

"Yeah, I guess it doesn't surprise me."

"Not everyone's into monotony—I mean *monogamy*—like you are. But you had a good time too, I hope."

"I'm not in a relationship, Ron. If I were, then you wouldn't catch me in there."

"Then I'll have to hope if you ever find someone else, you end up with the most understanding, unjealous guy ever. Because I'm sure we'll need you in the trenches again." Ron leaned forward and punched Brice's arm playfully. "Look, I know what will cheer you up. Why don't you go over the contract again and make sure everything's shipshape before Cathcart gets here. I know legalese gets your motor racing!" Ron chuckled as he walked out of Brice's office and all the way down the hall to his own.

Brice got up and shut the door. He settled into the chair and leaned back so he could put his feet up on his desk.

Someone else. Ron hardly ever mentioned Brice's ex. He'd been with Greg since law school. Then a couple of years ago, Greg got an offer he wasn't about to refuse: partnership in his firm, but only if he transferred to their DC office. Brice had given up his own partnership-track job in a big patent law firm to join him, but the move had destroyed their relationship. Between Greg's additional job stress and Brice's inability to find a job in his field—there was nowhere near the demand for his particular type of legal expertise on the East Coast—they'd decided to call it quits. Brice moved back to Silicon Valley, but he'd lost his spot at his old firm, and starting somewhere new meant additional time to make partner. That was when Ron had made him an offer to join his VC firm. With Brice's patent expertise, he could help them avoid outsourcing certain legal tasks, and he'd come in with the promise of full senior partnership within two years.

Except for losing Greg, Brice had landed on his feet.

Losing Greg. Had he lost Greg, or had their inability to weather stress meant their relationship hadn't been very strong in the first place?

Brice had no interest in rehashing that mental debate. He pulled up the Cathcart contract and focused on work until a loud knock on the door startled him. He was surprised to discover several hours had passed.

Cathcart burst into the room, with Ron trailing behind. Cathcart flourished a bottle of pricey Champagne in each hand. "The party is here, fellas. Where do I sign?"

"That's great news!" Brice stood up and moved to the center of the room to shake hands with Cathcart, then Ron. "Assuming there are no changes to the contract, we can take care of all the paperwork right now." Brice glanced toward Ron, who shook his head.

"Terms we discussed this past week are acceptable to me, Brice. That's not what was holding back the decision…." Red Cathcart grinned. "You Silicon Valley boys know how to entertain a guest." He plopped himself onto the couch at the far end of Brice's office.

Brice leaned over to his intercom and buzzed his assistant. "Susana, can you print up a full set of the Cathcart contracts for us, please?" He moved toward the couch where Ron had also settled himself. "She'll bring the binders for your signature in about twenty minutes."

"Let's get started on these." Red thrust the bottles at Brice.

"Maybe we should wait until the business is concluded...," Brice started.

Cathcart shook his head. "No need. I'm gonna sign. You're gonna sign. We already know what's in there, right?"

Ron shrugged and nodded. "The man makes sense to me." He grabbed for a bottle, and Brice opened the cabinet where he kept a variety of glasses and two bottles of single-malt Scotch. He grabbed champagne flutes and brought them to the table. He tried not to remember the last time he'd seen one—the previous night as Sky Blue sipped at a glass of Champagne mixed with Remy's come before having Remy drink the rest.

As Ron popped the cork on the first bottle, Brice put the second one in the small refrigerator in the corner. Then he sat in the chair near the couch and waited for Ron to hand him a glass.

"To new partners!" Cathcart said as he raised his glass.

"New partners," Ron and Brice echoed, and they all sipped from the flutes.

"Once the paperwork is signed, how about we call in the rest of the senior team to share the second bottle?" Ron asked Cathcart.

"Great idea. Shoulda brought a six-pack of 'em." He grinned and drained his glass.

Brice sipped but raised an eyebrow toward Ron, who shrugged again.

"Yes, I've enjoyed my visit here. Especially last night. Thank you, Brice, for treating me to a real special evening."

"I'm glad you had a good time." Brice smiled.

"Oh, yes I did. Got myself a membership this mornin' before I left." He poured more bubbly into everyone's glasses. "Going back there again tonight. I wanted to schedule dinner with that sky blue boy who put on such a nice show last night."

Brice choked on his Champagne and started coughing so hard Ron jumped up and smacked him on the back a few times. When he'd stopped coughing, Brice took a few deep breaths to steady himself.

Cathcart hadn't noticed and kept talking. "Oh, but wouldn't you know, he's so popular he's all booked up, or so they told me. No surprise there." Cathcart made a sound so obviously sexual it had even Ron's ears turning red.

Brice wasn't sure he could speak and didn't quite know how to respond if he did. Thankfully, Susana arrived with an armful of leather-bound folders. "Here're the contracts. Thank you, Susana."

She eyed the Champagne bottle as she set the folders down on the table in front of the couch. She pulled three pens out of the inner pocket of her suit jacket and handed them to Brice. Then she turned on her heel and headed for the door again, but she directed a disdainful stare at the back of Cathcart's head.

"Wonder if she heard what I was sayin'." Cathcart laughed and emptied his glass. He didn't offer an apology in case she had.

Ron glanced over at Brice and raised his eyebrows. She'd heard all right. Brice just hoped Susana hadn't connected Brice with Cathcart's activities. He wouldn't want her to know he'd been at the Dinner Club.

"Brice?" Ron's voice cut into Brice's thoughts. "The man wants to sign."

"Yes, let's just go over a few points...."

Chapter TWELVE

JEREMY WENT to his lab Wednesday morning on autopilot. Despite the beers, he hadn't slept well. He'd put all the cash back in the folder and stuck it in a dresser drawer. He needed the money, but it still felt dirty to him. Eventually he'd deposit it in his bank account, but he wasn't ready yet to accept how he'd earned it.

His cell phone vibrated in his pocket twice before noon, but he avoided checking the messages. At the third call, he turned off the vibration. After class, he walked back to the apartment for lunch, and while he waited for toast for his tuna sandwich, he pulled the phone out. Ten texts, all from Thomas. The last one: *Call me, you idiot.*

Jeremy chuckled and dialed.

"Jeremy, where the hell have you been?"

"Working in my lab."

"Okay, fair enough."

"What's up?" Jeremy's stomach gurgled, and he didn't know if it was from hunger or something else.

"Dude, I've had ten requests for you already this morning. Can you work tonight?"

"Tonight? No. I'm scheduled for the lab every night this week."

"Well, reschedule something. Everything. You're a hot commodity, and you want to take advantage of it while it lasts."

"I don't understand." Unfortunately, Jeremy worried he understood too well.

"After last night's little performance, members are requesting you. Some of them are very keen, and they're offering bonus tips just to get on your schedule."

"Really?" Should he be flattered? That a bunch of rich guys wanted to get their hands in his pants? "Just for dinner? Or you mean nightcaps?"

"Dinner only. The nightcaps are up to you. I couldn't schedule them in advance, not legally." Thomas's voice somehow conveyed a wink, and Jeremy tried not to laugh.

"Ten?" Jeremy's curiosity bubbled in his gut. Was Green one of them? He wouldn't ask, no matter how much he wanted to.

"Yes. No. Actually four more came in while we've been on the phone. You'll need to decide who you want to serve, and when. Do you want to come by and check their profiles?"

"Profiles?"

"Yeah. Once you start getting requests, you get to choose, instead of it being random. Usually it takes longer for new boys to collect a clientele, but you're already a star."

Jeremy didn't feel like a star. He felt like a whore. What if someone at Cal found out what he was doing? Fuck. Maybe he should look at the profiles so he didn't end up serving a Cal faculty member. "Okay. I can come by this afternoon. Give me an hour and a half. My bike got stolen and—"

"I'll send a car to your apartment to pick you up. Forty minutes."

Jeremy gave Thomas his address and hung up. The toast had popped while he'd been talking, and it was cold now. He slid two more slices into the toaster and mixed mayo into a can of tuna while he was waiting. He ate, changed into a nice pair of jeans and a decent shirt, and was dragging a comb through his hair when he heard a car horn out in the street. A sleek limo waited for him at the curb. He grabbed his backpack and raced down the stairs.

THOMAS OFFERED him a drink when he arrived, and Jeremy chose coffee over alcohol. He pulled up a chair next to Thomas at the desk so he could see the monitor clearly.

"I'll scroll through the photos and give you some information about each guy. It's completely up to you how you choose. I don't care. It's important for you to feel comfortable with the clients and not feel obligated to serve anyone. If you do, then you won't enjoy it, and the gentleman won't either."

"Okay." Jeremy felt overwhelmed. Thomas had a list of twenty men requesting Jeremy, and it hadn't even been twenty-four hours since the last dinner.

The first photo showed a middle-aged man with a nice smile. He looked like he could be a high-school principal.

"That's Mr. Chamois."

"Is chamois a color?"

"Not exactly. He's a member of the Leather Couch Club, an offshoot of the main dining club."

"Leather Couch?"

"We have leather nights, BDSM-themed dinners, that sort of thing."

Jeremy knew next to nothing about BDSM. He swallowed, but it sounded more like a gulp and echoed through the office.

Thomas turned to him. "I don't suggest you select him, if you don't mind me saying."

Jeremy shook his head. "I appreciate your advice."

"Okay. I don't want to overstep here, but Chamois does like the Dom/sub and S&M aspects of the leather group. I suspect you're not interested in—or ready for—that right now."

Jeremy didn't know how to respond. "Let's see the next guy."

They scrolled through ten profiles, and sure enough, Jeremy spotted one of his old professors. He hadn't even known the man was gay, much less interested in a place like this. Such a small, perverted world.

By the end of the list, Jeremy had selected three maybes. "When do I have to decide?"

"Tomorrow at the latest for Sunday, unless you want to add any more dinners before then. I can match up your approved list with their schedules and consult you if there are two requests for the same night."

Jeremy chewed his bottom lip. "I need to check my schedule."

Thomas sat back in his chair and turned to Jeremy. "What's the problem here? You have plenty of offers, and you can't reject all of them. Not if you want to keep working here. I am running a business. I need servers who want to work and who I can rely on. I want clients to have a good time and come back. That usually is because they like a specific boy. It makes your life easy because you know who you're going to get in advance."

Jeremy nodded. What was holding him back? Had he really expected Mr. Green to be on the list? "Are those all the requests?"

Thomas shook his head and let out a loud sigh. "I'll check." He picked up the phone. "Liza, any more request for Remy? E-mail me the list." He turned to Jeremy. "A few more. Ah, here's the e-mail. Hmmm."

"What? Some good ones?"

"Yes, actually. Quite a few I think would suit you well."

"I'm sorry if I'm being picky. It's just…."

Thomas turned back to him. "I know you're new to this, and you're still adjusting to how things work here. You want to be with someone who'll treat you well. A lot of the first group to call this morning probably expect more from you than you feel comfortable with at this stage. I understand, which is why I'm helping you choose. I know each one of these men and how they've treated boys in the past."

"I'm not like Kit or Rand."

"I know. Not every gentleman wants to be with a Kit or a Rand. Some never order from the menu or take nightcaps. But others would fuck you into the table if we allowed that sort of thing."

"Isn't there another subset of dinners that do? The Roman Orgy Club?"

Thomas laughed. "They'd probably be popular with a certain set of clients. Maybe I'll consider it. Thanks for the idea."

"I don't think I'll sign up for that one." Jeremy grinned, feeling more relaxed. Thank God Thomas understood what he was thinking and didn't hold it against him.

"I wouldn't expect you to."

THE CELEBRATIONS with Cathcart included him ordering in a nice lunch from a local sushi bar for everyone in the office. Once the food had arrived, Brice slipped away from the festivities and locked himself in his office.

Cathcart had joined the Dinner Club and asked for Remy. Brice had seen how he'd treated Kit the night before—like a piece of meat—and he dreaded how Remy would feel sitting on Cathcart's lap with his hand on Remy's dick the whole meal. Sure, Sky Blue had played with Remy, and despite the exhibitionist aspects of the evening, he'd treated Remy with more respect than Cathcart had shown. He hadn't crammed his tongue down Remy's throat or dry-humped him at the table. He'd even held Remy on his lap as he recovered, and hadn't expected him to jump up and serve the next course.

Given the venue, such treatment was consideration. And Sky Blue hadn't even asked for a nightcap. Instead, he had asked if any of the other gentlemen wanted to offer Remy an additional tip.

What would Cathcart do to him?

And apparently, Remy was in high demand. Maybe Brice had misjudged him after all.

Maybe.

But he wouldn't know until he saw Remy again. He grabbed the phone and dialed the club.

"Men's Dinner Club," the woman answered.

"I'd like to make a reservation for dinner, with Remy please. This is Hunter Green."

"Hello, Mr. Green. I'll have to check Remy's schedule and call you back with his next available date. Did you want to book a spot even if he's not available? Would you accept another serving boy?"

The question gave Brice pause. He overheard Remy saying he was working on Sunday. Should Brice book Sunday, just in case? Could he deal with the possibility of being forced to watch Remy with someone else again? He didn't think he could manage that.

"No, just Remy. No one else. Let me know when he's available. I'm not interested in coming in until then."

"Yes, sir. I'll get back to you today or tomorrow." She hung up.

Brice put the phone in his pocket and kicked at the leg of his desk. How long would he have to wait? He could have had Remy the night before, but in his stupidity he'd avoided him, thinking that would preclude any possibility of an attachment. Now, Brice was worse off than before. Not only didn't he have much chance of seeing Remy again, but by the time he did, Remy would have been pawed over by a bunch of men who didn't understand there was more to him than a gorgeous body and an innocent smile.

Brice no longer thought Remy's charming naïveté an act. He wouldn't be able to prove it, but he felt certain Remy wasn't at the Dinner Club because he wanted to let a bunch of strange men take liberties with him. Maybe he needed the money, and maybe he did enjoy some of the activities, but there was something special about Remy compared to the other boys.

LIZA BUZZED Thomas while they were still looking through the second set of clients.

"Yes, Liza, thank you. I'll let him know." Thomas put the phone down. "One more to add to the list."

Jeremy didn't want more choices. He wanted fewer. He hadn't seen the one face he'd hoped to see in the second group of gentlemen. Thomas would demand he make a choice or fire him. His popularity did Thomas no good if Jeremy wouldn't accept any of the clients willing to pay extra for him.

"I'm not sure how you'll react. This guy isn't interested in anyone but you. He'll only make a reservation if he can have you."

"Is that good or bad?"

"He's the first one who's given that condition. As much as the others are dying to get paired up with you, they'll take someone else because they like coming here. That's why I don't mind if you reject most of them. I won't lose any clients. But this guy is different."

"Isn't that kind of stalkery?"

"I've seen some stalkers over the years, but I would bet this guy's no stalker." Thomas grinned, which surprised Jeremy.

"What? Who is it?"

"Your Mr. Green. Hunter Green, officially."

Jeremy sat up straight in his chair. "Mr. Green? But he...."

"Yes, I know." Thomas smiled, more to himself than to Jeremy. "Are you willing to forgive him?"

The question made Jeremy pause before answering. He'd been about to say of course, and then he took a moment to consider. If Green only wanted to see Jeremy, what did that mean? Had Green been so turned on by Jeremy's public orgasm he wanted Jeremy to himself and wouldn't be such a gentleman this time?

Jeremy also remembered Green had watched him the night before, paying him more attention than Law. He'd barely touched Law at dinner, though he'd had the chance. But he couldn't forget seeing Green walking upstairs with tented trousers. Clearly he hadn't rented a room to masturbate. He'd booked Law all night. Why did that get Jeremy's blood boiling?

Well, he wanted whatever Law had gotten. Jeremy wouldn't deny his attraction to Green, his own desire to have Green's hands on him and his hands, mouth—whatever—on Green. If they'd met in a bar or club, he wouldn't have second thoughts about fucking the guy. Why question his motives when Green clearly wanted him too?

"Put him at the top of my list." Jeremy smiled and got up.

"Do you want to serve him Sunday?"

"Yes." Hell-fucking-yes, but Jeremy wouldn't admit as much to Thomas. He grabbed his backpack.

"Hang on. I'll have the car drive you wherever you want to go. But first, what's your schedule for next week?"

"Wednesday and Saturday."

"Okay. Can I schedule these other gentlemen you approved?"

Jeremy stopped in the doorway. "Sure." He could always have Thomas or Liza reschedule those guys, depending on how Sunday went with Mr. Green.

He walked out to where the limo waited for him. He'd ask to be dropped off at his favorite bike shop to pick out a new set of wheels.

The prospect put him in an excellent mood.

Chapter THIRTEEN

BRICE HADN'T expected to hear back from the club so quickly, so he was taken aback when he heard a familiar female voice greeting him when he answered the phone as he packed up to leave the office on Wednesday.

"I've tentatively booked you with Remy for Sunday night, Mr. Green. If you can't make Sunday, he has openings on Wednesday and Saturday of next week."

Brice heart pounded. Somehow he'd managed to secure a dinner with Remy. "Y-yes. Sunday's fine. I'll take that."

"I'll put you in the schedule. I need to remind you that with special requests, we charge your account in advance."

"Oh." Shit, he didn't want this visit showing up on the corporate account. He didn't have a client to justify this visit. "Let me give you a different card to charge this time." He dug his wallet out of his pocket and read off the number on one of his personal credit cards.

"You're all set, then, sir."

"Oh, wait...."

"Yes, sir?"

"Can I book Wednesday and Saturday with Remy, too? While we're at it?"

"Three nights, sir?" She sounded like she'd swallowed a pillow.

"Yes. Charge everything to the new card."

"Yes, sir. We'll see you Sunday and Happy Dining!" She hung up.

Sunday. Brice would be with Remy on Sunday. Just four days away. He put his wallet back in his pocket and leaned back in his chair.

How the hell would he manage for the next four days?

He'd try to keep busy at work. He'd been avoiding a company review Ron wanted him to sit in on, but he decided to attend. He'd need to devote a good bit of time to read up on the company—one his firm financed but that hadn't been showing the results they'd expected. Ron had been scaling back new funds, and the outcome of this meeting would decide whether or not to completely pull the plug.

The review process would occupy him for the rest of the week. But how was Remy occupying his time? If men were lining up to reserve him, he'd probably be working every night now. Brice didn't want to think about that.

He just hoped he could call on his willpower.

BRICE SAT in the meeting, listening to the officers from LKB explain the delays. He'd pored over the binder summarizing their research and the financials from the past four quarters. They seemed no closer to a marketable product than they had a year ago at the last official review.

But the medicine they were working on was important. It would extend the lives of kids with a rare type of leukemia. The founder's son had died from the condition, and it gave him the drive to keep this from happening to other kids, as quickly as possible.

Brice's expertise was in software, though he'd gotten an introduction to pharmaceuticals during those unbearable months in DC, where he had worked for a firm representing companies dealing with the FDA. Now Christie, Parker, and Lane—CPL to those in the Valley—wanted to leverage his broad tech knowledge and experience, which is how Ron had made the case to bring him on.

After the presentation, the company officers left and Ron led a discussion among the assembled partners about the prospects for this particular investment. Most of them were negative.

Then it was Brice's turn.

"I vote to keep them in the portfolio. Maybe even increase their funding levels. It might help them overcome the setbacks that have put them behind in the research timetable."

A chorus of disapproval greeted him.

"What about all the kids this product will save? Diagnoses are on the rise, and the latest research looks very promising."

Ron shook his head. "Brice, you haven't been in enough of these to know, but they all come in with the same song-and-dance routine. They're always just one set of experiments away from the Eureka moment."

"Focus on the numbers first." Parker added. "Follow the money. How are they spending it? This company's balance sheet is too rich.

They've been buying a lot of unnecessary equipment when they should be investing in the right personnel, or funding university researchers to overcome the shortcomings in their products."

"I hadn't spotted those details," Brice admitted.

"It takes time to learn the ins and outs of each industry. We don't expect you to pick it up in only six months with us," Christie said. "Besides, you're here for your legal expertise, not your financial acumen."

Despite Christie's conciliatory tone, the remark sounded like a criticism to Brice.

"And don't let them fool you about how important the product is. They are all important, or we wouldn't be investing in them. We believe in every single product. What we need to discern is which companies will make profits for our investors." Ron smiled, maybe so Brice wouldn't feel like he'd put his foot so far into his mouth he'd be tasting it for weeks.

After the others left, Ron pulled Brice aside. "The senior partners will vote to dump this company, and for the right reasons. They all have excuses. The execs don't always tell the whole truth."

"Thanks, Ron."

Brice went back to his office and pored over the financial statements again, so he'd know what to look for next time Ron asked his opinion in an investment review.

After such a failure of a day, Sunday couldn't get here soon enough.

JEREMY'S WEEK went by slowly. He attended the two tutoring sessions he had and spent the rest of his time in the lab. Now he had a small financial cushion so he could spend more time on research instead of low-paying hourly work. He'd keep doing that as long as he worked at the Dinner Club. In the big picture, it was a small price to pay for the opportunity to further his research. He didn't even care about his dissertation and doctorate. Sure, he wanted those, but it wasn't why he spent hours in the lab.

If his research was successful, he'd be able to save the lives of millions of people.

Assuming he got the necessary results before his funding ran out. The latest news from PharmaTek said this might be the last semester, but he wasn't allowed to start looking for a new sponsor until they released him from the confidentiality restrictions. He could only discuss his project in academic circles. If he wanted to publish or speak at a conference, he had to get approval in advance.

He had plenty to write about and had produced research leading to several patents. PharmaTek seemed to have patent papers for him to sign or approve every month. With the emphasis on the paperwork, sometimes it seemed they were more interested in the patents and potential money-making opportunities than in saving lives. But this was how the research game was played between academia and technology firms, and he had to play by the rules in place. With government funding for scientific research so scarce, researchers scrambled to find companies to fund their projects.

The cuts in his funding for instrument time had slowed his progress, which led to further cuts when he couldn't keep with PharmaTek's expected timetable. How the hell could he succeed under these conditions?

It was one reason he'd broken down and taken the job at the Dinner Club. He hoped the Sunday dinner with Hunter Green would go well, and then next week he would meet two of the men on his approved list. They were both regulars, though neither had a favorite boy. If he liked one of them, he could stop worrying about money and focus on his research instead of trying to build a financial safety cushion in case his project got dropped completely by PharmaTek.

It also meant he could do volunteer shifts at the Berkeley AIDS clinic, which he'd dropped in order to take on more tutoring. It was a slippery slope of tradeoffs.

Just a few more days until he'd see Hunter Green.

Picturing the handsome face and bright smile made concentrating on work difficult, especially when his pants felt three sizes too small. Yes, Mr. Green was good-looking and sexy, and he got Jeremy's motor racing. That night they'd spent together had been so strange. He would happily have jumped into bed with the guy under other circumstances. And Green was turned on by Jeremy too. But neither of them had acted on their desires until the middle of the night, in the dark. It could have been so much more.

Sunday night would be different. Jeremy would do what he wanted. And for the first time, he wasn't ashamed to admit he wanted a lot from Mr. Hunter Green.

Chapter FOURTEEN

LATE SUNDAY afternoon the limo driver tooted the horn to let Jeremy know he had arrived.

Jeremy wasn't sure why he suddenly merited a personal driver when he could take his new bike and BART the way he had before. Maybe they didn't want him showing up with sweaty balls and bike grease on his ankles, though there were plenty of showers at the club if necessary. But he couldn't deny he liked the idea of being driven around.

Sunlight twinkled off afternoon waves on the San Francisco Bay as the limo sped across the Bay Bridge. It was a view Jeremy rarely saw. Bikes weren't allowed to cross this bridge, and BART went under the bay. He could get used to this and reminded himself not to. The Dinner Club might not work out as a permanent solution to his money troubles.

Once in San Francisco, the limo had to pick up two other boys scheduled with Jeremy: Law and Rand. Jeremy felt a momentary pang of guilt over Green not wanting Law again, then got over it as soon as Law sat next to him.

"Remy, I hear you're on the A-list now. Congrats, dude. Been busy since the other night?"

"No, this is the first dinner I've worked since then."

"What's holding you back? Didn't Thomas tell you about the booking tips?"

"Yes, but I couldn't rearrange my schedule this week."

"For that much money, I'd rearrange my face." Law made a crazy, cross-eyed face that had Jeremy laughing.

"Let's hope no one takes you up on the offer," Jeremy replied.

They were still laughing when Rand opened the door and hopped in the back with them.

"Hey Remy, Law." He knocked on the glass separating them from the driver. "Rick, how about unlocking the booze?"

"Not supposed to, Rand. You know better than to ask."

"Just one little shot each. That's all." Rand grinned as a compartment in the back of the limo clicked. He opened a small door and pulled out a bottle of single-malt and three glasses. He poured a healthy splash in each and put the bottle back. "To Remy!"

"Thanks, but I'm not sure I've done anything that merits a toast."

"Sure you have," Rand replied. "Most guys don't start getting requests right away. I hear you may already have a couple of regulars in line."

"That's great, Remy," Law sipped his whiskey.

Jeremy took a sip. "Wow, what is this stuff?" He'd never tasted anything like it. Very smooth, but smoky and dark. He reached for the door, but it was locked.

"Lagavulin," Rand replied. "Islay whisky is the smokiest. This is pretty good stuff. Not super expensive, since it's in the car and they can't keep the clients from drinking it all up."

"You know a lot about whisky?" Remy asked.

"You'll learn. The gentlemen offer it, or they might have a bottle in the room."

"I try something different every time I can," Law said. "The club only has the best stuff, things I wouldn't order myself when I go out. One of the perks of the job."

"Along with good meals and rich, clean gentlemen to wait on." Rand sighed and leaned against the dark leather seat, clearly enjoying the luxury. "Not to mention car service on nights you get a request."

"It's just for requests?"

"Yes. There's an extra booking fee. You get half, and the club gets half. They want to encourage us to get the bookings."

"So the other guys tonight aren't requests?"

"Not necessarily," Law replied. "Some clients send their drivers to get you."

"One or two," Rand countered. "That hardly ever happens."

"It happens for Kit." Law grinned, and Jeremy laughed. Apparently Kit was quite a character, infamous among the clients and the boys.

"So who requested you guys?" Jeremy asked.

Law shrugged. Rand replied, "Burnt Siena."

"How can you not know, Law?"

"I didn't ask. I don't really care. Thomas knows who's a good match for me, and I trust him. I'd sure like to get Sky Blue, though. You totally lucked out, Remy."

Jeremy nodded. He agreed. If only because Sky Blue had clearly gotten Hunter Green a little jealous. "I did, didn't I?"

The limo made a sharp turn, descended into an underground parking structure, and stopped.

"We're here," Law said. He grabbed his overnight case and opened the car door.

"Where are we?" Jeremy had never been here before.

"It's the club's private parking." He pointed to a line of parking spots along a far wall. "The men can drive here and take the inside elevator. No one sees them come in or go out. The garage entrance is through the alley. It's all very discreet."

On the ground level of the club, the boys exited and headed for the dressing room. Kit was already there, along with two other boys: Rico, a Latino guy with thick black hair and the most beautiful mouth Jeremy had ever seen, perfectly shaped lips that made Jeremy wonder what it would be like to kiss, and Taylor, who had milky-white skin and long silky blond hair. He looked about twelve to Jeremy, which probably made him popular with some of the clients.

"Hey hey, Julia!" Kit gave Jeremy a full-body hug and held on longer than was necessary or appropriate, especially since he was naked. Kit was pretty much always naked, except when he wore the skimpy little costumes.

"Why're you calling me Julia? It's really Jeremy."

"Oh, he thinks you're Julia Roberts' character in *Pretty Woman* and you landed the big fish in his fantasy version of reality." Rico grinned. "Hasn't shut up about it."

Taylor nodded, causing his fine hair to flutter and float around his face. He didn't say anything.

"I'm not Julia Roberts. I don't even know how this is going to go. It's one dinner."

"I heard you're an Only for Hunter Green," Kit replied.

"What's an 'Only'?" Jeremy asked.

"Means he'll only make a reservation if he gets you," Law explained. He dumped his case next to one of the mirrors and went over to the wall where the assignments were posted.

Green only wanted Jeremy? That certainly brightened up his mood. He picked a mirror and joined Law at the wall. "Hey, Sky Blue is gonna be here tonight!"

"Oh, this should be interesting," Kit said.

"Hey, guys, what do you do when a guy you've, uh, served before is there and you're with someone else?"

"Sure, I can see how it might be awkward, since Sky Blue jacked you off last time." Kit giggled and came up behind Jeremy and gave him another hug, while reaching around for his dick.

Jeremy swerved out of Kit's grasp. "It's not funny." He felt his cheeks heating up, which was even more embarrassing.

"It happens all the time because there are more gentlemen than boys," Rand replied. "And it's a good question, Remy. Just smile and say 'Hello, Mr. Blue' or whatever. If you're not with a regular or a request, you can give them a hug or kiss or touch their shoulder when you do the first circuit. Especially if you want to serve them again."

"Thomas is good about seating so you don't end up next to a guy who couldn't keep his hands off your junk a few days earlier." Law chuckled.

"Okay, thanks. I feel really weird about seeing Sky Blue after the other day."

"What's the theme tonight?" Rico asked when Thomas arrived.

"Public servants. Cops, firemen, paramedics." He had an armful of costumes on hangers and put them on hooks marked with each boy's name. On Jeremy's hook he put a cop outfit, and he had a female nurse's uniform for Taylor. *It would look perfect on him*, Jeremy thought. "You guys can switch around if you don't like what I've chosen for you. Tonight's colors are ties, or scarves, depending on what works best with your costume."

The boys pulled the costumes down and held them up for the others to critique. Jeremy remained a cop, and a few others swapped costumes.

Taylor was next to Jeremy. He watched as Taylor stripped down to nothing. The guy had no hair at all on his body. Either he waxed or he just didn't have any, not even on his balls. It reinforced the childlike appearance, and Jeremy thought it was a little too childlike not to be creepy. Kit came over to put some makeup on Taylor before he put on the nurse's skirt and white thigh-high stockings.

"You want me to paint anything, Jules?" Kit singsonged to Jeremy.

"I don't know. What do you think?" Jeremy watched Kit paint Taylor's nipples pink with the baker's colors. He pinked up Taylor's pale cock too, a dusting around the head to make it look appetizing to his client. He finished up with some pink on Taylor's round ass-cheeks before Taylor bent over and Kit pushed a butt plug into him with a wet pop.

"Your turn." Kit came over and made Jeremy strip down. "Hmm. Let's start with a little trim." Kit grabbed a pair of barber scissors from Jeremy's vanity and knelt between his legs.

"Not too much. I don't want to look all bald or anything." Jeremy tried not to glance in Taylor's direction and realized he was trusting Kit an awful lot down there. "And be careful."

"Don't worry. I've done this a million times." He chuckled and snip-snip-snipped a few times, making every excuse to play with Jeremy's cock at the same time.

Jeremy had to admit he looked pretty good with his pubes trimmed close to the skin. Enough to give a good view of everything, but retaining enough coverage so he didn't feel like a prepubescent boy.

"Hon, with that dick and those long balls, no one's gonna think you're a kid." Kit apparently read Jeremy's mind. He stroked Jeremy's ball sac so it swung back and forth. Jeremy hated that it felt so good. "Bend over now."

"Why?"

"See if you need a trim or anything."

Jeremy hadn't really thought much about how his ass looked, but now he was self-conscious. He bent over.

"You're good. Nice and smooth. Want some lube or a plug, or you want me to open you up with a dildo?"

Would Mr. Green like that? Jeremy didn't think so. "Not this time." He'd let Green do it, if they got that far. In the mirror he watched Rico pushing a dildo into Rand. No one had gotten dressed yet. They were all still naked as they prepped their bodies and hair. It was as if the costumes were just an afterthought. They were, to some extent, since the purpose of the evening was to get them off the boys.

"I'm with Mr. Pearl Gray. He always goes for the shorts first," Kit said, handing Jeremy a dildo. "Open me up, then push in that big plug. I need to be hard right out of the gate."

But still, there should be some playfulness and excitement surrounding the undressing. Otherwise they'd just take everything off during the first course. It should be fun for the men to peel off the layers, at least Jeremy wanted it to work like that. He noticed most men didn't take the shorts off till the boys were hard, not the other way around. The men worked to get their boy excited, then showed him off to the room.

"Take a pill, Kit," Rand said from across the room. "Pearl Gray'll probably keep him hard the whole meal and not let him come, which is no fun."

Kit shook his head. "No. One of you want to put me out of my misery?"

"What do you mean?" Jeremy asked.

"He'll ask his client if he can play with one of us, and we get him off. Then he can take a pill upstairs if necessary."

"I don't need no stinkin' pill!" Kit said. "I'm Iron-cock!"

The phrase sent everyone into peals of laughter.

"Hey, Iron-cock!" Thomas stood in the doorway. "Fifteen minutes. You better get dressed."

Jeremy pulled on tight, dark blue shorts. They were just like the white ones he'd worn last time. Button flies so they could be unbuttoned slowly, and not as dangerous as zippers against bare cocks. He figured out how to arrange his balls, then put on the shirt. It was a button-up in a cotton/Lycra blend so it hugged his body like it was painted on. Good thing he went to the gym. He wrapped the belt around his waist, noticing a pair of handcuffs, and in place of a nightstick, a large black dildo swung from a hook. Vials of lube were placed in the bullet holders. He tied a green tie around his neck and put on a shiny silver sheriff's badge and a hat. Last, he slipped his feet into a pair of black boots that were loose enough to be comfortable without socks.

The gong sounded.

Chapter FIFTEEN

BRICE MADE awkward small talk with the other men at the table and sipped a glass of bourbon. He recognized the Sky Blue man from the previous visit and recalled how he'd felt watching him with Remy. He certainly didn't want to see that again. At least tonight Remy would be on his lap.

At the mere thought, Brice became aroused. Startled by his strong response, he gulped more bourbon to steady himself. Not too much, though, or he risked dulling his senses. He was here to indulge them—all of them. Sight, taste, sound, smell, and especially touch. He intended to experience Remy with all of them.

By the time the gong sounded, Brice's nerves were raw. He couldn't recall the last time he'd been so anxious about seeing someone. Not even on those first dates with Greg. What was wrong with him?

Then the door opened and the boys streamed in. A hunky Latino fireman led the group, followed by cops, a paramedic, a nurse, and Remy, wearing some semblance of a police uniform with a green tie. Brice smiled. Remy was here, wearing his color tonight. He flashed Brice that familiar nervous smile as the boys made their first circuit of the room.

"Hello, Mr. Green," Remy said in a whispery voice against Brice's ear. Then he swept a hand across Brice's back and continued around the room. The warmth of the touch, the pressure of Remy's fingers against his back, and Brice's pulse raced and his throat tightened. He noted that Remy kept his gaze locked on Brice as he moved around the room toward the door again, then shifted briefly to Sky Blue. Remy gave his past client a friendly smile and a wave. Law put a hand out and squeezed Brice's shoulder as he went past, which made seeing Remy's greeting more tolerable.

Less than five minutes later, Remy returned with the first course of shrimp cocktail. Large pink prawns were arranged around a bowl of cocktail sauce. Tonight's meal was old-fashioned steak-house fare, featuring food from Harris', the top steak house in the city.

Remy put the plate down and settled on the bench next to Brice. "How are you tonight, Mr. Green?"

Their thighs touched, and Brice looked down at Remy's leg, the thick cyclist's thigh against his, and found himself tongue-tied. "Good."

"I hope you're hungry." Brice couldn't take his eyes off Remy's lips as he spoke. He nodded, and Remy smiled. "Do you like it hot?"

"What?" Brice's brain had turned off, but his body was overheating. "Hot?"

"The cocktail sauce? Mild, spicy, or extra hot?"

Brice gulped as he watched Remy's lips form the word "cock." "Medium hot, I guess. We can always add more."

"Right." Remy grinned and splashed some hot sauce into the cocktail sauce. He dipped a finger in and brought it up to Brice's mouth. "Hot enough?"

Brice sucked sauce off Remy's finger and fought the urge to keep sucking. His cock was already swelling. How could Remy get him this damn excited so quickly? "Mmm. Good, but maybe a little hotter." Brice hoped it came out sounding playful and not as needy as he felt at the moment.

"Hotter." Remy practically purred the word, then nodded and splashed more hot sauce in and repeated the finger tasting. This time he tickled the roof of Brice's mouth, and Brice laughed.

"Perfect." He grabbed Remy's hand and sucked the finger a few seconds longer before releasing it.

Remy gave him that charming little smile and plunged a shrimp into the sauce before bringing it to Brice's lips. He held it over the palm of the other hand so as not to drip onto Brice's clothing. Brice opened and took a bite from the shrimp. Remy put more sauce on and fed Brice the last portion.

"Do you want another drink, sir?" Remy asked.

"What do you like to drink?"

"Vodka martinis."

"Order one. We can share it."

"Okay." Remy waved the barman over, and Brice let him choose the vodka. "Belvedere."

When the drink was ready, Brice handed it to Remy. He liked the way Remy's lips looked pressed against the glass. He couldn't wait for them to be pressed against him—his lips, his body, his—

Another shrimp headed in his direction. "You have this one," Brice said.

Remy took a bite and dipped more sauce, getting some on his fingers. As he brought his hand up, Brice moved it toward his own mouth and took the shrimp and Remy's fingers inside, licking off the spicy coating.

"Hey, not fair. You said it was mine," Remy teased.

They shared more shrimp. Feeling particularly uninhibited, Brice put the very last piece between his teeth and let Remy bite it away, but he didn't take the opportunity to kiss him. The brush of Remy's lips against his sent fire throughout Brice's body. He thought his cock might tear through his pants if he actually kissed Remy.

Remy stood up. "Time to take something off. Did you want to or—"

Brice took hold of Remy's tie and pulled him between his knees. He noticed Remy's smile widen. He loosened the tie a little and then started undoing Remy's shirt, one button at a time, slowly, prolonging the contact. Then he pulled the tails out of Remy's shorts—damn, those shorts were so small, and Brice saw the distinct outline of Remy's erection beneath the thin fabric. There would be plenty of time for that, he reminded himself and peeled the shirt back off Remy's sinewy shoulders.

He felt and saw Remy's intake of breath as Brice yanked the shirt the rest of the way off him. His nipples budded tight. He guessed they kept the temperature in the dining room a bit low because there was so much body heat and because the cool air made the boys' nipples look so pretty. Brice pulled Remy closer by the tie and flicked the tip of his tongue over one nipple, then pulled it into his mouth. Remy's hands went to Brice's head, tangling in his hair.

Then the gong sounded, and the boys left to bring the next course.

IN THE kitchen Kit came up to Jeremy. "Damn you learn fast. I'm going to remember your hot-sauce line." He smacked Jeremy's ass.

Jeremy realized he hadn't even noticed any of the other boys or their gentlemen during the whole shrimp course. He'd only had eyes for Mr. Green. It had been fun realizing how nervous he was at first. Jeremy felt exactly the same way. Like it was a first date and neither of them knew what to say or do after they'd cleared the hurdle of expressing interest in the other.

But thankfully, the food gave Jeremy an opportunity to play. And Mr. Green loosened up and became playful too. When Mr. Green sucked on his fingers, Jeremy got so hard he thought he'd pop some buttons on his shorts. Yes, he'd put his fingers in Mr. Green's mouth, but he hadn't anticipated the surge of arousal Mr. Green's tongue had produced. Then the little trick with the shrimp between his teeth. But Green hadn't taken the kiss, which had Jeremy even more aroused. He liked the game.

"I didn't expect your guy to go for the shirt first," Rand said as he grabbed a plate of salad. "Very interesting choice. But hot. You look good in just the tie with the dildo swinging off your belt."

"I thought I was gonna come when he sucked your nipple," Kit added. "Fuck me, that was hot!"

A chorus of approval from the rest of the boys echoed Kit's sentiments. Jeremy wondered why he was the center of attention. Had they all been watching him?

"How's Mr. Gray, Kit?" Rico asked. "You're still wearing your shorts."

"Barely," Kit replied. He'd removed his shoes, but all the buttons of his shorts had been undone and his dick stood out in front of him. Law tossed a ring of onion from his salad at Kit's erection and even though he missed, everyone laughed. "He had his hand in there pulling at me the whole time, and I'm ready to explode here."

"You wanna get off this round?" Taylor asked. "Salad is boring; they usually want some games before the main course."

"Yeah. I don't think I can last all the way past steak." Kit shook his head. "Any volunteers?"

All the others raised their hands. Jeremy felt guilty he didn't offer.

"That's okay, Jules," Kit said. "You play with your client. I wouldn't ask anyone with a request anyway. Focus on him unless he wants you to play with us. But I don't think Mr. Green wants anyone else's hands or mouth on you!" He winked.

Jeremy felt a little thrill the way he and Mr. Green were getting on so well. Not that they'd spoken much. Salad *was* boring. There would be time to chat then, before the steak, when they'd be chewing a lot. Odd how the courses seemed to dictate the interactions.

As he entered the room with the salad, he felt his chest—and his dick—swell with pride. Mr. Green's gaze bathed him in a heated glow. He set the plate down and sat beside Green.

Green's thigh next to his was hot, but now he was seated, the room's chill hit him, and Jeremy felt his nipples peaking and tingling. They throbbed in time with his cock at every beat of his heart.

"Salad? Caesar." Jeremy presented the bowl with a flourish and placed it on the table. "Or you can have just a green salad."

"No thanks."

"Another drink?"

"Okay."

Jeremy motioned to the bartender who came right over.

"Another Belvedere martini, please." Green didn't even look at the bartender. He kept staring at Jeremy.

"Yes, sir."

"There's no anchovies in the dressing, in case—"

"Come here." Green took one of Jeremy's hands and pulled him onto his lap, facing Green, thighs pressed outside of Green's.

"Today you're not wearing a tie, and I am." Jeremy couldn't think what to say or do. Too much of his body was in contact with Mr. Green. And his cock was nearly pressed to Green's abs, while Jeremy could feel Green's hard-on against his ass. He put a hand out to play with Mr. Green's collar. He wore a pale green button-down oxford and putty-colored chinos. Despite the casual attire, he didn't look particularly relaxed. He looked like the kind of man who belonged in a suit with a beautiful silk tie around his throat.

"I wear them all the time, but you look *very* good in a tie, Remy."

"Don't you like ties?"

"Yes. I do. And I like suits, too."

"You're very handsome in a suit. Out of one too." Jeremy felt his cheeks heating. "I meant.... Oh, hell. Yeah, I meant that too."

"Would you unbutton my shirt, Remy?"

Jeremy was glad for something to do, a task to occupy his hands, though he noticed them shaking as he worked on the first button. He smoothed his palms across Mr. Green's shoulders, squeezing just a little. He felt firm and solid. He felt damn good.

Jeremy got three buttons opened and traced his fingertips down Mr. Green's breastbone, then back up along his collarbone. He felt him shudder under the touch. It was nice, having that effect on him. It balanced everything out because, until now, Green's touch, his scent, even his words had Jeremy so on edge he wondered how they would get through five more courses. Now he understood why some men took their boys upstairs before the end of the meal. Would Mr. Green suggest that? And would Jeremy go?

Movement at the other end of the table caught his attention. Green shifted him so they were back to front, and they watched as Kit stood up. Rico's client said something to him, and Rico walked up to Kit and pulled Kit in for a kiss.

"So much better than salad," someone said.

Jeremy glanced across the table to see Taylor sitting on his client's lap. The man had a hand under Taylor's nurse's skirt, exposing his thighs and the lacy white garters holding up sheer white stockings. A nurse's cap atop Taylor's flowing hair completed the illusion. Add in the pink lipstick and he looked so much like a young woman. Then the client's hand slid higher and Jeremy could see Taylor's cock. The client stroked it up and down. No doubt Taylor was a guy from this angle. To Jeremy's surprise, Taylor's cock was huge. Thick and long, with a very pink head where Kit had painted him. But the shaft was dark and hard, in stark contrast to his pale thighs and the white stockings.

Taylor glanced up at Jeremy and smiled, and Jeremy glanced away, embarrassed to be caught watching the client's hand on Taylor's dick. His *enormous* dick. Certainly no one would think he was a girl with a big red hard-on.

Sounds from the other end of the room captured Jeremy's attention again. Now Rico was on his knees with Kit's cock in his mouth. Rico slid his mouth off, giving everyone a nice view of Kit's wet cock before he slurped it back in. The rest of the men in the room were enthralled by the sight.

Jeremy sat on Mr. Green's lap, watching the boys play. Mr. Green traced circles around Jeremy's navel with a fingertip and occasionally reached up to pinch or tug at a nipple. The little blue shorts felt like they would explode or cut off Jeremy's circulation. He almost asked for Mr. Green to take them off, or at least unbutton them, but he didn't. He'd been playful and a little slutty already. He didn't want to overdo it so early.

On display, Rico worked on Kit's cock, sucking at it, skillfully moving on and off it to give the men a show. He made a lot of noise, and so did Kit. Then Law moved behind Kit, squeezing his ass and pressing up close so he could reach around to play with Kit's nipples. Kit made more noise. Next Law and Rico played a kissing game that included sharing Kit's cock. Then Rico got up and pulled something from Kit's set of toys on the sideboard. He held it up behind Kit to show everyone it was a medium-size red dildo. He reminded Jeremy of a magician holding up his props before the trick.

Rico got down on his knees behind Kit and, with as much flair as possible, pushed the dildo in. Kit's eyes popped open, and he made lots more noise.

"Now we're talking!" he said and leaned forward, shifting his position so the men could see what Rico was doing but still watch Law sucking him.

Then Taylor got into the game. Kit wrapped his arms around Taylor's waist and took his huge cock into his mouth. This thrilled the gentlemen, except for Mr. Green, who tugged on Jeremy's tie and kissed his shoulder while playing his hands along Jeremy's thighs, too close but too far from his ever-expanding cock. Now it stood up over the waistband of his shorts and the top button popped open on its own.

"Mmm, telepathy works," Green whispered against Jeremy's ear.

Jeremy chuckled and gently ground his ass against Mr. Green's cock.

At the other end of the room, the party went on, Kit sucking Taylor while being sucked by Law. Behind him, Rico was using the dildo until suddenly Law pulled back and Kit spurted all over his chest and costume. The men—except for Gray and Green—clapped and shouted. Gray did not look happy his boy shot his load all over another boy.

Green nudged Jeremy off his lap. "I think it's time to put your shorts out of their misery, don't you think?"

"Oh, yes, sir."

Green had Jeremy stand slightly to the side so the others at the table could watch as he popped each button slowly, allowing Jeremy's cock to spring free with a bounce that got some applause. He shifted his weight and cocked his hip just right so the shorts slid down on their own. Kit had taught him how, and he'd had to practice, but the gentlemen loved it. Now he wore just the hat, tie, cop's utility belt, and black boots.

Mr. Green curled one hand loosely around Jeremy's cock as if admiring its shape and hardness before sliding his hand lower and playing with Jeremy's sac. He pulled Jeremy between his legs and stared down at Jeremy's cock as if he wanted to taste the tiny clear bead of precome glistening in the slit. Green moved his head a fraction of an inch lower.

And the gong sounded, ending the course.

Green gave Jeremy a wistful glance as he picked up the untouched salad and paraded around the room, his cock and balls swinging.

IN THE hall outside the kitchen, Thomas gave Kit a sharp look. "Mr. Gray isn't very happy."

"It wasn't on purpose…. Blame Law." Kit batted his eyelashes.

Thomas smacked Kit's ass so hard he left a handprint, but Kit just grinned.

"Remy, I guess I don't need to ask if you're doing okay with Mr. Green," Thomas said as he eyed Jeremy's erection. "Think you'll make it to dessert?" The other boys laughed along with Thomas.

Jeremy shrugged but secretly he hoped he wouldn't have to.

A THRILL zinged through Brice's entire body as Remy came back in with the steak. He looked even more delicious than the main course as he made his way around the room, cock still at attention and the black dildo on his belt swinging back and forth. He barely noticed the other boys and suspected some of the other men had their gaze on Remy. At least for tonight, Remy was all his.

The question was what to do with him. Or to him. And when.

Remy sat down on the bench next to Brice and cut a few bites of steak. "Is this to your liking? Medium rare?" He fed a bite to Brice.

"Delicious." It was. He'd never expected much from the food here, but it was always top notch. The plate held a steak large enough for both of them, plus several roasted vegetables and crispy potato wedges.

"This course is two pieces of clothing, sir. If you like, you can take them off me now."

"Good idea. Come here."

Remy stood in front of him while Brice decided what to remove. "Okay, the boots can go."

Remy sat on his lap and Brice slid a hand down each leg, unzipped the boots, and tossed each away. What next? The tie looked so damn hot on him, pointing down to his cock. And the utility belt just perched on his hips was pretty hot too. And the hat. *Mmmm.* Brice pictured Remy wearing the hat and nothing else.

"You don't have to decide right away." Remy grinned.

"Yes. How about some more steak?"

Remy fed him more dinner, and they took a break with Remy straddling Brice's lap, facing him. He unbuttoned the rest of Brice's buttons, and now his cock pressed against Brice's torso, a clear, thin line of precome trailing from the end of his cock onto Brice's stomach.

Up close Remy wasn't as young as Brice had thought. Midtwenties, maybe a bit older. He was in good shape. Brice slid his palms along those thick thighs.

"You cycle a lot?"

"Yeah."

"The thighs give it away."

"No secrets when you're naked, huh?"

"None." Brice sucked in a breath and reached down for Remy's cock. Then Remy sucked in a breath. "I like how you touch me, sir."

"Is that your way of telling me I should keep going?"

"If you like."

"I would like. What would you like?" Brice took another firm stroke and felt Remy's body tense. His nipples were hard, swollen. Just inches from Brice's mouth. He leaned forward and flicked his tongue against one.

Remy gave a soft moan.

"Please keep going."

Brice grinned. Remy's eyes were half-closed.

"This won't be a show for everyone. Just for me, okay?"

"Oh, yes. Just for you."

Brice slid Remy back a few inches so he had room to move and to look. With one hand he worked Remy's cock, and with the other he loosened the tie a little, then traced along Remy's shoulder and collarbone.

"This belt keeps getting in the way. I'm going to remove it."

"Yes," Remy said.

But Brice couldn't unfasten it, and Remy helped, his hands over Brice's. Long slim fingers, heated touch. Brice couldn't wait for the end of the meal. Once the belt was unclipped, he laid it down on the bench next to him and went back to Remy's neglected cock.

He slid his hand slowly as he leaned in to taste the other nipple. He pulled this one into his mouth and sucked hard, shocked it could swell even further. Remy made soft little moans as he reached out and put his hands on Brice's shoulders to steady himself. Brice could tell he was in the pleasurable zone where his brain was no longer in control and his body simply reacted to stimuli.

Brice scraped his teeth gently as he pulled back on the nipple, and Remy let out a beautiful moan that ended on a needy whimper. Remy slid his hands inside the collar of Brice's shirt and along his shoulders before working them into his hair and holding on, keeping Brice's mouth on the nipple. Brice was happy there as he slowly stroked and pulled at Remy's hard cock. He worked on the other nipple for a while, feeling Remy's heartbeat accelerating.

He leaned back to gaze at Remy's cock, dripping and swollen in his hands. He used both of them now, still moving slowly and exploring the new terrain. He loved the sound of Remy's raspy breaths and the little catch in his throat when Brice stroked a certain spot near the base of his erection. The flesh was hard and hot, and he sensed Remy was close. Should he make the boy ask for this? Or should he give Remy the final push into bliss?

Carefully Brice leaned down far enough to swipe the tip of his tongue across the slit and collect the salty drops. Remy's fingers tightened in his hair. Had anyone seen him? Was this allowed? Did it matter? As another tremor traveled through Remy's body, Brice leaned down once again and took the entire head of Remy's cock into his mouth.

He heard the gasp a fraction of a second before his mouth was filled with hot, salty proof he'd made the right decision. He pulled off and let Remy spurt on both their chests. Brice enjoyed a money shot as well as the next guy, and he liked the way Remy's come looked dripping down his chest. He fought the urge to lick it off. He hadn't swallowed yet and considered leaning up to kiss Remy, letting him have a taste.

No. He wanted their first kiss to be different. It would be special, not here and not like this. He felt some sense of embarrassment he'd sucked Remy off before he'd ever kissed him.

Brice swallowed and held Remy as he came down from his high, clutching at Brice's hair, knees tensing against Brice's legs. Brice slid his hand around Remy's waist to support him.

"You okay?"

"Yeah." Remy was grinning, eyes still closed. "Oh yeah."

Brice leaned both of them toward the table and grabbed the martini glass. "Here, have a sip."

Remy let Brice help him drink. "Thank you."

"More?"

"No. That's not what the thank you was for."

Brice looked away. Not that Remy could see the expression on his face. He glanced around to see what the others were doing, and they were all focused on their boys or their meals, or both. That was just the first of many meals he'd enjoy here, Brice thought. He wouldn't share that decision with Remy either. He didn't even know if Remy wanted to spend the night with him.

"Do you want more to eat, Remy?"

"Oh, that's my job." Remy rotated toward the table, and Brice eased his arms away. Remy fed them both a few bites of food.

A flash of white caught Brice's attention. It was the blond boy's skirt. He glanced over Remy's shoulder to see what the man across the table was doing. The boy was standing up on the bench, one foot on either side of the man's thighs and facing away from Brice. The white skirt was hiked up, and the man was squeezing the pale ass as the boy fucked the man's mouth. Brice hadn't seen anything like this so far. It made his quick taste of Remy's cock seem tame. A few other men were watching.

Every few strokes the blond boy turned around to smile at the others. When he finally came, everyone around the table heard. Possibly even people in the building across the street. He pulled away from the man and spurted all over his shirt and trousers. The man pulled him back close and loudly sucked at his cock for a few minutes.

A tug at Brice's elbow caught him off guard. He turned to see the man to his right. "You gonna do anything with that dildo?" He pointed to the cop's belt that lay on the bench between them.

"Why?"

"How about if my boy Kit here fucks your pretty boy with the dildo?"

"How does that sound, Remy?" Brice asked.

"Would you like to see that, sir?" Remy asked. His lips were full, and the bottom one swollen. He'd bitten or bruised it during his orgasm. He looked so young again.

"Not particularly. At least not right now," Brice replied to Remy, then he turned to the other man. "Not now. But we'll keep this. We might still use it later."

"Okay." The man smiled. He didn't seem offended that Brice and Remy turned him down.

"Sir, what can I do for you now?" Remy slid a palm down Brice's bare chest, and Brice's cock ached and throbbed. It was against the rules for the gentlemen's cocks to be visible in the dining room, but there were plenty of ways for the boys to get the job done.

Brice did not want to wait another hour until after dinner, so he nodded. "Anything you want."

Remy nodded and went to work. He licked and kissed his way around Brice's chest, repaying the treatment he'd gotten on his nipples until he had Brice squirming. At the same time, he unbuckled and unzipped Brice's trousers. Brice was already so close, and the nipple play had him near the edge. Then Remy slid a hand into Brice's pants and stroked the underside of his cock through his boxer briefs. It was a good thing, because Remy's hand directly on his cock would have been the end.

Remy leaned toward the table, grabbed a spare cloth dinner napkin, and spread it over Brice's lap. He repositioned himself, back to Brice's chest, and slid along Brice's lap until his cock fit in the groove of Remy's ass. Remy settled down and began a smooth back-and-forth motion along the length of Brice's cock. Up, a little wiggle, then down, up, a little wiggle, then down. It wasn't perfect and it wasn't skin-on-skin, but the pressure and the sight of Remy's ass sliding along his lap got Brice just to the edge. He grabbed onto Remy's hips to control his movements and thought about how good his cock had tasted and how hot and tight Remy's ass would be later if he got the chance to fuck him.

That image was all it took. Brice held Remy against his lap and came, leaving a hot, sticky blob in his shorts. He couldn't remember the last time he'd come in his pants, but it probably hadn't been as much fun—or quite as frustrating—as this.

Remy turned around and peeked under the napkin and planted a soft kiss on Brice's cock through his damp shorts before trying to blot away some of the mess. Brice cursed himself for not wearing dark pants. The spot would show through once he fastened his pants again.

"They have dry cleaning here," Remy whispered, clearly reading his mind, before zipping and buckling everything back up.

Brice would have been happy to leave his pants undone for the rest of the meal and was about to ask Remy to unzip him when the bell sounded. The main course was finished. And so was Brice.

"WOW, KIT, the napkin thing worked. I didn't expect it to, but it did."

"Remy, you are on fire tonight!" Kit pinched Remy's ass. "I have plenty more things to teach you. Just you wait."

Dessert flew by. Jeremy settled his policeman's cap on Mr. Green's head and fed him cheesecake. Then during the last course, after-dinner drinks, he sipped the smoothest brandy he'd ever had while Mr. Green slid the tie from his neck. Jeremy barely paid attention to anyone else.

"Thank you, Remy," Mr. Green said as the last course ended. The words sounded so final, and Jeremy wondered whether he'd been too complacent thinking he'd be invited for the night. His stomach was in knots as the boys all stood for the last parade around the room, this time all naked. They'd all come during tonight's dinner and were at least half-hard again now, the stirrings of interest in a second round that should encourage the gentlemen to stay for more.

Back in the dressing room, Jeremy paced.

"What's wrong, sweetie?" Kit asked.

"I did something wrong, but I don't know what."

"Why do you think that?" Taylor asked.

"He thanked me, like I wouldn't be seeing him later," Jeremy said. He wasn't sure if he'd been too slutty or not slutty enough. "I don't know if I acted like he wanted."

"Remy, one thing to remember is that you only go so far to please them, but never past the point where you please yourself," Law said.

"What does that mean?" Jeremy's brain wasn't working at full capacity.

"Do you want to spend the night with him to make him happy or for yourself? And if you didn't do what he wanted, do you still want to try? You did what you wanted tonight, right?"

"I guess. Yeah. I had fun. I did what felt good," Jeremy replied. He hadn't been thinking about it at all, just being and doing, enjoying Mr. Green's company and attention.

"That's good. Do what you like, and if they ask for something, you can always say no," Taylor said. "They can say no, too. If he didn't, then he loved it."

Thomas came in a few moments later. "Call backs, boys! Kit, Mr. Gray isn't interested, but Mr. Brown is. Sorry, Rico."

"No problema, Tomas." Rico grinned. "I think he was wondering which end of the dildo he was going to be."

Everyone laughed.

"Taylor, you're on. Remy?"

"Yeah?"

"You have two choices: Green or Sky Blue."

"Sky Blue?" the boys chorused.

"He *never* stays over," Law said. "You really made an impression on him."

"Sorry." Jeremy shrugged at Law. He hadn't intended to have Law's gentleman paying attention to him. Again.

"No sweat, dude," Law said. "There's more where he came from. I wasn't up for anything tonight anyway."

"So, Remy, who do you want? Sky Blue offered double the usual. Or you can have both. Each for half the night."

"You do that?" Jeremy wasn't interested, and frankly the idea of hopping from one man's bed to another's horrified him.

"Sure. In some cases, two will share a boy in the same room. We have all sorts of options."

"I'll just take one. Green." Jeremy couldn't imagine how it would be to have one guy watching him with the other one and maybe taking turns. That wasn't *his* fantasy, no matter how much it paid.

"Okay." Thomas gave the boys their instructions, and Jeremy grabbed his duffel and headed upstairs.

They were in Room 4 again.

Chapter SIXTEEN

BRICE PULLED his hand away from the key when he realized he had been assigned Room 4 yet again. His original memories of the night with Remy there had been overshadowed after spending the night with Law. Of Law's body and mouth on him. Brice liked what Law had done to him. He hadn't felt any guilt at the time.

But now, spending the night with Remy in the same room felt wrong. He wanted something entirely different for him. At least he thought he did. Dinner had been nonstop arousal until they'd gotten each other off during the main course. Remy had pushed all of Brice's hot buttons. It had been fantastic, but now he wondered just how inexperienced the guy really was. The thing with the napkin trick couldn't be a beginner move. He'd known exactly what he was doing and how Brice would respond.

That's how whores worked, Brice reminded himself. Why had he ever thought Remy was more? Brice was willing to pay for attention and pleasure, and that's what he'd gotten so far. Everyone was happy, right? Why did it disappoint him so much?

He took the elevator upstairs, slowly opened the cage at the top, and then moved down the hall. He could still go home. Would it be better to waste the money he'd spent for staying the night, or to have his illusions shattered about who Remy really was? He stopped and turned back toward the elevator. He was inside and about to push the button for the ground floor when he stepped out again.

Until he experienced the disappointment he expected, he would always wonder about Remy. Best to go in, get it over with, and then be done with this place for good. He didn't want to be lured here again. He felt like Dorothy in *The Wizard of Oz*. She believed right up until she looked behind the curtain.

Brice had to look behind the curtain.

He unlocked Room 4 with an ache in the pit of his stomach.

"Mr. Green." Remy stepped out of the bathroom. He looked up at Brice as if unsure how to act, now they were alone.

Brice felt the same way. He reached a hand out for Remy's, and Remy stepped close enough for Brice to embrace him. He wanted to kiss Remy so badly, but now wasn't right. Not yet.

"Shouldn't we discuss....?" Brice stopped, unsure how to continue.

"Discuss what? You mean condoms?"

"No. Well, yes, but I meant...." Brice pulled back a few inches, reluctantly. "Uh, money?" God how he hated bringing up that topic. When Remy let go and leaned away, Brice wished he hadn't. He didn't know how this worked.

"I don't want your money. I didn't come up here with you for money." Remy's eyes darkened, and he drew his eyebrows together slightly.

"Isn't this your job?" Shit, why did he keep throwing gasoline on the fire?

Now the hurt was evident in Remy's expression. "No. Serving dinner and taking off my clothes is the job. Anything else I do beyond that is my choice. For me, at least, money has nothing to do with it."

"Then why did you come up? With me?" Asking might ruin everything, but Brice needed to know. He could easily leave, walk away from Remy and this place forever—but he didn't particularly want to. "This time I'm not staying just to save face with a coworker."

"I want to spend the night with you, even if we do just the same as last time. I like how you touch me, how you make me feel, and I'd like to reciprocate." He looked away from Brice for a moment, then looked directly into his eyes. "I don't know what you're expecting."

Brice stared at Remy, standing in his sexy-cop costume, shirt unbuttoned, shorts half undone. He let his gaze wander down the muscular legs dusted with pale hair, then back up, taking in every tantalizing inch of exposed skin and admitting how much this man got his motor running. Then he stepped forward, took Remy's hand in his, and played with his fingers for a moment before pulling him in and doing what he'd wanted to do practically since the second he first laid eyes on Remy.

He drew him close and pressed his mouth to Remy's for a sweet, simple kiss. No tongue, no teeth, no heat, just the pleasure of soft lips against his and the delightful little gasp as Remy understood Brice hadn't come here to fuck him.

Brice put a hand behind Remy's neck, stroking the heated skin as he pulled him closer. Remy parted his lips, but still Brice didn't enter, just continued the kiss, tasting Remy, feeling him relax into Brice's embrace. This unexpected gentleness was more arousing than a deep, needy kiss, though that would come later. But for now he wanted to take things slowly.

Not that his cock was in agreement. He was fully hard again, and he felt Remy's cock thicken and press against his in response. But they stood there kissing like teenagers on a first date. After what could have been two minutes or two hours, they pulled apart for air.

"The bath is almost ready," Remy said. "Would you let me bathe you?"

"Yes, please."

Brice watched as Remy undressed. He did it slowly, but deliberately, with no teasing or playfulness. Did he really want to be here?

REMY WAS naked, and he looked uncomfortable, hands together and hovering over his crotch as Brice, still fully dressed, looked at him. "The tub's probably full now."

"Good." He'd requested a bath first. Nice of them to have it nearly ready when he arrived rather than waiting for the huge tub to fill. He couldn't fault the service around here.

"Let me take your coat and—" Remy reached for the jacket and hung it in the wardrobe, then he fell to his knees, then into a sitting position, and reached for Brice's foot. Brice let him slip the shoe off, leaning on Remy for support. Remy helped him out of his pants and shirt. "Shall I leave the pants outside for the laundry? They'll be ready by morning."

"Ye—" Brice stopped himself. If he let the pants go, he was committed to spending the night. He couldn't leave without pants. He glanced down at Remy, slightly shivering in the cool room, goose bumps evident on his arms. He seemed so different up here, so vulnerable. Even the plump hard nipples weren't enough to dispel this new impression of Remy. "Yes, please."

Remy nodded and stood up. He put the pants on a hanger and hung them on a hook in the hallway. Brice had wondered what that hook was for. Then Remy came back in and knelt in front of Brice, fingers in the waistband of his boxer briefs. The dark wet spot was kind of embarrassing.

Remy slid the shorts down, and Brice stepped out of them. "Can I...?" Remy didn't elaborate, but Brice nodded. Remy leaned forward and licked at Brice's cock, washing away the last traces of his semen with soft, gentle strokes of his tongue. His cock wasn't hard, and Remy easily got the whole thing into his mouth as Brice watched, enjoying the wet heat and glad the boy seemed less skilled at this simple task. Then Remy glanced up at Brice and tugged on his cock playfully. The stimulation sent the blood flowing, and it swelled in Remy's mouth.

"Mmm. Should I keep going?" Remy mumbled around Brice's growing erection.

"After the bath."

Remy glanced up again, warily this time, and pulled off Brice. "Yes, sir." Remy stood, and Brice was surprised to see his cock was hard and jutting away from his body at a very enticing angle. Brice had barely touched him, and Remy hadn't touched himself. That hard-on was real. The thought put a little spring into Brice's step. He let Remy take his hand and lead him into the bathroom.

It was much warmer in there, with steam rising from the woodsy-scented bubbles.

"I can wash you if you like," Remy suggested, perching on the edge of the large tub.

Remy helped Brice into the tub. The water was heavenly, not so hot his skin nearly melted when he got inside. "Mmm, perfect." He leaned back and slid down so his shoulders were below the surface.

"I'm not sure what you're expecting from me, sir."

"First off, please don't keep calling me sir."

"Okay."

BRICE HAD let Remy peel away his clothes with tentative trembling fingers. It was so different from the seductive way Law had undressed him last time. Remy didn't touch Brice to arouse him, but simply to remove each item, letting only his fingertips graze Brice's heated skin. When he dropped to his knees to pull Brice's pants and shorts off, he made no move to touch Brice's cock when it sprang free of the confining fabric. He had just gazed at Brice's body, not hungry or appraising, but with what felt like simple appreciation. That lasted a moment before desire flashed across his face and he asked to taste Brice.

Now, Remy helped Brice step into the tub and sat on the edge as Brice sank into the warm suds. He took a washcloth from the towel rack and plunged it into the water, then squirted some body wash on. The tub smelled as fresh and green as a hike through Muir Woods, and Brice relaxed as Remy rubbed the cloth against his shoulders and back. He leaned into the strokes and let out a sigh.

This wasn't at all how he expected things to go tonight, but it was really what he wanted.

JEREMY LEANED down and soaped Mr. Green's back and shoulders. He had a nice body. He took care of himself, and touching him was a pleasure. Jeremy would enjoy doing just about anything with Mr. Green, and he'd expected to be bent over the sofa by now or have Mr. Green's cock down his throat. Both possibilities would be enjoyable, but Jeremy was pleased Green had slowed things down.

And that kiss! It had thrown Jeremy for a loop. It had been so unexpectedly sweet, so gentle, and it made him want Green even more. But whatever they ended up doing would be so much more enjoyable without rushing in. He couldn't remember the last time anyone had treated him with such consideration. Mr. Sky Blue had been a real gentleman in a different way. He hadn't used Jeremy for his own pleasure, but for Jeremy's. It had been intimate despite having been in public. But Jeremy hadn't felt used, the way he thought some of the other boys might.

But Green had been more gentle even than Jeremy's last date. Was this simply kindness, just an act before he would expect Jeremy to do things he might not want to, lulled into a sense of comfort and security?

"You could do a better job if you got in here with me," Green said. He took the cloth out of Jeremy's hand and got him to stand up. He felt his cock stiffen as Green looked at him.

"You have the same effect on me," Green said with a charming smile as he held his hand out and helped Jeremy into the tub.

Green grabbed the cloth and started washing Jeremy's back and chest. The water was a perfect temperature, and there was plenty of room for both of them in the oversized tub. They were facing each other and

Green scooted forward so his legs were on either side of Jeremy's body. They took turns soaping each other's arms and chests and legs.

Then Green moved closer until his lips were less than an inch from Jeremy's, and as if pulled in by a magnetic field, Jeremy closed the distance until they kissed again. Arms circled his waist, and he reached out for Green. They kissed for a long time. It was delicious. He felt Green's cock pressing against his leg, as hard as his own. His nipples ached, and he wanted Green to touch him, hold him, do something to ease this building tension and hunger.

Jeremy opened his mouth and licked at Green's lips, at the tip of his tongue, drew his tongue across the tops of his teeth, wanting to explore but not wanting to break the sensual spell. Green's tongue met his, and they deepened the kiss, still slow and unhurried. Then Green slid a hand along Jeremy's chin, down his throat, and across his collarbone, sending tremors through his entire body.

When Green's finger slid down his chest and grazed a sensitive nipple, Jeremy sucked in his breath and let out a soft moan. Green slid his hands lower, along Jeremy's torso, but before they reached where he most wanted to be touched, Green eased them around to Jeremy's back, and down the curve of his hips and ass, pulling him in close. One hand came around to cup his balls, carefully, tenderly, testing, like a blind man wanting to see everything with his perceptive fingers.

Jeremy moved his own hands to mirror Green's movements, enjoying the hard muscles under the slippery, smooth skin, the curve and swell of Green's ass. At his touch Green's balls moved in the loose skin of his sac. Jeremy gently brushed one nipple, and Green shuddered at the touch, groaning into Jeremy's mouth.

"Am I clean enough for you now?" Jeremy whispered.

Green's response was a hand sliding back behind his balls to brush against Jeremy's hole, igniting the sensitive nerves and causing Jeremy to reach up to embrace Green more tightly. God how he wanted this man. With another partner, Jeremy would be saying good-bye after half an hour, not wondering when Green would finally touch his cock.

He liked not knowing. He liked taking it slow.

"Clean enough. Maybe too clean."

Jeremy looked into Green's eyes.

Green laughed. "Bubble bath is not my favorite flavor."

"The shower?"

"Good idea." Green stood up, the lingering bubbles settling onto the curls surrounding his cock and sliding down his powerful legs.

Jeremy stared up at him and moved to stand, careful not to slip. Green steadied him with a firm, warm hand, and they moved together the few feet to the large shower. Green reached in and turned the water on. He pulled Jeremy close and kissed him until the water was hot, only a moment or two, but the kisses made Jeremy drunk with desire for Mr. Green.

Green slid the door shut and grabbed the detachable showerhead. He sprayed water all over Jeremy and then himself before leaning down to lick a stripe down Jeremy's abs.

"I think you're soap free. Just turn around...."

Jeremy turned, and Green angled the water between his thighs. The stream was just strong enough to generate a nice sensation. He leaned forward enough to give Mr. Green a nice view of his ass. In response Green treated him to a soft, warm pulsing spray that tingled against his balls and hole. He let out a little moan, and Green kept the spray on him.

"Ready?" Green asked.

"For what?" Jeremy wished he hadn't asked such a stupid question because Green clammed up and turned off the shower without replying. He slid open the door and cool air rushed in making Jeremy shiver.

"Here you go." Green grabbed a thick pale blue bath towel and wrapped it around Jeremy, giving him a tight squeeze. But he looked a little nervous again, perhaps just as unsure what to do next as Jeremy.

Jeremy let Green mop him dry for a moment, then pulled the other towel off the rack and began drying Green, letting his own towel slip to the floor. He was still hard, and so was Mr. Green. Jeremy enjoyed letting Green set the pace, but he wanted more soon. *Now*.

He stepped over the towel on the floor and moved toward the bedroom, and Mr. Green followed, towel around his shoulders and hair dripping, leaving thin rivulets sliding between his smooth pecs.

"Do you want me to put on the costume again? Or wear anything special for you?"

"Costume?" The question seemed to surprise Green.

"The cop costume? The hat? The belt?"

Green shook his head. The movement made his cock swing back and forth, and Jeremy couldn't help staring. Green had a gorgeous cock. The head was plump, and Jeremy recalled its taste. He wanted more, and he hadn't been allowed to see or play with it in the dining room. Now he could.

Green met Jeremy's gaze, questioning.

"Would you mind if I…?" Jeremy ran his tongue across his lower lip and moved to kneel at Green's feet. He licked at the glistening slit before Green could choke out a no.

Jeremy held onto Green's thigh as he licked his cock, enjoying the way it bobbed out of reach. Green shuddered with every touch of Jeremy's tongue, gasping softly and running the fingers of one hand through Jeremy's damp hair.

He sucked the head in and explored it with his tongue, letting it slide in and out of his mouth before taking more and more in. He couldn't get enough of it.

"Mmm, no, slow down," Green said, tightening his fingers in Jeremy's hair. His knees buckled slightly, and Jeremy moved with him toward the bed, not letting go of Green's cock as Green settled onto the edge with a grunt and a chuckle. "You're gonna kill me," Green said, his voice husky from the warm bath and arousal.

The sound got Jeremy even harder. He bent between Green's legs and resumed his task.

"Seriously, Remy, please slow down."

The gentle insistence stopped Jeremy, and he pulled off and settled onto his heels, looking up into Mr. Green's brown eyes for just a moment before glancing away.

"Sorry, Mr. Green, but I—" Jeremy paused, licking his lips. He could still taste Green, and he couldn't really think clearly. "My name's Jeremy. I'm not sure if we're supposed to say, but I want you to know."

BRICE LOOKED down on Remy—Jeremy—and saw all of the confidence of a moment ago melt away until Jeremy looked simply like any earnest young man. A wave of relief flowed over Brice at Jeremy's words.

"Jeremy. Thanks." He stopped himself from saying "nice to meet you"—since thirty seconds ago Jeremy had had Brice's cock down his throat—and watched some of the unease drain from Jeremy's face. "And in here, at least, please don't call me Mr. anything. Call me Brice."

"Okay, Brice." Jeremy gave Brice his sweet, shy smile, the one he remembered from their first night together.

Brice scooted away from the edge of the bed and reached a hand out to pull Jeremy up next to him. Jeremy laughed as he lay next to Brice, slightly out of breath. God, he was beautiful when he laughed, when he relaxed. Even though Brice had seen Jeremy plenty of times without his clothes, and had touched him intimately in the dining room, this was entirely different. Here they weren't playing roles or games—at least Brice hoped they weren't anymore. He wasn't, and he hoped this was the real Jeremy.

Now Brice was free to do whatever he wanted with Jeremy— whatever Jeremy wanted. Brice rolled onto his side, up against Jeremy, who lay on his back. Jeremy's plump nipples just begged for attention, and Brice leaned down to suck at the nearest one. He loved Jeremy's little gasp of pleasure, and he slid his hand along Jeremy's abs and down one hip, feeling for his hot spots and enjoying the reactions as he found them. He felt Jeremy's shudders and gasps and wanted him all the more.

But Brice avoided taking hold of Jeremy's cock. He didn't want to rush things, wasn't sure what Jeremy wanted. When Jeremy took hold of Brice's hand and pulled it onto his hard-on, Brice got the message loud and clear. He closed his fist around the hot, hard length and felt Jeremy tremble beneath him.

Jeremy bucked his hips up, increasing the friction of Brice's hand on his cock. Brice slid down Jeremy's body and took his cock into his mouth, savoring the clean, hot taste. Jeremy rotated toward Brice, and a moment later, Brice felt Jeremy's mouth close onto his cock, and they lay facing each other, sucking, stroking, feasting on each other.

Sixty-nine had never been one of Brice's favorite positions. It always felt like too much work, requiring coordination and concentration rather than enjoying either role, but he and Jeremy balanced each other. When Brice took a pause for breath, Jeremy increased his efforts, so they could both enjoy giving and receiving.

Brice took little detours to suck and play with Jeremy's balls and trace a finger around his entrance. Taking the time getting to know a new lover rarely happened with the casual sex he'd had since Greg. Despite the awkward start to their night together, Brice felt comfortable with Jeremy and wanted to give him as much pleasure as he hoped to take.

"Do you want me to finish you like this?" Jeremy asked when Brice was hovering in a zone of equilibrium, keeping himself from getting too close to the edge. "I like to bottom, but I can top if you want...."

Brice hadn't allowed himself to contemplate how much he wanted to sink into Jeremy's sweet depths and lose himself. He feared there would be nothing to look forward to if he had what he most desired so easily. He'd save that pleasure for later.

"Keep going," Brice said in a breathless whisper. The brief thought of Jeremy's tight ass had him hard as a rock again and a little disconcerted.

"Lemme do you first," Jeremy said and shifted position so his cock and ass were nearly out of Brice's reach. Brice reached for Jeremy's cock as he settled onto his back, and Jeremy lay across one thigh, putting in 110 percent effort with hands, mouth, and as much skill as enthusiasm. Jeremy worked Brice right back up to a crescendo and took him just to the edge a couple of times before pulling him over in a whirlwind of an orgasm that took away Brice's breath and most of his strength until he gave in and shot his load down Jeremy's receptive throat.

While Brice caught his breath, Jeremy licked his balls and planted kisses on his thighs and hip. Then he leaned over and planted a feathery kiss on the head of Brice's cock.

"I could suck your dick all day."

The comment took Brice aback. Was this Jeremy the hustler again? Flattery never worked on Brice. "Really?" He couldn't keep the skepticism from his tone.

"Probably not, but I could think about it all day. I like your cock a lot. The shape is kind of perfect, and it's a good fit for my mouth." Jeremy lay on his back again and clamped a hand over his mouth for a moment. "Fuck, I don't know why I said that. Maybe it's the cognac. I don't drink much, and it makes me run off at the mouth." He rolled back onto Brice's thigh. "You must think I'm full of whore shit."

"That's a colorful statement. I don't know much about whores. Or their shit."

Jeremy released a soft chuckle. "Me neither. But suddenly, I don't care. I just want to have a fun night with you."

"In that case, it's your turn. What would you like?" Brice shifted so he could reach out and take hold of Jeremy's cock. The guy was still hard, the flesh swollen and dark. Maybe he really had enjoyed sucking Brice off as much as he'd said. Most guys didn't stay this hard unless they were getting additional stimulation—or were incredibly turned on. Brice's mood lifted. "Well, name it. Anything you want."

"Anything?"

Brice questioned the wisdom of his offer. He'd been in such a good mood, flattered how aroused Jeremy was. What could the guy ask? Maybe the erection was just the result of popping a little blue pill when Brice hadn't been looking. God, when would he learn not to fall for these hustler tactics?

"Well, there's something I wouldn't mind, but if you don't want to, just let me know, okay?" Jeremy took on a nervous look again, but on him it was so endearing Brice was ready to agree to anything.

"I'll do my best."

"Okay." Jeremy got up and went over to the little love seat across the room. He picked up something and brought it over to the bed. Only then did Brice see what it was. The dildo "nightstick" from Remy's cop costume. "Would you use this on me? I've been wondering about it since that guy offered during dinner." Jeremy gave a little shrug. "And since you didn't want to top just now."

Brice kicked himself mentally. He could have had Jeremy with no fuss, but he'd put it off. And now the kid wanted Brice to fuck him with the dildo? Brice took the thing out of Jeremy's hands and looked at it. It wasn't huge as dildos went. Pretty similar to Brice's own cock in girth, if a few inches longer. It might be fun to watch this after all.

No, he'd be doing more than watching.

"You sure about this?" Brice glanced at Jeremy, who was still hard. Very hard.

Jeremy nodded.

"We're going to need a lot of lube," Brice said with a smile. He had the feeling Jeremy didn't do things like this very often. That would make it more fun for both of them, and he appreciated how Jeremy trusted him for a new experience.

"Probably in the drawer."

Brice pulled the drawer open and removed the bottle and held it up. "You want me to….?"

"Yes, please." A teasing tone crept into Jeremy's voice, and he curved one corner of his mouth into an impish half-grin.

"My pleasure." It would be too. Brice would enjoy this almost as much as Jeremy. He pulled the box of condoms out of the drawer and unrolled one onto the dildo. It appeared new and still smelled of silicone, but he preferred not to take chances. He couldn't be sure, even with a good scrub, and he could tell Jeremy wasn't in the mood to wait much longer for his turn to play.

Brice drizzled lube on a couple of fingers and approached Jeremy, who had rolled onto his side, one leg bent forward. This way, Brice could see Jeremy's face, which would be nice. He circled Jeremy's pucker, feeling the little shudders beneath his fingertips. Once the whole area was slicked, he pushed just the tip of his index finger inside. Jeremy let out a little moan. He was really tight. Apparently he didn't bottom much, or at least not recently.

To his surprise, Brice started getting hard again. The sound of Jeremy's obvious enjoyment and the way his ass clenched Brice's finger so tightly made it difficult for Brice to catch his breath. He took his time playing, getting a feel for what Jeremy liked—which seemed to be almost everything. When he was prepped, Brice rolled him onto his back, not missing the fact that Jeremy was hard as a rock. He'd get to that soon.

After adding more lube to the condom-coated toy, Brice lined it up with Jeremy's hole.

"You ready?"

Jeremy nodded. His eyes were already unfocused, and he was hard, nipples tight buds. Brice reached up to tweak one, and Jeremy let out another blissed-out sound. Brice slid the tip of the dildo inside and watched Jeremy's eyes widen and heard his breath catch.

"You okay?"

"Go slow."

"Sure." Brice eased the toy in a little, then out, then in a little more, adding more lube so it slid easily. Jeremy relaxed and opened up nicely, and soon Brice had most of the thing inside. "Ready for some action?"

"Is it in?"

"I think you've totally offended this dildo." Brice chuckled. "Yeah, it's in. Can't you feel that?"

"Hell yeah, I can feel it. I thought it would hurt. You're really gentle."

"I'm a little offended now." Brice grinned, but he saw Jeremy's eyes flicker a little. "Too gentle?" Jeremy shook his head. "Feel good?"

"God, yes."

Brice slid the toy in and out and watched and listened as Jeremy responded enthusiastically. It was almost as good as really fucking him, Brice decided. Jeremy didn't hold back with groans and moans and suggestions.

"Faster? Deeper?"

"Yes, yes." Jeremy's eyes were closed, and he lay with his legs splayed wide.

Nice view. Very nice view. Brice used his free hand to play with Jeremy's balls, but he really wanted to grab onto his cock, now thick and red and dripping. "Let me know when you want me to finish you off."

"Keep fucking." Jeremy panted between the words.

Brice chuckled. He imagined how much fun it would be to have his cock this deep in Jeremy. Would he enjoy it as much? Brice sure as hell would. He leaned forward and grasped Jeremy's hard length and wrapped his fingers around it, feeling the heat and hardness.

Jeremy's breath sputtered, and then without warning, his cock spasmed and he came in a powerful spray across his chest. Brice slid the toy out and tossed it out of their way as he lay down next to Jeremy and leaned toward his torso in order the lick the pearly strands away.

Jeremy held Brice's head against his chest, and Brice listened to Jeremy's heartbeat slow. Little aftershocks shook Jeremy's body as he fought to catch his breath. After a few moments, Jeremy let go.

"Oh, God, that was incredible. I had no idea what I was missing." Jeremy opened his eyes, and when his gaze met Brice's, Jeremy turned away. "Fuck, this is so embarrassing."

"Why?"

"I can't explain it. But it is." Jeremy rolled away and curled himself up into a ball.

"Hey, don't be. It's great that you liked it. Much better than the opposite reaction." Brice propped himself up on one elbow. He understood how Jeremy might feel embarrassed or vulnerable at letting himself go so completely. Maybe he'd grow to feel more comfortable with Brice. Hopefully this wasn't their only night together. He enjoyed Jeremy's pleasure as much as his own.

To give Jeremy some privacy, Brice went into the bathroom and soaked a washcloth with warm water. There was a whole stack of washcloths and small towels on the counter. This place thought of everything the guests would need or want.

When he walked back to the bed, Jeremy was asleep, sprawled on his back. Brice gently cleaned him up with the warm cloth, then slid into bed next to him and turned off the lights.

IN THE morning, Brice woke up to find Jeremy plastered against his chest. He made a soft moaning sound, and Brice wondered if he were actually awake and playing with him. Jeremy had one arm curved over Brice's chest and his mouth a few inches away from a nipple. When Jeremy shifted, his cock—nice and hard—pressed into Brice's thigh.

God it felt good to wake up with someone in his arms—or close enough. Someone clean and warm and willing. Brice stroked Jeremy's wheat-colored hair, enjoying its silky softness.

"What time is it?" Jeremy whispered huskily against Brice's chest. The slight movement of his lips did crazy things to the lower of half of Brice's body.

Brice leaned up to see the clock. "Not quite seven."

"We have an hour to kill, don't we?"

"We do," Brice agreed and rolled onto his back, pulling Jeremy on top of him.

Jeremy opened his cornflower blue eyes and smiled, lids still heavy with sleep. The look was good on him. Jeremy shifted an arm so he could tweak Brice's nipple. The quick, almost painful motion surprised him, but the pinch and lingering tingle had him immediately hard and hungry. He pulled Jeremy up and gave him a rough kiss, pulling his head back by his hair. Possessively, not violently. Jeremy opened his mouth and let Brice take what he wanted. Almost. Brice wanted much more.

Jeremy kissed back, matching Brice's eagerness. They kissed deeply for a few moments, and Brice forgot to breathe. He was light-headed, giddy, so fucking hard he thought his dick had turned to stone. He pressed up against Jeremy's body, and they spent a few pleasant moments grinding against each other.

"Let's let the dildo sleep late," Jeremy said, meeting Brice's gaze. His meaning was crystal clear.

"Let's."

Jeremy reached for the lube, still on the night table. He handed it to Brice.

"Why don't you do it this time?" Brice suggested. "Shouldn't take much work, and I want to watch."

Jeremy blinked shyly and nodded. He gave a languorous feline stretch, giving Brice a good view of chest, abs, and best of all, his sturdy morning wood. His cock bobbed against his torso, leaking a clear glistening trail. He put some lube into his palm and slicked a few fingers, then pulled one knee up and traced his hole with a slippery fingertip. He rolled over onto his other side, ass toward Brice, so Brice could watch.

After the dildo action the night before, Jeremy's ass was still a little slick and loose. He wouldn't need much prep, but he made a good show of it, plunging his fingers in deep and making noises that drove Brice wild. He nearly pulled Jeremy's hand away so he could shove his cock in there, but that wasn't how he wanted this to go.

This would be the first time he'd be in Jeremy, and he wanted to remember every single second of it. He'd thought about this for weeks now. He admitted it. The whole time since the first night they'd met, Brice hadn't been with anyone else. Hadn't *wanted* anyone. No one else would satisfy him until he had Jeremy.

Being with Law hadn't given Brice what he wanted or needed. He acknowledged that he wouldn't have been satisfied with anyone but Jeremy. Now he'd get his wish.

But then what? How anticlimactic would that be?

"You need me to put this on you?" Jeremy flapped a condom packet in Brice's direction.

"No, unless you want to." Brice hadn't realized Jeremy was finished lubing up. He'd been so caught up in what he was about to do, he wasn't paying enough attention to actually doing it.

He remembered how hot and tight Jeremey's ass had been the night before when he slid his fingers inside. He only hoped he could last long enough to give Jeremy enough pleasure. With the dildo, Jeremy had been hard, and he'd enjoyed being filled up. How would Brice feel in comparison?

"You going to fuck me by telepathy?"

"Hardly." Brice lay next to Jeremy and pulled him close for a deep kiss. Jeremy wrapped his fingers around Brice's cock and gave him a few good tugs, then rolled the condom over Brice's erection.

"Hard. Perfect." Jeremy rolled away and pulled his knees up in case Brice needed any additional encouragement.

Brice knelt so he could line his cock up with Jeremy's slick hole. He took a breath as he pressed inside. He'd intended to slide in slowly, but it felt so damn good he couldn't stop himself and pushed in all the way.

Jeremy gulped. "Ah, you're gonna kill me."

Brice started to pull out. "Sorry."

"No, don't stop. Kill me in a good way. Keep going."

Brice let out a pent-up breath, relieved that he felt good to Jeremy. Because Jeremy felt like absolute heaven. Taking his time, Brice slid in and out a few times, enjoying the way his cock looked entering Jeremy. He noticed how hard Jeremy was again, even without Brice touching him. Jeremy really liked getting fucked. Good thing, because Brice really liked fucking Jeremy.

He closed his eyes and concentrated on the heat and pressure and the way it sent sensations all the way to his toes and made his nipples tingle like they'd been pinched. He played around with speed and angles, listening to Jeremy's breath and moans as an indication of what he should do. If anything, Jeremy was as loud as he'd been the night before.

Brice felt Jeremy's legs wrap around his waist, heels digging into his ass to push Brice in deeper and faster and harder. When he felt a tug at one nipple, he opened his eyes. Jeremy was watching him, eyes glazing over, one hand reaching up to play with Brice's nipples and stroke his torso, as if Brice needed any more stimulation.

It took sheer determination not to come. Just as Brice neared his limit, Jeremy shuddered beneath him and came. That sent Brice over the edge, and he let himself come, crashing hard into absolute bliss. He couldn't hear or see or feel anything for a few moments as the world went white-hot and intense pleasure gripped him from head to toe.

When he finally opened his eyes, he was lying on top of Jeremy, who was looking at him with a touch of concern.

"You okay, Brice?"

"No." Brice rolled over and pulled Jeremy along with him so they were on their sides, still wrapped together. "I'll never be okay again."

"I know what you mean." Jeremy leaned in and kissed Brice. It was mostly soft lips and just a little taste of the tip of his tongue. "I think we can retire the dildo."

Chapter SEVENTEEN

EVEN AFTER Brice got home, he couldn't stop thinking about his night with Jeremy.

Having sex with him had been everything he'd expected—and so much more. It had been as satisfying as he'd hoped and even more fun. Jeremy was sexy and inventive, but best of all, he was genuine. He'd had the same mix of fear, trepidation, and shyness Brice did. It hadn't felt like he was fucking a whore. It felt like having good, clean sex with a hot friend he'd always wanted but worried it would ruin their friendship.

But to Brice's relief, the sex hadn't ruined things with Jeremy at all. It meant their relationship—however it was defined—had just moved to a new level.

FOR THE next month, Brice met Jeremy for two dinners and overnights per week. Jeremy didn't work at the club at any other times. Some nights they only kissed during dinners, and other times they went much farther. One night they went upstairs after the first course.

One Wednesday morning, Brice was trying to tie his necktie and get to work for a meeting certain to be far less interesting than another hour with Jeremy, who sat on the bathroom counter naked, sliding a hand along an erection he insisted needed Brice's immediate and urgent attention.

"You are going to kill me," Brice said and flipped the tie over his shoulder as he bent down to help Jeremy with his problem. He spent an enjoyable fifteen minutes making Jeremy squirm, scream, and squirt, in that order. By then he was so hard Jeremy reciprocated, on his knees, promising not to spill a drop of anything on Brice's trousers. Brice watched Jeremy in the mirror, round ass and balls bobbing as he sucked Brice off—still wearing shirt, tie and freshly pressed trousers. And true to his word, Jeremy swallowed down everything.

He sat back on his heels with a grin. "Think of this while you're in your meeting."

"You make me want to…. Damn, you know what you do to me!" Brice teased as he cupped Jeremy's chin in his hand and leaned down for a spunky kiss. "I can't wait until Saturday." They shared another long, deep kiss.

"Brice, you like baseball?"

The non sequitur took Brice aback for a moment. "Yeah. Love it."

"GIANTS OR A's?" Jeremy asked, not wanting Brice to leave.

"Giants. And not just because they might actually win the pennant this year."

"Beats another nail-biter hoping they get a wild-card spot." Jeremy grinned and kissed Brice again. "Now go to work. I have to get to the lab."

"I hate leaving."

"I know." Jeremy waved, still on his knees, cock at half-staff as Brice left.

During the cab ride to the office, he flipped through memories of the last twelve hours with Jeremy. His phone rang, and he put a hand into his breast pocket to retrieve it, encountering an envelope he didn't recall putting there.

"Yeah, Ron, I'm on my way. Ten minutes."

"Don't rush. Meeting's postponed a week."

"Fuck."

"You weren't really looking forward to it that much, were you?"

"What? No. Something else. See you in ten anyway."

Brice exhaled loudly. He could have stayed with Jeremy…. He put the phone away and picked up the envelope, which had fallen onto his lap. A small white envelope, the kind used for thank-you cards, with nothing written on it.

He ripped it open, and a single small piece of cardboard fell out.

A ticket to the Giants game on Friday night. One ticket.

Now Jeremy's strange question made sense and brightened Brice's day and the rest of the week. He wasn't sure if it meant what he thought it did, but he hoped like hell it did.

Chapter EIGHTEEN

FRIDAY AT six thirty, Brice made his way to the Giants' ballpark, AT&T Park, or whatever they were calling it this week. He headed for the lower infield seat indicated on his ticket. It was a good seat, close enough to the field to see the players' faces. Brice preferred these seats to the fancier Club section or the exclusive Sky Boxes high above the action and the crowd.

The park was packed for a Friday-night home game, even though they were playing the Padres, currently at the bottom of the entire National League. The fair-weather fans always showed up in droves after a World Series win and with the great season they were having this year. The teams warmed up on the field while the seats filled. All but the one next to Brice. He glanced around, searching the walkway, hoping he hadn't gotten his hopes up for nothing.

The first inning came and went, and so did the second. The seat next to Brice was still empty. The Giants were winning, but the game held no appeal for Brice on his own, even though the ticket had been a gift from Jeremy. Brice got up and made his way inside, ready to go home to an empty apartment and something from the freezer or take away from the diner or Indian place around the corner.

Then he smelled the aroma of grilled onions. Even the lower levels had decent food here, so he decided to grab a bite at the ballpark, then go home.

JEREMY HAD gotten stuck in the lab later than expected. If he didn't wait for the instrument sequence to finish, he'd have to start the whole thing over, which meant at least two wasted days and wasted resources. He gave it fifteen more minutes before he'd bail. He could still get to the ballpark during the first inning.

Five minute later, the samples still hadn't finished running, but thankfully his undergraduate lab assistant, Rhoda Bering, came in to check on another of Jeremy's experiments.

"You're here late, Jer. You smell great." She winked.

"I miscalculated, thought they'd be done. I'm late for a date." He smoothed his shirt.

"Anyone I know?"

"Someone I've had my eye on a long time. It's kind of a first date. Giants."

She glanced at the clock. "First pitch is in five minutes."

He nodded.

"Get going. I'll take your stuff out when it's finished. Tell me what I need to do. You go now. Call me from BART with instructions."

"I love you, Rhoda."

"Yeah, I know. Always a bridesmaid, never a bride. Go have fun. Kiss and tell?"

"It might scar you for life." He hoisted the messenger bag over his shoulder.

"God, I hope so."

He planted a kiss on her cheek and ran for the door.

Of course, BART was fucked up. It was crowded even going into the city, thanks to the game, and they got stuck in the transbay tunnel for no reason. When they finally arrived at Embarcadero, Jeremy raced to the MUNI platform, wondering whether it might be faster just to run the mile and a half. Why hadn't he brought his bike? He'd run a hell of a lot farther in triathlons, so he hoofed it.

It was the top of the fourth inning when he got to his seat, only slightly winded, but the one next to it—Brice's—was empty. It was still before eight, and Brice worked late a lot, though rarely on Fridays. Hopefully he was still coming. Jeremy would stay till the end. He didn't have Brice's phone number, didn't even know what company he worked for. Those were the rules. Even seeing each other here at a baseball game was against the rules. But Jeremy had only given Brice a ticket; they hadn't actually made a plan to meet outside of the Dinner Club. Technically, they hadn't broken that rule. Brice was a lawyer; he'd explain the logic behind that if Thomas found out.

The fifth inning started. Jeremy couldn't concentrate on the game. His stomach was still in knots, half from the excitement of seeing Brice, and half from fear they'd get caught. Add in another half of worry Brice wasn't coming. He must have seen the ticket. Jeremy had put it with his cell phone. Why hadn't he checked the number while Brice was sleeping?

Jeremy couldn't help glancing back to the steps more often than toward the field. He lost track of the score and the game.

"You waiting to meet someone?" the guy next to him finally asked during a lull in the game.

"Yeah."

"He left in the third inning. Had the same look on his face, though, and kept checking the entrance." The guy turned his attention back to the field and shouted as the ref made a bad call on a pitch.

Jeremy's mood lifted momentarily: Brice had come after all! But then it plummeted. He'd left.

"Thanks." Jeremy got up and began to climb the steps to go inside. No point in sticking around. He had his head low, shoulders slumping, when he heard someone shouting above him. The words sounded familiar, but there was a roar of the crowd drowning out the voice. Then a lull.

"Jeremy! Wait!"

He turned to see Brice elbowing his way through a crowd of guys chugging beers while waiting in line for more.

"Brice?" Jeremy stood there like an idiot as Brice rushed up and pulled him into a hug.

The crowd roared again, like they were cheering for Brice and Jeremy. They kissed and kept kissing.

"I'm sorry I was late."

Brice pushed hair back from Jeremy's eyes and grinned. "I should have waited. I just wasn't sure you were coming. I thought I had misunderstood the ticket."

"Let's go back and watch the game. Sounds like we're missing something good."

"We can watch the highlights later. Let's not waste tonight on baseball." Brice put his arm around Jeremy's waist. Jeremy's heart pounded like it would take off right out of his chest. He nodded, and they headed for the exit.

They walked back to the Embarcadero and strolled along the bay, watching the twinkling lights of the Bay Bridge reflected in the choppy waters below. An icy breeze chased them north, and they stayed close for warmth in the autumn evening chill.

They were approaching the Ferry Building when a man and a woman stopped them on the street.

"We're trying to find Boulevard. Can you help us?" the man asked. The woman had her arm in his and looked particularly windblown. She was wearing strappy high heels and had the look of a tourist about her— probably surprised how cold Northern California could be even in early autumn.

"Sure," Brice said. He pointed across the street. "Just there, on Mission."

"Thank you," the woman said, and they walked off.

Jeremy could hear him saying "I told you it was over there."

"Honey, it's our anniversary. For once, let's not argue," she replied, voice fading as she moved in the opposite direction.

"Did you eat?" Brice asked, pulling Jeremy close again.

"No. I didn't have time."

"Have you eaten at Boulevard?"

Jeremy shook his head. He'd heard of it, one of the best—and most expensive—restaurants in the city. It wasn't on a grad student's budget.

"You're in for a treat. Come on." Brice tugged Jeremy's arm, and they raced across the street, outrunning approaching traffic when the light changed as they were only halfway across.

They landed on the other side of the Embarcadero, winded and laughing. Brice opened the door to Boulevard for Jeremy, and warmth and a wall of sound greeted them as they entered.

"This place is packed." Jeremy glanced around at several people waiting to be seated, including the couple they'd just met. "And people are wearing ties and fancy clothes." He looked down at his jeans. Even the best pair he owned wasn't good enough for this place.

"Those are tourists. This is San Francisco. You're fine." Brice's smile put Jeremy at ease.

Brice approached the hostess stand.

"Good evening, Mr. Martin. How are you? How many in your party this evening?" She smiled, and her tone made it sound like Brice was a regular. She looked down at her reservation book.

"You booked a table?" Jeremy whispered.

Brice put an arm around his waist and replied to the hostess, "Just two tonight, Shelly. Do you have a quiet little table?"

She nodded. "Absolutely."

"And if you can, will you see if you can seat the couple waiting at the end of the bench fairly soon?"

"They don't have reservations, but I can do some rearranging for friends of yours."

"Thank you. And add their check to my bill. It's their anniversary."

Shelly led them to a table off to one side, away from the flow of servers and customers, and handed them menus. "Do you want to order drinks or start with a bottle of something?"

"You come here a lot?" Jeremy asked once she'd left.

"Business dinners. I've never been here on a date before."

A date. The words warmed Jeremy even more. He hadn't thought of the ball game as a real date, even though that's what he'd told Rhoda. But now it felt official.

They had wine with dinner, and after the waiter served the first course, Jeremy picked up his fork, then paused. "It's strange sitting across from you at dinner."

"Would you rather feed me?" Brice asked.

Jeremy shook his head, feeling his cheeks warming.

"Well, come sit here next to me anyway." He scooted Jeremy's chair closer so they were shoulder to shoulder, knees touching.

Dinner was delicious and romantic, and Jeremy never wanted this evening to end. For a few hours, it felt like a real date. They were having coffee when the out-of-town couple stopped by their table.

"Thank you so much for making our evening. We can't possibly thank you enough for dinner and the Champagne." The woman leaned down and gave Brice a hug. The man nodded and shook Brice's hand, and the woman hugged Jeremy too. "You're very lucky," she whispered in his ear.

Jeremy felt very lucky tonight. At least so far. She would never dream what his real relationship with Brice was. But for now, Jeremy could pretend they were just like any other couple.

After Brice paid, they walked outside into a biting wind coming right off the bay.

"Thank you for dinner, Brice. It was lovely."

"My pleasure." He paused. Jeremy wondered if Brice was thinking the same thing he was: how odd for Jeremy to be fully clothed at the end of the meal. If he was comparing tonight to their usual dinner interactions, he didn't mention it. "Do you need to get back to Berkeley?"

"Not right away. BART goes till around one. I've got plenty of time."

Brice's smile drifted away. "BART?"

"The train."

"I know what BART is. I thought you might want to stay in the city tonight. With me."

Jeremy hadn't wanted to get his hopes up, but he certainly did want to stay with Brice.

"We could stay at a nice hotel. Any place you like. The Fairmont? The Mark Hopkins? And I'll cover whatever you get for overnight—"

Jeremy pulled away and shoved his hands into his jacket pockets as he turned toward Market Street and the BART entrance. "No thanks."

"Wait. Jeremy… please wait." Brice reached for Jeremy's elbow, but Jeremy shook the grip off.

"Sorry. I really made a mistake here, Brice. I need to go."

"No, Jeremy. I'm the one who made a mistake. I said it wrong. I just thought maybe the money was really important. I want to spend time with you, and it isn't about sex. I just… aw, fuck. I'm sorry. I don't know what *you're* expecting. Maybe I'm just a wallet to you. I have no clue."

Jeremy hadn't considered the possibility Brice might also feel used, but in a different way than Jeremy did. "No. You're not a wallet. Yeah, the money is important, and I took the job at the club for the pay. But I'm not working tonight, and for me, nothing about tonight was about money." He paused. "And I don't want it to be."

"Good. Shit, now I sound like I want it for free." He put his hands over his face and looked like he wanted to crawl under a rock.

Jeremy reached out for Brice's arm, pulling his hands away from his face. "This got way too complicated tonight."

"If we'd met at some bar, we wouldn't be having this discussion, would we?" Brice made a weak smile.

"You want to pick me up at a bar?" Jeremy teased. "I'm not easy. You'll have to work for it."

"How about the bar at the Fairmont?"

"Is there one near your place?"

"No."

"I can stand under the streetlight, but then you will have to pay."

"Okay. No sex tonight. Or at least no obligation or expectation. How much for you just to stay over and keep me company?"

"That's extra." Jeremy glanced up from under his lashes, the way Kit had taught him.

"You're worth it, no matter the price."

Jeremy smiled and nodded. Brice sounded like he really meant it, and Jeremy's throat became unbearably tight. Anyone listening would think they were nuts, but Brice's comments meant a lot to Jeremy.

Brice flagged down a taxi, and they slid into the backseat. Jeremy leaned his head on Brice's shoulder as Brice put his arm around his waist. They didn't speak on the ride as the taxi stopped and started in San Francisco traffic and poorly timed stoplights. The ride didn't take long. Brice lived on Russian Hill, affording a spectacular view of the bay and the Golden Gate Bridge.

The taxi stopped in front of a classic Victorian with a circular tower extending from one corner of the upper level. The street was quiet, residential, and exclusive, and each house had a patch of lawn or landscaping between the entrance and the street. Even the cars lining the curb were expensive.

Brice unlocked the front door, and they took a small elevator—not unlike the one at the Dinner Club—to the third level.

"Here we are," Brice said as he unlocked the door. He waved Jeremy in with a gallant flourish, and Jeremy glanced around the entranceway, where two old Japanese woodblock prints hung. An enormous and intricate Oriental carpet covered most of the smooth dark wood of the hallway. Jeremy didn't even hear his footsteps as he moved into the living room.

"It's lovely."

"Thank you. Make yourself at home." Brice helped Jeremy out of his jacket and hung it up in a closet on a real wooden hanger.

Jeremy sat on the plush couch and looked around at the room. Brice made good money as a lawyer, but now Jeremy saw what good taste he had as well. The art and furniture in the room were exquisite. A few of the pieces would be right at home in a museum.

"Would you like something to drink? I can open a nice bottle of wine or...."

"No thanks."

"Cognac or brandy? Armagnac?"

"I don't know what the difference is." Jeremy paused. "I'll have whatever you're having."

Brice nodded and went behind a bar at the far end of the room and pulled glasses out of a cabinet.

"Before you think I robbed the deYoung or something, the art is mostly my parents'. They collected too many gorgeous things to fit in their house anymore. I was lucky enough to get their castoffs."

"These are castoffs?"

"Yes. They kept the best stuff for themselves." Brice handed Jeremy a glass and sat next to him on the couch, leaving about four inches between their thighs. "This is Armagnac. It's a type of French brandy."

Jeremy sniffed it, then took a tiny sip. It was like drinking electricity, unbelievably smooth electricity, tingling against his lips, tongue, and throat as he swirled it in his mouth and let the liquid spill gloriously down his throat.

"Wow. Oh, just wow. I'll never be able to drink beer or even decent whiskey again."

Brice grinned. "You like it?"

"Oh, yeah. But how's it different from brandy or cognac?"

"Do you really want to know?"

"Yes. But maybe not now."

"I'll be happy to tell you. Later."

"Later." Jeremy took another smooth sip and leaned in to kiss Brice. The kiss was tingly and delicious, and Jeremy found himself taking a more aggressive role than he usually did with Brice. He kicked his boots off and put his empty glass down on the table behind the couch, then straddled Brice's hips and settled himself into Brice's lap.

Brice slid his arms around Jeremy and pulled him in for another long, deep kiss. Jeremy threaded his fingers through Brice's hair. He could feel Brice's cock swelling beneath him, pressing against his balls through two layers of denim. They kept kissing, unhurriedly. Brice didn't glide his hands under Jeremy's shirt or grab his ass or even try to unbutton anything.

They made out for a long time. Jeremy's arousal increased, and his nipples tingled and ached as he moved against Brice's chest, but he didn't feel the usual sense of urgency and hunger, and apparently neither did Brice. It felt familiar and comfortable. He pulled away for a moment to replenish his supply of oxygen and rested his head against Brice's shoulder.

Brice caressed Jeremy's arm. "There's a guest room, if you'd like to stay there."

"A guest room?" Jeremy sat up straight again. "Does it have a big bed?"

A smile hinted on Brice's lips. "Well, I didn't want to make any assumptions or for you to feel any obligation."

"The guest room sounds fine." Jeremy peeled himself off Brice and slipped his boots back on.

Brice didn't give any indication if Jeremy's choice surprised or disappointed him. He stood and led Jeremy down a short hall. "This is the master bedroom." He indicated an open door on his left.

Jeremy glanced in to see a large bedroom decorated in dark reds, with an unmade bed.

"This is the guest room." Brice stopped at the end of the hall and flipped the light on, then waved Jeremy inside.

This room was smaller, but still spacious. It was done in dark blues, with cherrywood floors and a lovely Oriental carpet. The bed was a four-poster of shining dark wood with an elaborate canopy in midnight blue silk. It looked like something from the set of *The Tudors*.

"Wow. It's beautiful."

"Lots of blankets on the bed, in case you get cold. And a private bathroom." Brice indicated a door. "Let me know if you need anything."

"I will. Thanks." He stepped forward and kissed Brice, then grabbed his bag and headed for the bathroom.

BRICE WASHED up for bed and stared at himself in the mirror, noticing more than the usual number of silver hairs near his right temple. For two seconds he considered pulling a few out, finally deciding to leave it be. He wasn't vain. Then he glanced in the direction of the guest bedroom and wondered whether Jeremy thought of him as anything more than a rich older guy. Was that why he wanted to sleep down the hall? It wasn't what Brice expected. Was this the end of their—he didn't even know what to call it—relationship? They met twice a week at the Dinner Club. Did Jeremy want to keep their physical relationship confined to that? Or would Brice find himself with a different serving boy next time?

He undressed and threw everything into the hamper in his dressing room, then pulled on a pair of comfy blue sweats, leaving the string untied as he slid under the blankets in his suddenly too-large bed. He wasn't tired, but he didn't feel like reading a book. He switched the lamp off and closed his eyes. He was still wired with arousal from having Jeremy in his lap. He wouldn't fall asleep anytime soon unless he got some release. Maybe a shower would do the trick.

He heard something in the hallway and waited. Nothing. Just his imagination. Then he saw a shadow in the doorway. Then it was gone.

"Brice?"

This time Brice saw Jeremy outlined in the dim light from the hall. The curve of his hips gave the impression he might be naked. Brice felt a little jolt of excitement. "Yeah?"

"Do you have room in there for me?" Jeremy's voice was a low almost-whisper, but rumbly and sexy as hell.

"I might."

Jeremy walked toward Brice, and in the glow coming through the window, he could tell Jeremy wasn't just naked but hard. Moonlight outlined his cock as it jutted from his body, bobbing as he moved. Brice lifted the covers, but Jeremy didn't get in. He just stood at the edge of the bed while Brice took in his slim, athletic body and the perfect curve of his erection.

"You look beautiful in the moonlight." Brice sat up in bed and swung his legs over the side. He took one of Jeremy's hands and kissed the palm. Inches away, he saw Jeremy's cock stiffen even more and heard a soft moan. Brice pulled Jeremy closer and leaned forward so he could take just the head of his cock into his mouth, tracing the contours of the smooth crown with his tongue and using the lightest of suction. He played with Jeremy using just his mouth, unable to stifle his own groans. Jeremy had a handful of Brice's hair and pulled with exactly the right amount of pressure. He opened his mouth and took more of Jeremy in, moving up and down but still concentrating on the crown and the sensitive ridges.

"Slow down a little, Brice." Jeremy stepped back a pace so his cock slipped out of Brice's mouth. "I want to lie down with you, feel your arms around me."

"Yes." Brice moved in for one last taste of Jeremy, then got back into bed and made room for Jeremy.

Jeremy slid under the covers and pressed himself to Brice. "Let's get rid of these." Jeremy pulled Brice's sweats down his hips far enough for Brice to kick out of them. Then Jeremy pressed himself against Brice's skin, hot and hard, his cock head wet with Brice's saliva. In about three seconds, Brice was so hard it hurt.

"Jeremy, I don't actually have any supplies here…."

"Nothing?"

"Maybe a condom somewhere, but that's it. I don't entertain here." Fuck, why had he said that?

"Would you think I was too slutty if I told you I brought some?"

"Not at all."

"I'll get them."

"No. I will. In your bag?"

"Outer pocket. The bag's on the bed in the other room."

"Wait here."

He felt rather than saw Jeremy nod. Brice got out of bed and moved swiftly down the hall to collect the necessary items. He slid back into bed, and almost immediately Jeremy pulled him into another needy embrace, cock still hard and insistent against Brice's body.

Jeremy took the condoms from Brice while Brice drizzled some lube into his hand. "On your back?"

Jeremy obliged, and Brice knelt between his legs, eager for more of Jeremy's cock. He continued where he'd left off earlier, at the same time pressing a slippery finger to Jeremy's hole. When Jeremy groaned softly, Brice pushed a fingertip inside, enjoying the tight grip of muscle. He pushed in deeper, spreading lube and fingerfucking Jeremy until he had him squirming and moaning.

"You want to come now?" Brice asked.

"Not yet. With you inside me?"

"Mmm. Sounds good."

Together they rolled the condom onto Brice, and he pressed himself inside as slowly as possible. He liked watching Jeremy's expression as his cock filled him. Even in the moonlight Brice could see Jeremy's pleasure, cock still hard, nipples plump and peaked. Brice reached out to tweak one and felt Jeremy's sharp intake of breath as he arched his back.

"Real slow."

"Am I hurting you?" Brice started to pull out.

"No. I just want to make this last a long time—if you can."

Brice grinned. "I don't know how long I can last right now. You feel so incredible."

Brice started a slow, easy rhythm, moving in deep on each stroke, then shifted to shorter, shallower thrusts for a while, then alternating randomly. With one hand he pinched Jeremy's nipples or gave a firm tug of his cock. He wanted to make Jeremy feel good without taking him too close too quickly.

"A little faster now."

Brice obliged. He kept himself close to the edge, concentrating on the movements that made Jeremy moan and writhe.

When Jeremy finally gave him permission, Brice thrust slowly and steadily against Jeremy's gland, while using his hand in firm, even strokes, thumbing Jeremy's frenulum until he felt the tremors begin. He caught most of Jeremy's release in his hand, then smeared it onto his own chest. He liked the sticky heat on his skin, and only then did he let himself tumble into orgasm, with Jeremy beneath him, legs tight around Brice's waist.

Brice rolled onto his back, and Jeremy pressed against him, taking the condom off, then leaning down to lick Brice's cock nice and clean. The extra stimulation pumped out a few last drops that Jeremy enjoyed with a slurpy chuckle. Then Jeremy licked Brice's chest clean too, with extra attention to one sticky nipple until Brice had to push him away.

"I'll head back to the guest room now." Jeremy sat up.

"No, you're not." Brice gripped his wrist. "Once you leave this room, you can't come back. I don't have a revolving door around here."

"Oh no?"

"No. You're my first overnight guest...." Brice stopped. He hadn't meant to get onto this topic. Too late now. It wasn't something he'd wanted to talk to Jeremy about.

"Ever? Were you a virgin before you started fooling around with me? Or just don't like strangers in your bed?"

"I lived with someone for a long time... but since then, you're the first."

"Thank you." Jeremy snuggled up against Brice and didn't keep asking questions.

Brice appreciated Jeremy's unexpected tact and politeness. "Thank *you*."

They held each other tight until sleep overtook them.

Chapter NINETEEN

SUN STREAMED through the windows when Jeremy woke up next to Brice, who was still sound asleep, breathing deeply, one arm across Jeremy's chest. He didn't want to wake Brice and lay listening to him, feeling his heart beating as the sun warmed the room. The furniture in here was as beautiful as the rest of the flat, like a fancy bed-and-breakfast. No canopy on this bed, so Jeremy examined the coffered ceiling.

The drapes were still open, and even from bed, Jeremy could see out into the bay toward Alcatraz. From another room the Golden Gate Bridge would be visible. He'd get a proper look around later. He let out a sigh as he relived the night before. They'd had a few rough spots and misunderstandings, although the lovely dinner and Brice's lovemaking had all but eliminated Jeremy's concerns.

But it was crazy to think coming here meant anything. They still weren't on any equal footing. They'd gone from the Dinner Club bedroom, where Brice was nominally in charge because he paid for everything, to Brice's bed, where he had the home field advantage. Jeremy was guest rather than a paid companion, but nothing had really changed. Had Jeremy thought it might?

He wasn't sure what he'd expected when he'd given Brice the ticket. He wanted them to meet in a neutral location and do something that wasn't about getting into bed or getting each other off. Or not only about sex. It had been as satisfying as ever with Brice. But was there anything more? Jeremy didn't want to think about it, much less have a discussion on the topic. He'd been crazy trying to see Brice outside of the club. Tonight they would go back to their regular arrangement, and this would never need to be discussed.

The phone rang and Brice stirred. He grinned at Jeremy and answered the phone. "Myeah?" A pause. "Uh-huh." Brice kissed Jeremy's shoulder as he listened.

Jeremy felt self-conscious in the light of day. He didn't belong in Brice's real world. He was part of Brice's secret life. Time to go. He started to sit up.

Brice held Jeremy's wrist and shook his head.

"Can't make it this morning. I'm busy. ... All day. And tonight. ... I can meet for a late lunch tomorrow if it can't wait till Monday. ... Fine. Fine." Brice pressed his lips together and nodded. "Okay. Bye." He hung up. "Sorry about that." Then he leaned down and kissed Jeremy. "Good morning."

"Good morning. Sounds important. I can get going."

"Nothing that can't wait until tomorrow or Monday. My boss is under the impression I don't have a life outside of work. For a change, he's wrong."

Jeremy didn't reply, but Brice's comment cheered him.

"I make some decent waffles if you have time to stay for breakfast."

The intimacy of the invitation touched Jeremy. "I haven't had homemade waffles in a very long time."

"Please don't tell me your mom used to make them for you."

"I wasn't exactly thinking of my mom just now, but I'm a little disturbed that you were." Jeremy grinned.

"Point taken. You have to stay in bed—naked—until the waffles are done. Can you handle that?"

"I suppose so."

"I'll get some coffee going." Brice hopped out of bed, nude and gorgeous even in the harsh morning light. His cock was slightly thick, and Jeremy wouldn't have minded a little prebreakfast playtime. He watched Brice's firm ass as he walked out of the room and thought about what might happen later, since Brice had told him to stay undressed.

He heard Brice grinding coffee beans, and a few minutes later, the aroma of fresh-brewing coffee tickled his nose and made his stomach rumble. He hadn't given a moment's thought to food since dinner the night before, but now he was ravenous. They had expended a lot of energy, hadn't they?

Brice's bare feet on the wooden floor alerted Jeremy to his arrival a moment before he entered.

"What the hell?" He shook his head and stared.

"Today I'll serve you." He put a steaming mug of coffee on the night table. "What do you think?" He did a model's catwalk turn, showing off his outfit: a silk tie, an apron, and apparently nothing else. "Be kind, I only had about two minutes to come up with this."

Jeremy couldn't hold back the laughter. "I did say I liked you in a tie." He grinned, admiring Brice's round, bare ass. "Two courses, then?"

Brice gave a charmingly cryptic shrug as a reply. "How do you take your coffee?"

"Milk and sugar, please, if it's not too much trouble."

Brice pulled a spoon and sugar packets from one pocket in his apron, and a small container of milk from the other.

"Oh, and I thought you were happy to see me," Jeremy teased.

"But I am, sir." Brice sat on the edge of the bed and put milk and sugar in Jeremy's coffee, stirring it the way Jeremy did for him at the Dinner Club.

Jeremy started to sit up against the headboard, and Brice quickly rearranged the pillows behind his back, propping him up.

"Comfortable, sir?"

Jeremy felt his cheeks warm. He felt so out of place here, in Brice's bed, with Brice serving him. He just nodded and gratefully took the mug when Brice handed it to him. The coffee was incredible. Dark and rich and much more flavorful than the supermarket ground beans he used at home. After a few sips, he felt emboldened.

"So, Brice, what's on your menu?"

"Just about everything. How can I serve you?" Brice shifted position so he was facing Jeremy. The apron pushed away from his body.

"Oh, really?" Jeremy couldn't believe he was saying this. He also couldn't believe the way he slid a hand up Brice's thigh and noticed the apron push out farther. He liked that. He stroked Brice's thigh with one hand while drinking coffee with the other, trying to get up the courage to reach for Brice's now-obvious erection.

"I told you I was glad to see you, sir." Brice spoke in the soft, flirtatious way the boys at the club did. "Would you like to find out how glad?"

Jeremy's breath caught in his throat, and he slid his hand all the way up Brice's thigh until he could grasp his cock. Brice was aroused, but not fully hard. A couple of smooth strokes remedied that. It was nice to see how quickly Brice responded to his touch. Under the sheets, Jeremy was already pretty damn hard too.

From the kitchen came the ding of a timer.

"Waffle time," Brice said. He moved to stand up, and Jeremy realized he was still holding onto Brice's cock.

He pulled his hand away, embarrassment washing over him again. "Sorry."

"Don't be. I liked that." A pause. "Sir." Brice stood, and now the apron was much farther from his body. "Now you get to remove something before I go."

Jeremy debated. He would like to see Brice just wearing the shimmery necktie. But that wasn't fair if he was going to be cooking. He put the coffee down and sat up so he could reach up to loosen the tie, wanting to touch Brice's shoulders and chest as he did so. But he restrained himself, only letting his hands linger on his throat and collarbone. He slid the tie slowly from Brice's neck and gave in to the sudden desire to kiss one pink nipple.

Brice just stood there, not reciprocating, but the little shudders through his body indicated he liked it. "Thank you, sir." He made another quick turn around the room, showing off his body, before leaving the room, his tight ass barely bobbing as he moved out of Jeremy's sight.

"Jesus." Jeremy lay back against the pillows and tried to calm himself down. It was strange having someone wait on him, Brice letting himself be touched, displaying himself. Jeremy wanted to touch, but he didn't want to invade Brice's personal space. They'd spent several nights together, made love and fucked each other senseless, but this was something else entirely.

As his cock throbbed and desire coursed through his body, Jeremy finally understood the attraction of the Dinner Club. The luxury of having your own boy for the evening, to touch and play with practically however you wanted? No wonder men spent so much money to be there. It was a powerful experience and incredibly arousing. Perhaps it was even more exciting to have a total stranger at your complete beck and call.

Jeremy licked his lips and hoped the waffles—and Brice—would be here soon.

AS BRICE watched the last batch of waffles cooking, he thought about Jeremy, waiting for him in bed. He'd felt so self-conscious going in to serve him the coffee, not sure whether Jeremy would appreciate it or feel that Brice was demeaning his role at the club. When he saw Jeremy's initial embarrassment, he wished he'd never come up with ridiculous idea in the first place. But when Jeremy's discomfort turned to playfulness and arousal, Brice enjoyed the game. Maybe more than he'd expected. There was an amazing feat of surrender to give someone else liberty with your body. Even more so with a stranger.

Brice pulled the waffles out of the oven, where they had stayed warm and crispy, and plated them before garnishing with sliced berries and whipped cream. He set two plates, silverware, and syrup on a tray and headed for the bedroom.

Jeremy glanced up expectantly as he entered. "Smells fantastic."

"I hope you like it." Brice put the tray down next to Jeremy.

"Looks fantastic too. Thank you."

Brice was about to sit down when Jeremy stopped him.

"I'd like to take that apron off you first."

The confidence in Jeremy's tone sent the apron fluttering, reviving his slightly flagging hard-on.

"Yes, sir." He stood by the bed as Jeremy reached around to untie the strings, fondling his ass and getting him even more revved up. By the time the apron had been tossed away, Brice had an erection to be proud of. Jeremy had that effect on him normally, but now, in their reversed roles, being with him was even more arousing.

"That looks delicious too." Jeremy wrapped a hand around Brice and squeezed gently before leaning over and licking at the slit. "Mmm." He took the whole glans into his mouth, and Brice thought the wet heat would make him explode. Jeremy let Brice's cock slide out of his mouth and grinned up at him. "I'm starving, for more than your cock, at least for now."

"Yes, sir." The words came out shaky. Brice hadn't quite caught his breath yet.

"I'm not sure how we're going to eat this beautiful meal," Jeremy said.

"I have a plan." Brice grinned. He peeled back the sheets, pleased to see Jeremy's eagerness beneath. Then he straddled Jeremy's lap, balancing on his knees and lower legs. He scooted forward until his cock dueled with Jeremy's, their balls squishing together pleasantly. "How's this?"

The position gave easy access to play with each other during the meal.

"Perfect."

Brice cut pieces of waffle and fed them to Jeremy, occasionally dropping a piece onto his lap or chest, and he gladly licked away stray splashes of whipped cream and syrup.

"I think you're dropping things on purpose." Jeremy shook his head as a glob of cream landed on the head of his cock.

"No, I'm not." Brice's voice was muffled as he spoke around Jeremy's hard-on.

"I've had enough. Breakfast was really good."

"As they say, it gets better." Brice came up for air before going back down on Jeremy, pleased with the soft whimper his mouth coaxed out of Jeremy.

One sweet, sticky orgasm later, they were both messy from cream, syrup, and Jeremy's pleasure. They laughed and kissed, rolling around together until they were both breathless.

"Brice, stop." Jeremy's voice was suddenly serious.

Brice sat up and looked at him. He had the paleness of someone who'd suffered a fright. "I'm sorry. Did I hurt you?"

Jeremy shook his head and moved to get up. Brice caught him by the shoulders and kneeled next to him on the bed. "What? What's wrong?"

"This. You're spoiling me. Last night, this morning, it's all too… incredible. I don't want to get used to this. I can't."

"Don't you like being with me this way? Like this?" He swept his hand around the room, comfortable and lived in, unlike the old-fashioned but impersonal luxury of the rooms upstairs at the Dinner Club. Now Brice felt the warmth drain from his face and body. Had he overstepped with Jeremy? He thought they'd been getting along so well.

"I do. I like it more than I should. I can't get too attached to you."

"Why? Because you have other clients? Because you need to keep some distance from the clients?" Brice's tone turned icy.

Jeremy shook his head, blinking. "No. Because I don't want you to make me think we could ever be more than we are when we're at the club."

"Aren't we already?"

Jeremy glanced up, eyes questioning.

"Jeremy, when I first met you, you filled a void in my life—a physical need—in a fun and exciting way. But the more I spend time with you, especially like last night, where I can talk to you and get to know you, the more I realize you fill up the emptiness in my heart too."

As soon as the words were out of his mouth, Brice kicked himself. What was he saying? The thoughts just popped out, fully formed, without benefit of going through his brain. But he knew they were true. Something about Jeremy was different from anyone he'd met.

"But you don't know anything about me. How can you say that?"

"Because who we are when we're not together doesn't define who we are when we are together. We don't have ideas and expectations. We are just ourselves. At least I have been."

"Yes, Brice, this is me. I'm not putting on an act."

"Do you want to spend time with me, get to know me, and maybe progress to something more fulfilling for both of us?"

"You mean like…." Jeremy stopped and pressed his lips together. "What do you mean?"

"Like a real relationship, whatever *that* is. Not as your trick or a client. As your lover, unqualified, and maybe more."

"You're serious?" Jeremy suddenly looked so young again. Brice didn't know how old he was. Maybe he should have asked before he jumped in with both feet.

Jeremy nodded, and Brice pulled him in close for a kiss. His cock reminded him he hadn't come yet as it prodded Jeremy, stiffening as the kiss went on. Not such great timing, but every touch from Jeremy made Brice feel like he was seventeen again.

When they broke the kiss, their skin stuck together as they pulled away, and they both laughed, breaking the tension that had built up around their serious discussion.

"Since you cooked, it's the least I can do to clean up. How big is your shower?"

A few minutes later, they embraced and kissed under warm massaging jets.

"I'm going to have bruises from that thing," Jeremy said as he wrapped one hand around Brice's cock. "Let's start with this."

He pushed Brice against the wall and slid down to his knees.

Everything else disappeared as Jeremy sucked at him. If he wasn't a pro, he sure gave head like one, not that Brice would know. But his technique was so incredible, it must have taken a lot of practice to perfect. Dizzy from lack of oxygen, Brice reached back to steady himself against the wall and knocked the showerhead down from the clip. It swung back and forth, spraying Jeremy and leaving rivulets of water dripping down his face as he continued worked Brice's cock.

"Just leave it," Jeremy said around Brice's dick.

"You sure?" Brice hoped like hell Jeremy didn't want him to put the damn thing back right this moment.

Jeremy reached for the showerhead. "Can I try something?"

"Uh, I guess so."

Jeremy took the length of Brice into his mouth again, tongue writhing against Brice's most sensitive places. He'd learned well what Brice loved and was able to control when Brice would plunge over the cliff into orgasm.

Brice concentrated on Jeremy's talented mouth. Then suddenly he felt a soft, warm spray between his legs, striking his perineum and asshole in the most incredible way. He let out a groan that echoed around the shower and the whole bathroom.

"You like?"

"Fuck, yeah. Oh yeah." He couldn't think. The pleasant warmth and pressure on his sensitive skin combined with Jeremy's mouth on his cock, and he came hard and fast, like he'd been hit full force by a tidal wave of incredible pleasure. He rode, hoping it would never end. He gasped for air.

The sound of Jeremy choking brought Brice back to earth. He'd come down Jeremy's throat, and he didn't think he'd been very careful about it. Jeremy coughed and started breathing again.

"Oh God. Are you okay?" Brice fell to his knees beside Jeremy.

Jeremy nodded, holding his throat with one hand. He swallowed and began to pull air into his lungs. The color came back into his face. Then he smiled. "I couldn't tell. Did you like that?"

"I thought maybe I'd died and gone to heaven."

"Shut up." Jeremy chuckled. "Help me up?"

Brice gladly pulled Jeremy to his feet and drew him close for a long, possessive kiss. He held on tightly, taking everything he could from the moment.

How on earth could he handle the day this would all go to hell and Jeremy would walk out of his life?

He glanced down into Jeremy's eyes and saw his own strong emotions reflected there, and decided he wouldn't worry about that just yet.

Chapter TWENTY

ON WEDNESDAY, Jeremy rode in the back of the limo to the club for dinner, alone this time. He and Brice had spoken once on the phone for a brief, awkward conversation until one of Brice's associates called him into a meeting he couldn't duck out of. But since Brice had called him, Jeremy thought that was a good sign. Brice must not yet regret anything he'd said or done with Jeremy the previous weekend.

What would tonight be like? If his racing heart was any indication, he couldn't wait to see Brice. If only he could calm himself down. By the time they arrived, he thought he had himself composed enough. But when he walked into the dressing room, he had second thoughts.

Kit came barreling up to him before he'd gotten ten feet inside.

"Look at you, all glowing! What did you do over the weekend? Dish, girl!"

A few of the other boys looked up expectantly.

"I, uh." Was that judgment or disapproval on their faces? Not on Kit's, at least. "Nothing."

"You lie like a cheap rug. Whatever that means. I can tell something's different about you. In a good way. In a very good way. You have been having some amazing"—he drew the word out into several extra syllables—"sex."

Jeremy shook his head and stared at his feet. Was he so transparent?

"You do look a lot more relaxed than usual," Law said over his shoulder as he applied some eyeliner.

"Mmm, mmm, mmm, mmm." Kit ran a finger across Jeremy's cheek. "Who is he?"

"He's... no one."

"So there is someone!" Kit just wouldn't give up.

"I have to get ready, Kit."

"To be continued, sweet potato pie!" Kit sashayed over to his own mirror as Jeremy's mood took a major downturn.

He rushed to his mirror and wondered what Brice would like tonight? Should he paint his nipples? Use a butt plug? Better not. Kit was perceptive enough to notice if he did anything different for Hunter Green tonight. But as soon as he was alone with Brice, Jeremy would ask him what he'd like next time.

Thomas came in to hand out costumes. Tonight's theme was sports night. Everyone got jockstraps and uniforms of various sports and wristbands color coded for their gentlemen. There was a box of sports gear for them to play with.

"Oh great. I love big balls night!" Kit announced as he grabbed a basketball from the box and bounced it a few times.

"The jokes just don't stop all night. And we've heard them all." Rand groaned.

"For some reason they think it's carte blanche with *our* balls too," Taylor said, cupping his sac. "I *hate* sports night!" He directed his comment to Thomas's back.

"I heard that," Thomas shouted back. "You don't have to work tonight, Taylor."

Taylor mumbled under his breath as he donned a tennis outfit with a tiny swinging skirt instead of the tight shorts everyone else had. He put his long hair in a ponytail and dug a tennis racquet out of the box. He shook it menacingly in Thomas's direction.

Jeremy laughed as he put on his soccer uniform. Tiny white shorts—practically a staple for him—that rode up so much the straps across his ass were visible even if he didn't bend over, a red-and-blue skintight jersey that made him feel more like Spiderman than David Beckham, and sheer, silky knee-high socks. He had to admit they looked good on his legs. He stepped into sport shoes and pulled a soccer ball out of the box. He'd played in high school, so he kicked the ball around the dressing room a few times till he got the hang of it again.

"You got some moves," Law said. "Not bad."

"Time to go, boys," Thomas said from the hallway. "Do a couple of circuits playing with the balls. Toss them—"

"We know the drill, sergeant," Kit said, fluffing Thomas's hair as they filed out of the room. Thomas wasn't deserving of a pastry name.

The gong sounded, and Kit pranced in wearing a version of a basketball uniform, bouncing the ball. They jogged around, tossing balls to each other or to the gentlemen. Jeremy came in dribbling his soccer ball, but he lost control of it as soon as Brice's gaze locked on him. It was such a soft, sweet look it made Jeremy's chest ache with joy to see.

"Oh sister, you are in for it." Kit smashed into Jeremy from behind, and the gentlemen laughed, thinking it was part of the show. "You didn't, did you?"

Jeremy didn't say anything as he tried to retrieve his ball, which had rolled up against Brice's chair. Brice leaned down to pick it up and smiled. Jeremy gave him a shy smile back and followed everyone else out of the room.

"You did!" Kit whispered loudly when they were back in the dressing room. "You better hope Thomas doesn't see you and Green making schmoopy eyes at each other."

"Schmoopy eyes?" Jeremy tried not to laugh, though the warning jarred him. "What will he do?"

"He might fire you. Or kick Green out of the club for violating the… policies."

"Oh."

"You better hope you do turn out to be Julia Roberts in this little show…. Or—"

"You two, get the first course!" Thomas snapped at Kit and Jeremy, and they raced into the kitchen and ended up last into the dining room. Kit usually wanted to go first, but he didn't say anything about losing his prime spot.

The first course was melon with prosciutto. The chefs had gotten into the theme and, instead of the more traditional honeydew wedges, had made and wrapped individual melon balls with the thin cured ham. Jeremy settled next to Brice and offered him a ball, trying not to smile too much or make schmoopy eyes.

Brice took the morsel and Jeremy's fingers into his mouth, giving the fingers a suck before letting go in order to chew. Having Brice suck his fingers got Jeremy instantly hard. The jock strap was tight. Maybe it would come off soon. If he asked, Brice would do that for him.

"Come sit on my lap, J—Remy."

Jeremy sat across Brice's lap and fed him another melon ball.

"That's not what I meant."

Jeremy stood up, and Brice put a hand on his ass, then slid it down his leg slowly before moving up again. Then he slid his finger under the ass strap. The touch was electrifying. Thank God he hadn't gone for the butt plug. He'd be in big trouble now. As it was he could feel his cock poking out over the top of the jockstrap. The thing was so damn tiny, probably designed that way.

"You know what I'd like, Remy."

Jeremy smiled and straddled Brice, the way he'd sat on Jeremy feeding him waffles just a few days earlier.

"You look a little warm, Remy."

Understatement. Jeremy's whole body was on fire.

"Let's fix that." Brice took hold of the hem of Jeremy's jersey and started to peel it up, sliding his hands along Jeremy's back and abs. When the shirt had Jeremy's arms trapped over his head, Brice sucked on each of Jeremy's nipples for a moment before he finally pulled the shirt off completely. "Cooler now?"

The air on Jeremy's wet nipples made them peak, but the rest of his body was overheating. He couldn't get enough air. Damn Brice for doing this to him during the first course. How would he last through four more? He bit his lower lip and fed more melon to Brice.

"Mmm. Delicious. Would you like one?" Brice fed some melon to Jeremy. His other hand explored the straps across Jeremy's ass.

"You do know we're supposed to be seducing you, and not the other way around? Sir."

Brice nodded, a mischievous light dancing in his eyes.

Then the gong sounded, ending the course, and Jeremy had to force himself to get out of Brice's lap.

In the hallway, Law came up to him. "What's gotten into Mr. Green? I've never seen him play that hard, that fast."

"More like what got into Remy," Kit chimed in. He swiped a hand across Jeremy's shorts. "Oh, and he's that hard, that fast. Watching the two of you is like a spectator sport. We're taking bets on which of you will come first and when."

"I don't think they'll make it through another whole course," Taylor said as they picked up the next dish, a salad of cherry tomatoes and bite-sized mozzarella balls. Jeremy shook his head at the sight of it. He noticed Thomas watching him closely as he entered the dining room. Did he suspect? What would happen if he discovered Brice and Jeremy had seen each other outside of the club?

The jokes kept up as they served the main dish, some kind of meatballs in a tomato sauce. No spaghetti.

"Are all the dishes going to be balls?" Jeremy asked, and everyone just laughed. It was going to be a long, hard evening, he thought as they marched back into the dining room.

During this course all but one of them was down to the jockstrap and accessories, except for Taylor, who was bare under the little white skirt. Just as he'd predicted, his gentleman couldn't keep his hands off Taylor's balls. They were sitting next to Brice and Jeremy, so he had a prime view of everything going on. Even Brice seemed enthralled by the way the man kept pulling at them.

"Does he think they'll get longer if he tugs hard enough?" Brice whispered.

Jeremy shrugged and tried not to watch.

"You seem awfully interested in Taylor's balls," Jeremy said.

"Oh, am I? Are yours feeling neglected?" Brice teased. "Let's remedy that." He pulled the jockstrap until he could get a handful of Jeremy's sac. It tickled. Jeremy squirmed, and a meatball rolled out of the dish and down Brice's shirt and pants.

"Oh, I'm so sorry, Br—Mr. Green." Jeremy hopped off Brice's lap, and the jockstrap slid off.

"Forget it. They have dry cleaning. Now come back here."

Jeremy tried to pick up his jockstrap—he'd already lost his shorts during the course—but his erection made it difficult to bend down. When he straightened up, he felt the gazes of the other men in the room.

"Let's see that boner, boy. C'mon!" one man called from the other side of the table.

Jeremy let Brice turn him around. For the first time since he started here, he felt self-conscious. He'd forgotten his arousal wasn't a private thing between him and Brice when they were here. He put a good face on it and did a little twirl.

"He's got a nice set of balls on him!" another man shouted. He'd had several drinks from the sound of it. "Hangin' nice and low."

Brice slid an arm around Jeremy's waist, then reached down to cup his balls. "Not feeling left out now?"

Jeremy wanted to smack Brice. Not from anger, but because Brice's other hand was exploring some very sensitive spots around Jeremy's ass and making his dick even harder.

"Hey, which of them has the biggest balls?" the drunk guy shouted. "Let's line 'em up."

Everyone else yanked his boy's jockstrap off and examined their balls. Taylor lifted his skirt up and shook his head as he caught Jeremy's eye. "Told you," he mouthed.

All the boys were lined up, and the men filed past, examining their equipment—hands off, Brice made it a rule before he let Jeremy participate. Jeremy liked how Brice didn't want anyone else's hands on him, though a few guys got far too up close and personal in other ways.

Jeremy won lowest balls, Kit had the tightest sac, and it was unanimous that Taylor had the biggest balls. Jeremy also came away with the best hard-on honors, and Brice had to make sure no one else got a handful of anything.

The contest threw off the usual pattern of the dinners, since all the boys were naked by the third course, and there wasn't much left to reveal. Most of the other men ignored dessert—sorbet balls—in favor of exploring the naked flesh all around them.

Kit and Law provided entertainment as Law stood on a small pedestal and let Kit shave his balls.

By that time, no one was paying any attention to Brice and Jeremy. They got each other worked up so much they left before the cognac was served.

Upstairs in Room 4, Brice had Jeremy in his arms before he closed the door behind them. They made love fiercely until they were both exhausted. Still sticky, sweaty, and out of breath, Brice pulled Jeremy up close.

"I'm sorry about tonight, Jeremy. Really sorry. I shouldn't have showed you off like that. It wasn't respectful."

Jeremy's chest was heavy and tight. "There's not much respectful about this place. Don't think about it." He paused. "In a way, it's probably a good thing it happened tonight."

"How could me treating you like a piece of meat be good?"

"Thomas knows about us, or suspects. Kit figured it out almost immediately. If you'd been too nice to me, they would know for sure. Now, they won't be so suspicious."

Brice took in the information without responding. He closed his eyes for a moment and let out a sigh.

"Even so, can you forgive me?"

"Didn't we just make love?" Jeremy wouldn't look at Brice.

"No, Jeremy. What we just did wasn't making love. It was barely even fucking. It was something else I can't even define."

"Then don't—"

"Don't tell me not to define it. Don't say that." Brice's voice sounded tight and sad. Hearing it made Jeremy's heart break a little bit more.

"Come here?" Brice gathered Jeremy to his chest and held him.

Jeremy lay in Brice's arms and listened to him fall asleep. Until tonight, that had been one of his favorite things. Now, he had a lump in his throat, and even breathing felt like a chore.

Which had been the worse mistake, spending time with Brice outside of the club, or coming back here after their relationship had shifted?

He stared at the ceiling as if the answer were written there.

His heart told him one thing and his head another.

Chapter TWENTY-ONE

WHEN BRICE woke Thursday morning, he was alone in the big bed. A wave of fear washed over him.

"Jeremy?" He sat up and looked around. "Jeremy?" Then he noticed Jeremy's bag on the floor near the wardrobe and the light coming from under the bathroom door.

"In here," Jeremy shouted. A moment later he came out, fully clothed, hair damp. "I have to get to the lab. Sorry."

As he walked over to pick up his bag, the scent of shampoo and shower gel wafted toward Brice. It usually made him feel good because it was associated with Jeremy. But as he watched Jeremy walk out the door without as much as a kiss, Brice felt a chill creep into his body that wouldn't go away, even when he pulled the covers up to his chin.

He'd wanted to have his cake and eat it too. A relationship with Jeremy and playtime here, knowing the steady money was important to Jeremy. There were alternatives, but the way things stood, if Brice offered Jeremy help with his expenses, it would come across as trying to pay for forgiveness.

How could he be so competent at work, and such a fuck-up when it came to his personal life? Again. For a change it wasn't his job that doomed his nascent relationship with Jeremy. The irony felt heavy in his gut.

He had to get to the office. It was the end of the third quarter, and they had to conduct performance reviews on the portfolio companies that hadn't come in yet. Ron wanted him to attend a few of the discussions as they decided which firms to continue to support and which to cut back or drop funding for altogether. Brice would scrutinize the contracts for the terms of each deal if a change was necessary.

He'd spend the next week looking at pie charts and listening to a bunch of blah, blah, ROI and blah, blah earnings per share. Right now, the only thing to keep his attention was Jeremy.

They had a date scheduled for Saturday: first a walk on the beach at sunset, then dinner at a divey joint that served the craziest sandwich combinations in San Francisco. Greg had hated everything about the place and made it known every time they'd gone. Brice thought Jeremy would like it. It had a Berkeley feel to it. Old Berkeley, not the new gentrified Berkeley.

But would Jeremy show up?

JEREMY'S LAB work kept him so busy he didn't have time to think about Brice during the days. But at night it was a different matter. Even though Brice had made it clear he thought of Jeremy as more than an object to display, he still couldn't wipe away the unexpected sense of humiliation when Brice spun him around to show him off to the other men. It gnawed at him, day and night.

But the loneliness each night as Jeremy wondered what Brice was doing served as a powerful reminder that the emotional attachment he'd developed hadn't changed as a result of Brice's single moment of insensitivity. Nothing would stop him from keeping their Saturday date. He dressed with particular care to his appearance and headed for the city.

He'd been to the Java Café before, but he'd forgotten how bad the delays on the N-Judah line were, and the longer the ride took, the worse his stomach knotted. Finally, he arrived and glanced in the window, knowing how much it would hurt if Brice wasn't there. The clock on the wall told him he was ten minutes late. The coffee shop buzzed with activity. People who had just been to the beach had the rosy-red glow from the brisk salty breezes that washed over Ocean Beach in the afternoon.

His gaze went from table to table. Then his heart trembled when he spotted Brice in the far corner. A nearly empty glass of tea sat in front of him. He wore a tan zip-up jacket, and he had the fresh windswept look, chestnut hair mussed. It was the look of someone who would be right at home at the helm of a sailboat skimming across the waves, heading out to sea under the Golden Gate Bridge.

Brice had come. He really wanted Jeremy, wanted something besides what they had at the club. Excitement made him race inside, and the look of joy on Brice's face as he spotted Jeremy meant he'd made the right decision.

Brice stood and pulled Jeremy to him and planted a definitive kiss on his lips. It stayed tame, but no one in the place could doubt Brice's feelings. Certainly not Jeremy. He let himself be swept up in the moment.

When they separated, Jeremy noticed the creases around Brice's bloodshot eyes, mostly from the same sleeplessness plaguing Jeremy.

"I didn't think you'd—" they both began, then self-consciously stopped and sat down.

Jeremy didn't want to rehash their last meeting. Instead, he said, "You promised me a romantic walk on the beach and a beautiful sunset."

Obvious relief flooded Brice's face. "If the clouds cooperate. But I can't guarantee the sunset won't be more than a red glow."

"I won't hold the weather against you." Heavy fog typified this westernmost part of San Francisco. Even in the summer, there were days the locals never saw the sun.

"Let's go." Brice stood and put some cash on the table before threading his arm around Jeremy's.

They crossed the street, heading into the strong breeze coming off the ocean. Little billows of sand blew across the Great Highway as they made their way to the beach. It was a lovely day, or at least it was to Jeremy. They strolled hand in hand, Brice stopping practically every ten feet to kiss him. On Jeremy's romance scale of one to ten, it hit eleven.

Kids flying kites raced past, and a few windsurfers in wetsuits braved the elements for the last waves of the day. When they reached the end of the beach near the zoo, Jeremy didn't want to start back. He was too happy here and now.

Streaks of pink, orange, and red spilled across the sky as they made their way along the beach. The families and surfers had left, replaced by others strolling and enjoying the evening spectacle in the sky. Soon the evening fog would take over again, but for now it was clear and beautiful.

"You're cold." Brice stopped walking and pulled his jacket off.

"I'm fine." Jeremy hadn't even noticed the wind had picked up until now. He was wearing a long-sleeved shirt, but it wasn't particularly warm. He dug in his messenger bag for a jacket and found only a dark blue Cal sweatshirt.

"You're shivering. That's not enough. The jacket's warmer." Brice took the sweatshirt and tugged the bag off Jeremy's shoulder. Then he helped him into the tan jacket. It had a thin lining of something incredibly warm. The fabric was smooth and felt wonderful. Like all of Brice's clothes, it was high quality and probably cost what Jeremy earned in a week.

"Thanks. What about you?"

Brice pulled the sweatshirt over his head. Jeremy reached up to draw hair out of Brice's eyes, and Brice grabbed his hand and brought it to his mouth for a sweet kiss. "I'm perfect. That jacket looks good on you."

"Really?" Jeremy had never paid much attention to his own clothes. Not many grad students did, especially in the sciences. It had never been an issue before. Now he was suddenly conscious of how much separated his life from Brice's.

"Yeah. Now let's get moving. I'm famished." Brice took hold of Jeremy's hand and tugged him along as they broke into a slow jog. With the wind whipping across his face and the sand soft beneath his feet, he found the sprint exhilarating. His heart was pounding, and he was a little winded when Brice slowed down. "It's a block from the beach. Let's cross."

"Good. Now I'm starving too." Jeremy's words came out between short breaths.

"God, you sound so damn sexy when you're breathless. Gives me chills."

"I told you not to give me your jacket."

"That's not the kind of chills I meant." Brice put an arm around Jeremy's waist as they waited to cross the Great Highway. When the light changed, Jeremy pulled Brice into a run, even though they had plenty of time to cross the six lanes.

At the other side, Brice slowed. "Why'd you go all Usain Bolt on me?"

"Maybe I like it when you're all breathless too. Especially when it's my fault."

"Mmm. Maybe we should get dinner to go."

Jeremy laughed. It felt good, great in fact, to be joking around with Brice. Just like a real couple on a real date. The stress and uncertainty of the past few days melted away, and he let it all out in peals of uncontrollable laughter.

"I hope your laughter's not a critique of my bedroom skills." Brice chuckled but hadn't joined in with Jeremy's giddiness.

"Not at all. I'm just… just having a great time tonight." Jeremy bit his lip. "Oh, God, I probably sound really lame. Like a sixteen-year-old girl or something. I'm sorry."

Brice stopped and turned to Jeremy; then he brushed stray hair out of Jeremy's eyes with a gentle touch. "It's not lame as long as it's honest. All I want is to know who you really are. No lies and no games." He caressed

Jeremy's cheek and pulled his face close to plant a soft, sweet kiss on Jeremy's lips.

The gentleness of the kiss and Brice's fingers on his face flooded Jeremy's entire body with desire. He was breathless again, feeling dizzy, and all entirely due to Brice.

His brain might be responding to oxytocin, but his body and heart told Jeremy he was falling in love. It felt wonderful, like flying. Jeremy had never experienced anything quite like this headiness before. But the higher Brice took him, the harder he would crash.

AFTER DINNER, when they were out on the street in front of the restaurant again, Brice took Jeremy's hand. "Would you like to come over?"

Jeremy glanced up sharply. "What? I mean, I...." He smiled. "I'm kind of a sure thing, but it's nice to be asked."

His reaction was so sweet and genuine Brice wondered how he'd ever thought Jeremy was a hustler. The memory of his initial mistrust hurt. It wasn't the only thing he needed to make up for.

"Is that a yes? Because you don't have to, unless you want to."

"Of course I want to. After this evening...." Jeremy left the thought hanging.

"I didn't take you to dinner so you'd feel obligated."

"It's definitely cheaper than a night at the Dinner Club."

"I don't need two hours of public foreplay to know I want to spend the night with you. And have you there when I wake up." Brice recalled the icy fear when he'd woken up alone in the bed at the club just a few days earlier. Jeremy had shown up tonight for their planned date, but Brice would be more careful not to insult Jeremy again.

"So what do you call your hand on my thigh during most of dinner?" Jeremy raised an eyebrow.

"Just making sure you didn't run off." Brice glanced up and down the street, and waved when he spotted a taxi on the next block.

"Did you think I would?"

"I'm prepared to chase you if you do." He squeezed Jeremy's hand.

The taxi stopped in front of them, and he opened the door for Jeremy, then slid in after him and gave the address to the driver. It was excruciating torture not to pull Jeremy into his lap. He just wanted to kiss him so much, hold him close enough to feel his heart beating. It wasn't about sex, just about needing to be close, to make sure Jeremy really was here with him.

Upstairs he poured two glasses of cognac, and they settled onto the couch.

Jeremy took off Brice's jacket and held it out. "Where should I put this?"

"Put it anywhere for now." Brice thought it looked good on Jeremy. He wanted to let Jeremy keep it. He just wasn't sure how Jeremy would take the offer. Best not to say anything just yet. They were barely back on solid ground, and despite the time they'd spent together, he really didn't know much about Jeremy.

He heard a beep. Jeremy's phone.

"I kind of need to get this, I'm really sorry. Just a couple of minutes." Jeremy answered and went into the kitchen for a short conversation.

"Was that your boyfriend?" Brice asked when he returned a few minutes later beaming. "Your other boyfriend?" Brice chuckled when he realized Jeremy hadn't known he was joking.

"Uh, no. One of my lab assistants. She had some really good results on the latest set of experiments and wanted to tell me right away."

"You have assistants?"

"Most people in my program do. I couldn't do all the lab work myself, or I'd be there twenty-four hours a day."

"Or late on Saturday nights."

"I've done my share of those, believe me."

"So you mentioned you're getting a PhD in biochemistry?" Brice had been surprised when he'd found this out a month into their Dinner Club relationship. He had no idea Jeremy was that smart or that committed. Now, he saw a light in Jeremy's eyes at the question. Clearly his work was important to him. "What are you working on?"

Jeremy sipped cognac, then glanced up at Brice. "Microbiology, actually. But you don't really want to hear all the boring details, do you?"

"Yes, I do." He wanted to know more about anything Jeremy was passionate about. Until now they'd avoided details about their work. It put them on more equal footing, not comparing who they were in their everyday lives.

"Right now?" Jeremy slid up close to Brice and put a hand on his thigh.

It was just enough contact to derail thoughts of anything but Jeremy right here and so close.

"You're right. Tell me at breakfast." He put his glass down, then reached over and took Jeremy's before pulling Jeremy into his arms and finally giving him that kiss he'd wanted so badly in the taxi.

They kissed for a long time, the desire building and surging through his body. He leaned back for a break and saw the arousal in Jeremy's eyes. When Brice brushed hair back from Jeremy's temple, sand rained down.

"Ah! Sand in my hair. Sorry." Jeremy brushed at his scalp. "Lots of it. I'll clean it up."

"Mine too. Don't worry about it. But I think we both need a good scrub." He paused. "Bath or shower?"

"Shower. Too long to run a bath."

"I like how you think."

Jeremy stood up.

"You want to go first?" Brice asked.

Jeremy shook his head and reached for Brice's hand. "Waste of water."

"I *love* how you think."

They undressed each other, more sand falling out of their hair and clothes, while the water warmed up. Jeremy cast a hungry look at Brice, eyeing him up and down. Brice realized that while he'd seen Jeremy naked so many times, Jeremy hadn't seen him in such bright light until now.

At least he seemed to like what he saw. Brice was in good shape for thirty-five, though he was no cover model. He let Jeremy look; it was only fair.

Then Jeremy opened the shower door and beckoned Brice inside.

They fell into each other's arms. Jeremy slid a hand down Brice's body, but Brice stopped him. He didn't want to get off in the shower, and Jeremy could get him there all too quickly.

"Let's play a game. No sex in here. No orgasms. Just hands. Okay?"

Jeremy nodded and grabbed the shampoo. He squeezed some out and reached up to massage it into Brice's hair and scalp, pressing himself against Brice in the process. Full-body-contact shampoo. Any salon offering this service would be booked a year out. He sighed and gave himself up to Jeremy's firm touch.

Afterward, Jeremy washed Brice's body before making sure the really important equipment was clean. With one soapy hand, Jeremy sudsed up Brice's balls and ass while sliding the other soapy hand along the length of his dick. Brice leaned back against the wall, needing the cool tile to balance the heat building in his core.

"I know I said just hands, but I also said no one comes yet."

Jeremy gave an impish grin. "I can't help myself. Your cock is just very, very dirty." He practically purred the last word. He would kill Brice if he kept this up. At least Jeremy stopped stroking him, but he kept up the ball massage and slid a finger along Brice's perineum in a way that made his insides melt.

When he didn't think he could stand any more of Jeremy's touch, Brice reciprocated until he had Jeremy in a similar state of arousal, begging Brice to stop or finish him off. After, they barely took time to dry off before falling into bed and giving in to their desire.

THE NEXT morning after an enjoyable hour of fooling around that left them exhausted, Brice rolled over on his side to look at Jeremy.

Jeremy still hadn't quite recovered from the last orgasm, and the hungry look in Brice's eyes frightened him a little. "Not again?"

"No. I couldn't if I wanted to."

"Don't you want to?" Jeremy tried to sound insulted.

"I think you're hazardous to my health. I need to get to the gym more often. Build my endurance."

"You're in great shape. Do you cycle? You should come over to the East Bay for a bike ride?"

"I've got a road bike, though I haven't ridden it in ages. But I'd like to. Although cycling's not what I was thinking about just now."

"Do I want to know what you were thinking?"

Brice took Jeremy's hand and pulled him close for a tender embrace. It felt amazing being wrapped in Brice's arms. Safe, warm, and unreal. When would reality set in?

"I don't know about you, but I'm starving. And I'm too worn out to even open a box of cereal."

"I take full responsibility." Jeremy chuckled.

"Or full credit."

"I can cook for you, Brice."

"No. I'll order breakfast. Anything you particularly like or don't like for breakfast?"

"I'm easy. Anything is fine with me."

"Eggs, pancakes, bacon, smoked salmon, bagels? Don't make me choose, or you'll end up with everything I like."

Jeremy shrugged. He wanted to know what Brice liked, to discover more of his charming quirks. How he hated cappuccino but loved café au lait. How he always liked to sleep on the left side of the bed and how he had the coldest toes in the world.

"Definitely bacon. Otherwise, I'm easy."

"Fair enough."

Brice ordered omelets and eggs Benedict, fresh fruit salad, and two orders of applewood-smoked bacon from a fantastic diner around the corner. When the doorbell sounded, he got up, still gloriously naked, and went to the door. Jeremy was still thinking about what a fantastic ass Brice had when he came back with the food, still naked.

"Did you answer the door like that?"

"Like what?"

Jeremy landed a soft punch on his shoulder. "Idiot."

"No. I held up a pillow from the couch. You have nothing to be jealous about. Though the guy did seem to be staring at my nipples. Maybe the teeth marks caught his attention."

"I didn't bite that hard, did I?" Jeremy leaned in close to examine one, then flicked it gently. "I don't see anything." He frowned at Brice, but gave the nipple a kiss anyway.

Brice handed Jeremy a paper food container with a huge omelet and thick, dark bacon giving off a mouthwatering aroma. Jeremy's stomach rumbled, and he grabbed a piece and took a bite.

"Mmm. God, this is the best bacon ever in the history of the universe."

Brice took Jeremy's hand and bit from his piece of bacon. "You're right. Nothing beats post-coital bacon."

They had barely finished eating when Brice's cell phone rang. He looked at the caller. "I have to take this. Sorry."

Jeremy liked the way he apologized. Most people just answered and ignored the person sitting right next to them.

"Oh Jesus, is that today? But it's Sunday. We have to put into the contracts that they can't have meetings on Sundays. ... Yeah ... Yeah. ... Bye." He turned to Jeremy. "I'm sorry, but I have to go to a meeting. The guys are going out of town tomorrow, and we need to take care of some quarter-end details before they leave. I didn't realize it was past noon already."

"That's fine. Do what you need to."

"You're welcome to stay here. I'll be gone three hours, maybe. Catch up on your sleep?"

That sounded like a wonderful plan. Too wonderful. It would be easy to stay here and wait, but not a good idea. "I should get into the lab and check the results my assistant got. They were a little too good to be true."

Brice nodded. He looked disappointed. "I need a shower."

"You don't think your colleagues like the smell of watermelon lube and latex?"

Brice gave a little snort. "Probably not on me. No." He got up, and Jeremy couldn't help staring. "Join me?"

"That could be dangerous. Make you even later."

"Probably not a good idea." Brice headed for the bathroom and took a quick shower before coming back into the bedroom, hair damp, still naked.

Jeremy sighed and started to get up. "I'll be really quick."

"Take your time. You can let yourself out. The door locks automatically." He pulled on a button-down shirt, still nude from the waist down. He liked the look. It would be even sexier if Brice were wearing a tie. Just the shirt and tie, still naked from the waist down. Jeremy had never met anyone who didn't put their underwear on first. He'd never noticed that about Brice before. One more adorable quirk.

When the shirt was buttoned, Brice slid into silky gray boxers and pulled on a pair of chinos. Jeremy slipped out of bed and pressed himself to Brice, naked flesh against cotton. Brice slid his arms around Jeremy and held him close before laying a perfect good-bye kiss on him, one Jeremy knew would keep him thinking about Brice until the next time they'd meet.

"Help yourself to the leftovers or whatever you want." Brice waved and left.

Jeremy wandered around the apartment for a few minutes after Brice's departure. There was an office, the guest room, and another room at the end of the hall with the door closed. He put his hand on the doorknob, then let go. It wouldn't do to snoop. Brice had shown enormous trust by leaving him alone here. He wouldn't repay the trust by invading Brice's privacy.

He did pad into the office to examine the books on the shelves: mostly law books and some classic novels. One shelf had classic gay fiction, another held detective stories. Something else he'd learned about Brice. He moved behind the imposing carved wooden desk and settled into Brice's chair, one of those pompous-looking leather affairs reminiscent of port and cigars. Not exactly Brice's style. He felt the leather, cool at first against Jeremy's naked flesh, but it soon warmed to his body temperature.

He imagined Brice sitting here, dressed in a fancy suit and tie when Jeremy came in naked and sat on his lap before he knelt between Brice's knees and drove him crazy. The desk was an old-fashioned type with a closed front that hid the person's legs. Jeremy could kneel down there sucking Brice's cock while he had a meeting, and the other person wouldn't even see him. The thought got him hard. Would Brice enjoy playing games?

The possibilities were endless.

Jeremy's hard-on hadn't subsided, so he took care of it in the shower, remembering last night with Brice. Afterward, as he was leaving, he found an envelope taped to the door with money for a taxi back to Berkeley. It was a nice gesture, so he allowed himself the luxury.

WHEN JEREMY got back home, he changed and headed for the lab. Rhoda had called the previous night because the results of the weekend's experiments were particularly good. Earlier in the semester, he'd hit a wall on the transfer mechanism for one of the antigens. For some reason, once it entered the cell, it completely degraded, and he had proposed several explanations and devised experiments to test each theory. So far, none of the experiments had been informative. Until now. He thought he might have the answer. If so, he would be able to propose a solution to the issue.

"This is excellent work, Jeremy," Dr. Morrell said when they met first thing on Monday. "Let me take a look at the protocols and results. I think once we can overcome this problem, PharmaTek will be able to get back on schedule for the vaccine."

"Should I keep working on the other experiments?"

"Absolutely. Focus on this set, but continue the others; even negative results offer useful information. You'll need to repeat this experiment to ensure we can replicate these results. I'll have one of my other students perform the work. Then we can submit a status report to PharmaTek."

"I'll get started on the analysis as soon as I have the next set of samples prepared."

"Jeremy, you need to let your undergrads do more of the basic lab work. It's how they learn. Remember when you were my assistant? You were always asking to do more. Rhoda and Varan can do the work, can't they?"

"Yes, but—"

"So let them. Your time is best spent on designing protocols and analyzing the results. You have plenty of data analysis to occupy you for the rest of the week." Dr. Morrell nodded and stroked his chin, like a villain from an old matinee film.

"Yes, sir." The "sir" sort of slipped out. Morrell cocked his head slightly but didn't remark. Jeremy grabbed his notebook, stuffing it into his bag as he rushed out the door.

He spent most of the next three days in his office in the Life Sciences Building. He shared it with another grad student who was away working on a joint project with a team at Johns Hopkins. It was nice to have the cramped space to himself for a while.

Plus, the work was a welcome distraction from having to wait until Wednesday to see Brice again. They had texted and talked a few times a day since Sunday. Their next date would be at a restaurant Jeremy liked in San Francisco's Mission District.

"I can get over to Berkeley. You don't have to keep coming into the city," Brice had said when Jeremy suggested the spot.

"Nope. I love this place. It closed about two years ago, and there was such an uproar from customers, they found another location and opened up again."

"Okay, I can't say no to something that good."

"If you don't like it, it will be our last date."

"I love it already."

"See you Wednesday."

Chapter TWENTY-TWO

QUARTER-END MEETINGS kept Brice busy all day every day. It was time for his firm to assess the financial results or progress of the companies they funded, the portfolio companies. Any company failing to meet expectations might lose their funding. It was up to the partners to make sure their investors made profits, and this was the only way.

By Wednesday afternoon, Brice's head was swimming with facts and figures. He'd had to draw up two termination contracts by 3:00 p.m., and if he could get out a little bit early, he'd have time for a workout and a shower before he met Jeremy for dinner. He'd ducked out of the last meeting because he wasn't needed.

Ron knocked on his door around four and shut the door behind himself as if he were hiding. Then he plopped down into a chair.

"I take it you're avoiding someone?"

"Just trying to recover from that last one. Company's working on a cure for some digestive issue I don't want to think about if I can help it."

Brice chuckled and started tidying up his desk.

"So when are you going to tell me about this new guy of yours?" Ron sat down in one of the chairs in front of Brice's desk.

"Who says there's a new guy?" Brice slipped into his jacket, figuring Ron would get the message he didn't want to chat just then.

"Because you've had a huge smile on your face most for the past two months, except for the past week. But I guess you sorted the problem out."

It was scary how well Ron knew him. Or how poorly he disguised his emotions. He'd better be more circumspect in the future.

"I'll tell you when there's something to tell."

"Fine." Ron's cell phone rang, and he picked up. "They're here? … Sure, Brice is here … Yeah."

"Brice isn't here. You're simply experiencing a memory on your retinas." He put a few folders in his messenger bag, though he probably wouldn't have time to look at them that evening.

"Hey there, fella. Where do you think you're going?"

"I've had one day off the past week. I even worked Sunday when I had more enjoyable options."

"Give me an hour, Brice. I rescheduled this meeting so I could have you there. I need you as a tiebreaker. The partners have been arguing over it for the past year, and I need you to back me up."

"Fine. Give me a minute, and I'll join you in the board room."

"Don't even think about making a run for it. I've got security on speed dial. They won't let you out the front door." Ron grinned and headed for the door.

"Hey, which company is it?"

"It's Pharma—" Ron was too far down the hall to hear the rest.

"Pharma what?" Brice frowned.

Half the companies they dealt with seemed to be called Pharm-something, and the other half had "Gen" in their name. He glanced at the firm's online calendar: Pharm-Gen. This one used both. How creative. The value of firms that helped companies choose unique and relevant names finally sunk in.

He saw that meeting for Pharma*Tek* was the next morning, and he'd made a note to sit on that one whether he was needed or not. They were working on an HIV vaccine, and Brice was curious about their progress. He knew Jeremy's research was in immunology, but due to confidentiality issues on both their parts, they'd avoided details of their work.

He couldn't recall anything about Pharm-Gen, so he waited fifteen minutes before heading to the meeting, using the time to skim their binder, and avoiding the initial chitchat. When he arrived, one of the company's officers was pointing to data on a PowerPoint presentation. Ron started to hand him a binder containing reports and financials, but Brice held up his own. He took a seat near the far end of the table and flipped directly to the balance sheet and earnings reports, tuning out the speaker.

He glanced over the information, keeping in mind what he'd been told by Ron and Lane at previous similar meetings.

The numbers weren't good and hadn't improved at all over the past six months. The balance sheet didn't look right, but he wasn't sure why. It seemed an easy decision to drop them from the portfolio. Their expenses kept increasing, far beyond initial projections because they had entered into badly structured licensing agreements where they had to pay before they generated an income stream. They would never get back on budget, which meant the firm and their investors would never achieve the expected return on their capital. Brice wasn't a finance guy, but even he knew that much.

"Thank you, Bob. I appreciate you coming in today and being so prepared." Ron flapped his binder. "Does anyone have questions for Dr. Bartlet?"

A few people asked questions about research details Brice couldn't begin to understand. He couldn't help glancing at his watch and wondering whether he'd get to the restaurant on time. Images of dinner and the upcoming weekend with Jeremy flashed through his brain.

"Brice, did you have anything to add? Questions, comments, whatever, for Dr. Bartlet or the CFO, Trevor?"

"No. I'm good with what's in the report here."

"Thanks, Bob. We'll discuss the situation and get back to you with our decision. We've got a lot to think about this quarter." Ron stood and saw the two men to the door before returning to his seat.

"What's the verdict, gentlemen?" Ron glanced around the table to the three other senior partners and Brice. "Do we need a discussion?"

"You know my stand on this," Parker said.

"Mine too," Christie added, giving Parker a sideways glance.

Clearly they disagreed, but Brice hadn't been able to figure out who was for and who against. He should have paid more attention to the discussion and their reactions to the presentation.

"So I can see we don't have a clear majority one way or the other here. We'll have to vote."

Brice knew his opinion wasn't needed unless there was a tie or someone brought up a contract issue.

The vote was split.

"Brice, how do you weigh in here? You've got the tiebreaker after all." Ron looked expectantly at Brice. Ron had voted to continue funding, and he'd asked Brice to sit in because he thought Brice would back him up.

"My vote will determine the final decision?" He felt very uncomfortable. He didn't want to cut Ron down in front of the other partners.

"No, Brice." Parker shook his head. "But the senior partners will take these discussions into account when we have our own discussion on Friday."

Brice nodded, knowing the pressure wasn't on him. "Well, I hate to say, but these numbers don't work for me. It seems black and white. I'm not sure why there's even a question. Sorry, Ron, I can't support continuing the funding."

"It's more than figures here, Brice," Parker said. "You must see that. It's the reason these companies need us in the first place. The market would never fund this kind of expense. Sometimes we have to give more leeway to certain companies. I'm surprised you aren't more supportive of this research."

"You asked for my opinion."

"Well, glad to see someone's looking out for the bottom line after all, rather than making the decision personal." Christie nodded to Brice. As a founding partner, he wielded the most power, and for the first time, he seemed pleased with something Brice had done.

Ron, on the other hand, looked like he was ready to grab a pitchfork. "So we're going with the easy solution here, despite our commitment and personal connection to this company for years?" No one spoke. "I accept the vote, since I asked Brice to participate."

People started filing out of the room. Ron grabbed Brice's elbow. "Brice, I'll need you to go over the contract terms and draw up a separation agreement. Tonight."

"Tonight's not good. They're not meeting until Friday, so why the hurry?" Brice wanted to get out of the room. With its glass walls, people walking past could see his disagreement with Ron.

"Tonight, Brice." Ron spoke through pursed lips. "I'd like to see it before you leave. I'll be in my office."

It took Brice longer than expected to read the original contract, since he hadn't written it. Once he understood the terms, he drafted paperwork severing ties with Pharm-Gen and citing specific contractual terms regarding the timetable and ownership of the few patents the company had developed. By six, he knew he wouldn't be able to meet Jeremy on time. He tried calling, but there was no answer, so he sent a quick text and went back to work.

Twenty minutes later, Jeremy phoned. "Hey, I got your text. I'm already at the restaurant. Should I head home?"

"No. I'll be forty minutes more, I think. Do you mind waiting?"

"No. The bartender's really hot, and he's been giving me the look."

"Twenty minutes. I'm leaving now. Already out the door…"

"Jealous much?"

"Not until now. Seriously, though, it's going to be nearly an hour. I don't want to make you wait."

"Stop talking and finish your work. See you later."

Brice couldn't help smiling as he put the phone down. He finished up the contract and went to Ron's desk to hand it to him personally. He needed to smooth things over with Ron. When he got there, the lights were off. Ron had already gone home.

It took willpower not to call Ron every name in the book for making him late with Jeremy. If he wanted this contract, he could come and ask for it. Brice went back to his office, locked the contract in his desk, then grabbed his jacket and headed for the Mission.

Chapter TWENTY-THREE

JEREMY WAS sipping a glass of beer at a table on the sidewalk outside Ti Couz 2 on Valencia when Brice arrived. He looked exhausted, tie loose and a little crooked but very sexy. Suddenly Jeremy didn't care about dinner.

"Sorry I'm late." Brice leaned down over the decorative metal railing to give him a kiss. "Mmm. You taste good. Order me a bottle of the same thing. I'll be right in." He put his case down on an empty chair and came around through the main entrance. Before he sat down, he treated Jeremy to another kiss.

Jeremy could really get used to this.

"You're pretty bold, taking a sidewalk table. I thought you were worried someone from the club would see us together." Brice reached for Jeremy's hand, clearly not caring who saw them.

Jeremy shrugged. "It feels like we're doing something wrong. Illicit. A little danger adds to the fun."

The waiter chose that moment to arrive. He handed out menus and took Brice's beer order, then left.

"So you like taking risks?"

"Not usually. Until lately I played it pretty safe. My roommate couldn't believe I took the job at the Dinner Club. I couldn't believe it either, at first." Jeremy looked away for a moment as he recalled that first night, not knowing what to expect or how to act. Never expecting he'd meet anyone like Brice.

"Doug?"

"You remembered?"

"I remember everything you tell me."

"Should I give you a quiz?"

"Not till I finish this beer." The waiter arrived to place it in front of Brice, and he took a long draw. "Really good. What kind it is?"

"Something French. I can't remember."

They discussed the menu, deciding together what to order so they could share. It was easy, comfortable, with Brice. They had similar enough taste in food and the desire to trust the other with something new.

Later, at Brice's, Jeremy confessed his fantasy about Brice in the office. Brice straightened his tie and sat in the desk chair. Jeremy stripped in the hallway, grabbed a legal pad he found in the living room, and knocked on the office door.

"Come in."

He strode in carrying the legal pad. "I'm Jeremy, your new paralegal." He loved the look of surprise on Brice's face. "You have a project you require some… assistance with?"

"Uh, right. Come in and we can discuss the details." Brice had trouble keeping a straight face.

"They told me this project would be very, very hard. And that's why you needed some ass-istance." He whispered the last word, trying to make it sound dirty, but now he felt like laughing.

"That's right. You should come closer and take a look at the briefs."

Now Jeremy did start laughing. They sounded like bad porn. God, this was fun, especially now Brice was getting into the game. Jeremy went behind the desk and stood between Brice's legs, letting Brice look him over.

"Yes, I see you have excellent qualifications." He took hold of Jeremy's cock and stroked him a few times, transforming a half erection to a full-blown hard-on. "Now come sit over here." He pulled Jeremy into his lap, and Jeremy shifted so he was facing Brice, straddling him, cock pressing against Brice's pretty silk necktie. It felt good. He liked the way Brice's clothes felt against the sensitive skin of his upper thighs. He'd been on Brice's lap plenty of times before, but tonight was even more fun.

"I'm not sure the project is hard enough just yet. Any suggestions?"

"I do have an extensive skillset for just this situation," Jeremy replied. He slid down off Brice's lap and knelt in front of him, then opened his belt and trousers. He brushed his lips across the bulge and heard Brice's gasp. It turned into a moan when Jeremy took Brice into his mouth.

Jeremy brought Brice to the edge twice, backing off before going too far. Then Brice nudged Jeremy off him.

"I had a different idea for how to end this project."

Jeremy licked his lips. Brice liked that. "Yes?"

"I'll need very special ass-istance. Are you up to the task?"

"Oh, I haven't got all my office supplies with me." Why hadn't he brought condoms? Nowhere to hide them since he came in here naked.

"I grabbed a few things from the supply closet." Brice pulled a condom out of his pocket. "Can you help me wrap this project up?"

"My pleasure." Jeremy rolled the condom down. He stood up and lay face down across the desk.

"Is that how you want this?" Brice asked. He wasn't using his fake boss tone.

"Yes, sir."

Jeremy felt Brice's hands on his ass, spreading him wide, and felt a finger at his hole.

"You're already slicked up!"

Brice seemed pleased at Jeremy's second little surprise, if the way he slid right in was any indication. Given Brice's state of arousal, it didn't take long before the project came to a successful conclusion for Brice, while Jeremy thoroughly enjoyed every minute of it.

What he didn't expect was for Brice to put him in the desk chair and proceed to give him a blowjob that rated eleven on a scale of one to ten. It was extra exciting being completely nude while a man wearing a suit and tie went down on him. He hadn't known until then it was another of his fantasies.

WHEN JEREMY finally collected his clothes again, much later, he spotted a text from Dr. Morrell.

Big news. Come to my office first thing tomorrow.

No details on what the big news was. But they'd sent off a preliminary report that afternoon about Jeremy's latest results. Maybe PharmaTek would come through and restore the funding levels and Jeremy's stipend.

"You look happy, and not just from what happened in my office."

"Yeah, my advisor has some news for me. I need to leave early for a meeting with him tomorrow morning. Our sponsor must have been pleased with the latest results."

"Can you tell me about them?"

"I've been dying to tell you, but I probably shouldn't. It's covered under my nondisclosure agreement."

"I won't ask again, but when you can, I'd like to hear more about it."

Brice's interest and his easy acceptance of the constraints relaxed Jeremy. "Let's get to sleep so I'll be awake for the meeting."

"Good night."

"Good night."

They kissed briefly, then snuggled together under the thick comforter.

Tomorrow's meeting would only add to the perfect week he was having so far.

Chapter TWENTY-FOUR

THE MEETING went better than Jeremy expected. PharmaTek was thrilled with his latest data and wanted him to prepare a more detailed report. They also asked for some additional tests to be performed. The work would keep Jeremy too busy to see Brice except for the one dinner already scheduled at the club.

Brice would be just as disappointed they wouldn't have an overnight at his place, but he would understand. He knew how important Jeremy's work was to him.

He scheduled a meeting with Rhoda and Varun to discuss the project and the workload for the next week.

BRICE ENTERED his company's building in a great mood. He'd had such a great time with Jeremy the night before, playing another one of his fantasy games. Not usually his thing; he'd only played to humor Jeremy. At least that was how it started, though it quickly turned out to be sexy and fun. Jeremy took Brice out of his comfort zone, out of his staid, predictable world, and infused it with laughter and excitement Brice hadn't experienced in a long time.

He hummed a nameless tune as he rode the elevator and exited on the eighteenth floor.

"Morning," he said to Sarah, one of the associates. She nodded her head but kept walking.

Then he spotted Watkins. He almost felt like thanking Watkins for dragging him to the club that first night, though it had been practically kicking and screaming. "Morning, Charles," Brice said.

Watkins frowned and didn't respond or even look at Brice.

What the hell was going on? Had someone died? He glanced toward Ron's office as he went past, but the door was closed. Also unusual.

When Brice got to his own office, he found a note taped to the monitor:

Come see me.

Ron's scrawl was unmistakable.

Brice put his bag down, peeled the note off, and tossed it in the trash. He found the Pharm-Gen dissolution contract and headed down the hall to Ron's office. He rapped softly on the door.

"Come in."

Ron was seated behind his desk, looking more serious than Brice had ever seen him.

"What happened?"

"Sit down." It was not a request.

Aware that Ron's uncharacteristic hostility hadn't abated overnight, Brice hovered for a moment, then settled into a chair.

"We've been friends for a long time. Fifteen years?"

Brice nodded. He didn't like where this was heading; it felt like a breakup. Was he out of a job? Why?

"Or I thought we were friends. I thought I could count on you. But I'm really disappointed. I thought you were a different person than who you've turned out to be."

Brice was stunned. Had they found out about Jeremy? About the Dinner Club? He thought Ron knew all about it, even if he didn't know how many times Brice had gone. Had he violated some morals clause in his contract? He waited for Ron to give him more information before he asked any potentially incriminating questions. Law school had taught him more than practicing law.

"You don't even realize what a difficult position you put me in, do you?" Ron paused. "I'll be honest. At the end of the quarter, there's a vote to name new senior partners, and you've been nominated. But I can't vote for you. I thought it best to lay the cards on the table." He glanced at Brice, clearly expecting a response.

The partner thing was news, as was Ron not wanting to back him.

"I feel like I walked into a film thirty minutes late. What happened? How have I disappointed you?"

"I thought you had my back yesterday. It was the reason I asked you to attend. Of all people, I thought you would make the right decision, even if it wasn't the profitable decision. Did you even read the binder?"

"I skimmed the technical stuff, but I concentrated on the numbers. I listened to what you told me last time. Not to be too soft on the portfolio companies. I didn't think the first part of the meeting was that important, and I didn't read the statements from the officers."

Ron pushed air loudly between tight lips. "You don't even know what they're working on, do you?"

Brice hated to admit that he couldn't remember. Some of the companies produced things he couldn't even understand. "I got the impression it doesn't matter to the bottom line."

"You need to consider all the information before you can decide which to base your decision on and which to ignore."

The earthquake rumbling in Brice's gut told him he'd made a very big mistake. He pressed his lips together and shook his head. "They make the eardrops for—?"

"A vaccine against HIV."

"No. That meeting's at eleven today, isn't it?"

"I told you we shifted the schedule around. Those two meetings got flipped."

"Shit. The online schedule didn't get updated."

"Oh, well, that's a good excuse."

Brice felt sick. He'd been rushing rather than being thorough on this review, and if he'd gone to the meeting on time, he would have realized the mistake and voted with Ron when it might have swayed Christie's decision. It was an enormous blunder, worse than not being made partner or even losing his job. It meant people's lives. People he knew. Maybe even himself someday. There was nothing to say. He felt sick.

"It's why I wanted you there. Christie has wanted to cut ties to them for a while, and he's getting Lane worked up over the numbers. Parker and I have confidence they're close to a breakthrough with this new line of attack, the VLPs. I couldn't explain it if my life depended on it, but they gave an excellent layman's summary yesterday—which you missed. They've always been a special company around here and gotten special treatment, but not because they're friends. The officers have become friends because I've fought for them every year."

"I can understand Christie's perspective. They don't have a viable product on the horizon yet, do they? How long before they do? Why do you have such faith in this particular company?"

"Their vaccine works, in limited applications. The stumbling block is the delivery mechanism. Hit a wall. They've been funding some cutting-edge research at Cal for the past two years, and that team has made important progress in not only identifying the problem, but positing viable solutions. I think it's going to be less than a year before they have the missing piece and will be ready for animal trials."

"I didn't realize." An apology was useless, no matter how much Brice regretted not trusting Ron. "What can I do? I'll talk to Christie, tell him I made a mistake."

"You're going to tell him you got the companies mixed up?"

"Yeah. I'm not afraid to admit my errors." This was too important to care about his reputation.

Ron shook his head. "You'll lose any credibility with Christie if you do that. I'm not that mad at you. Well, yes I am. But it wouldn't solve the problem." Ron took a breath. "You know how Christie thinks. Take a good look at the review and progress reports, including the most recent update they sent us, and see if you can find an angle to appeal to his inherent greed." Ron never went in for sugarcoating a situation. He swiveled his chair around, a not-particularly-subtle dismissal.

Brice returned to his own office. Next time Ron asked him to sit in on a vote, he'd ask in advance if there was anything specific he should know about the situation. He was useless at office politics.

Then he grabbed the PharmaTek binder, intending to read it cover to cover and find something that appealed to Christie's obsession over the bottom line.

Chapter TWENTY-FIVE

One week later

JEREMY HAD another early morning meeting with Dr. Morrell. This time, as soon as he walked in the door, he could see the news was not good.

"PharmaTek presented your research to the VC firm, discussed timelines and expenses for continuing research in order to replicate the results sufficiently to integrate into the vaccine."

"But?"

Dr. Morrell frowned and shook his head. "The project's on hold. PharmaTek's funders have backed out. They intend to sell their share to other interested parties."

"On hold? What does that mean?"

"Discontinued immediately. No additional disbursements will be allowed. They're putting your latest results into the offer documentation and shopping around for a new VC firm."

"That's it? My research budget, fees, and stipend?"

"Your fees are paid through this semester, but you won't be able to order new equipment or supplies once you exhaust the remaining balance in this research account."

"Am I still in the doctoral program? Will I finish my degree?"

"I'm working with the MCB department to find resources for you. The problem is that it's the middle of fall term. The budget has been allocated, and the funding cycle works on the academic year. But I'm certain the department or college will find a solution by next fall. You've already received your stipend through the end of this semester, correct?"

Jeremy nodded, not trusting his voice. Every student in this department got university or NIH funding for their degree, unless they had an industry sponsor. Jeremy had been the envy of his colleagues because he'd gotten a bigger chunk of research money and a more generous stipend for personal expenses. At least it had looked that way two and a half years ago.

"I know this must come as a shock. It's unconscionable if you ask me. I'm happy to extend you some money if you need it. I might be able to find another project for you to work on in the interim, which will cover your fees, but it won't help with your dissertation. Until the legal issues are resolved, the research belongs to PharmaTek. I will work all my contacts to find another program working on VLP—"

"I'd like to find another HIV vaccine program, even if it's not VLP."

Dr. Morrell tugged his beard, his tell that he disagreed with Jeremy. "That could put you back at square one regarding your doctoral research."

"I understand. The project is that important to me."

Morrell made another two tugs at the beard as he considered the situation. "I'll keep that in mind. It might be next term before PharmaTek arranges new financing, and even then there's no guarantee they will allow you to continue your research here at Cal. That will also disrupt your progress toward your doctorate."

"Thank you. I appreciate the offer. I will take you up on a spot on another project if I can't find other arrangements."

"It is a good opportunity for you to write some journal articles until we can get back to your research. You've only got one more year here anyway, and you'll need more publications if you intend to go after an academic position or a top postdoc placement. And some early peer reviews for the PharmaTek research may sway the new owners to restore your financing."

"That's a great idea." Jeremy stood and shook his advisor's hand, then left.

He'd controlled himself in the office, but now he needed to shout or punch something to get rid of this pounding in his head. Why couldn't the VC realize if they cut funding now there wouldn't be any results, any improvements? Too bad they had finance guys making these decisions and not scientists, not real people.

It wasn't even the money, or the disruption to his degree that upset Jeremy the most. His research had brought the vaccine so much closer to realization—and to saving lives. Then again, the largest need for such a vaccine was in developing countries where the tech companies couldn't get top dollar for every dose. He'd work for free if he could just keep making progress on this research.

He ran the whole way home to burn off excess energy and tossed his book bag on the couch. He opened the refrigerator and spotted the container of leftovers from dinner with Brice a few days earlier. They were meeting again tonight, but Jeremy still had most of the day to kill.

In the bedroom he stripped and pulled on his cycling shorts and a black-and-green jersey and filled up a few water bottles. Then he carried his bike down the stairs and headed up the street. A few turns and he hit a steep uphill grade. He switched gears smoothly and had to stand on his pedals to make any progress. His thighs burned, and his throat was raw from pulling enough air. He recovered on a flatter patch but kept pushing himself higher and higher into the Berkeley hills, pushing his body to its limits.

He hadn't been on these hills in months, and his fitness had deteriorated. At least now he had plenty of time to get back in shape. He took breaks for snacks or hydration, but kept climbing until he'd nearly hit exhaustion. He still had to make it back home.

From the top of Grizzly Peak, he had one of the most amazing views of the San Francisco Bay, with the city dissolving into a foggy haze across the choppy, gray expanse of water. Cyclists know there are two good reasons to keep climbing any hill. First, the view, which he took time to appreciate. He watched sailboats skimming the surface of the bay and the traffic crawling along Highway 80 until his breathing returned to normal. The second reason to climb was the amazing ride down. On a good hill, you never needed to pedal until you hit the bottom. And Grizzly wasn't just a good hill; it was a great hill.

When he'd recovered enough to feel almost like himself again, he tightened his helmet strap, clipped his shoes into the pedals, and headed down, shifting into the highest gear. The road was narrow and winding, and around the next bend, he might encounter a car or a cliff. It kept a cyclist on his toes. Jeremy sped down the hill, zigging and zagging around parked cars and oncoming traffic. Wind rustled in his ears, and the breeze cooled his overheated body.

A block from home, he made the final turn onto Spruce. A car coming from a side street turned directly into him, and before he could react, he found himself sliding across the car's hood and onto the pavement on the other side.

"Oh my God. Are you okay? I am so sorry. I saw you, but I didn't think you were going so fast. Are you hurt? Oh my God!" The driver, a woman, hovered over him. From inside her car, he heard a baby's panicky cries.

Slowly he examined himself, testing every joint before he tried to stand. Nothing was broken. His head felt a little thick, and he'd ripped the jersey, leaving bloody streaks where the skin had been scraped raw by the asphalt. "Yeah, I'm okay. I'm okay. It's okay."

The woman seemed ready to hyperventilate. Traffic swerved around them, a few people stopped to ask if he needed help or an ambulance. He waved the assistance away.

"Let's go to the hospital. I want to make sure you're okay. We need to call the cops."

"I'm really okay. Just a little scraped, and I might—will— need a new jersey." He glanced at the bike. It would need some minor repairs. Again. It was better than the alternative.

The crying baby raised its voice an octave.

"Look, ma'am, I'm okay. Don't worry. Your baby—"

"Here's my information." She handed him a business card, and he stuffed it into a pocket in his jersey. "Send me any medical bills or bike repair costs. I live nearby. My home address is on here too."

"I will. Thanks."

She reluctantly got back in the car and drove off, still watching him.

Jeremy retrieved the bike. It was too damaged to ride, so he hoisted it over his shoulder. Ouch, better use the other. It was a short walk home. He just needed a hot shower and some ibuprofen.

A FEW hours later, he felt stiff and achy, but he was sure nothing was broken. He was supposed to meet Brice in the city, and even though he couldn't wait to see Brice, his body already resisted. He dialed Brice.

"Hiya."

"What's wrong?"

"What makes you think something's wrong?"

"You never call when I'm at work."

"I had a little accident today."

"Accident." Worry infused Brice's words. "Are you okay?"

"A little achy. I fell off my bike." He laughed so it sounded like nothing. He would not tell Brice about the car or risk freaking him out too much.

"Are you at home? Hospital?"

"Home. It wasn't that bad, but I'm kind of...."

"I'll go over to your place tonight. Get some rest till I get there."

"You sure?" Jeremy loved how Brice's first thought was to come here. Doug had a break in his lab work and had taken the opportunity to go skiing in Tahoe with some friends. They would have plenty of privacy.

"Don't argue. Do you need me to bring something?"

"Yeah. I'm out of condoms."

"That's the first thing you think of?"

"And some ice cream?"

"Now you're talking."

"Go back to work and don't worry about me."

"I will worry, until I see you." Brice made a kissy noise and hung up.

Jeremy laughed, but it hurt, so he tried to stop and couldn't. When they'd met, Brice was not the sort of guy to make kissy noises over the phone. Jeremy chuckled again, then swallowed a few more pills and lay down on the couch.

He woke to the sound of knocking.

"It's open."

Brice came in carrying several white paper bags.

"You didn't even ask who it was."

"Okay. Who is it?"

"Land shark."

"I don't get it."

With an exaggerated headshake, Brice put the bags down on the table, then planted a kiss on Jeremy's head. "Never mind." Brice sat on the couch next Jeremy and brushed hair out of his face before giving him a visual once-over. "How're you feeling?"

"Sore." He shrugged and wished he hadn't. His arm and shoulder stung.

"You need a bandage on that shoulder. Or do you want to eat first?"

"Food. Please. Thanks."

Brice had stopped at the Thai place Jeremy liked over on Hearst, and he'd also gotten a pint of his favorite ice cream at the shop around the corner. Pistachio. He couldn't believe Brice had remembered. They'd only been there once before.

"Anything else in your bag of tricks, Mary Poppins?"

"Right." Brice dug into the bag, pulled out a 12-pack of condoms, and tossed them to Jeremy.

"Twelve? Did you invite someone else over? Like a football team?"

"I'm making an investment in our future."

All Jeremy could do was smile. He'd probably say something sappy if he spoke.

It was nice having Brice fuss over him, helping him eat and then putting the bandage on Jeremy's shoulder. Once he had assured himself Jeremy really had only suffered a few scrapes and bruises, he gave Jeremy a special "healing" blowjob and refused to let him reciprocate.

Jeremy yawned and stretched his legs out over Brice's on the couch. "Why am I lying here naked while you're still fully clothed?"

"You said you liked that."

"Maybe not every single time."

"You're right." Brice carefully moved Jeremy's legs off his lap and got up, then proceeded to strip down. "Better?"

"Yes." At least the view was better. With the crash, Jeremy had put the morning's bad news out of his brain. But now it nagged at him. Hearing it would probably upset Brice as much as the accident had, so Jeremy decided to wait until another time to share the news.

They snuggled on the couch and watched a film on Netflix. It was something French Jeremy had wanted to see, but his head was too foggy for the subtitles, so they turned it off.

"Brice?"

"Hmm?"

"You're a lawyer for a VC, but you must know something about the investment side, right?"

"A little. What did you want to know?"

"How does it work? I mean, what's the process when the VC invests in companies?"

"It depends on the company. Did you have a specific question?"

"How does it work in biotech? How much control does the VC have over how the company uses the money?"

"Sometimes the VC buys an ownership share, and the company uses the capital as they see fit. Other times, they fund specific projects and offer management advice. Usually it's somewhere in between. Depends on the company, the product, stage of development.... It gets kind of complicated."

Jeremy was already aware of the complications. "Can they just pull out their money?"

"That's more in my line of expertise. It depends on the contract. Whether there are specific targets the portfolio company has to meet, for example."

"This is good information. Let me take some notes. I won't remember everything." He started to get up.

"What do you need?"

"A notebook from my bag."

"There's one in mine, right behind you." Brice started to get up.

"I can reach." Jeremy sat up and leaned over the arm of the couch to grab Brice's bag.

"Help yourself," Brice said.

Jeremy fished around and spotted a legal pad. When he pulled it out, a binder got stuck in the pages and caught his attention. His mind must be playing tricks on him from the meds and the crash. He took the binder out. The front cover read in big letters:

PHARMATEK
3RD QUARTER REPORT 2014

What connection did Brice have to PharmaTek? Jeremy had never mentioned them by name before so Brice couldn't already have heard about Jeremy's connection with them. He felt quicksand in his core, and he looked up at Brice.

THE LOOK on Jeremy's face when he pulled the PharmaTek binder out of his bag worried Brice. Jeremy had gone deathly pale. Probably just a delayed reaction from the fall, which appeared to be more serious than Jeremy believed.

"What's this?"

"A report from a company in our portfolio. Technically it's confidential, but if you want to take a look, go ahead. I can explain some of the terms in this particular contract."

"Brice...." Jeremy's voice shook. "Brice, this is the company sponsoring my research. Do you work for the VC that finances PharmaTek?"

Pieces clicked into place, and Brice understood why Jeremy was asking questions. PharmaTek must have told him their funding was being reviewed. No wonder he wanted to know whether they could pull out of sponsoring him. But if they had told Jeremy the worst of it, he would have let Brice know.

"My firm owns the majority stake in PharmaTek." That was public information, though the news that they were about to dump their share was not yet public.

"Oh. Interesting." Jeremy didn't say more, and Brice thought he might drop the subject. He saw Jeremy bite his lip for a moment, thinking, then he put the binder back in the bag.

Disaster averted? He wouldn't have to be the one to break the news to Jeremy about his research. Brice took a tentative breath, but his chest still hurt. It was the first time he'd had specific insider information someone else needed to know. Even though PharmaTek wasn't publicly traded, Brice was not free to discuss their financials yet.

He remembered how excited Jeremy had been the past week, talking about his research, his confidence that the latest successes would make a difference. Brice already knew the results hadn't changed a thing as far as Christie, Parker, and Lane were concerned. But how could he let Jeremy get blindsided?

Because it was his job to keep his client's information confidential.

There wasn't supposed to be any gray area on what was legal. But for Brice, everything about his relationship with Jeremy was gray area from the moment they'd met.

"Jeremy?"

"Yeah?"

"It's not public knowledge, but.... But the firm voted to discontinue funding to PharmaTek. Last week. The details are still being finalized, but I'm sure you'll be hearing from them soon. I'm really sorry."

"I know. I already heard." Jeremy's voice had gone flat. "Did you vote?"

Brice considered lying and rejected the option. "Yes."

"For or against?"

Brice had insisted on honesty from Jeremy, and despite the unpleasantness, Jeremy deserved the same. "Against."

"Why? Did you see the latest data? We're really close to making everything work. Really close."

"I didn't have the new data at the time. If I had, I would have voted differently. The senior partners reconsidered their decision when they heard about the new results, but I wasn't part of the final decision to sell." He paused, hating himself for not having fought harder before that last-ditch effort from PharmaTek. "I don't know what to say. I'm sorry it's affected you and your work."

"Not just me. Not just the PharmaTek people. Everyone who contracts HIV because of the delay while they find new funding and we get the research started again will be affected. A change in process or a gap in the data could slow down any eventual FDA approval."

It was a heavy burden to lay on anyone, and it hadn't been Brice's vote that sealed PharmaTek's fate. But Jeremy wouldn't want to hear Brice's excuses.

"If the latest results show the vaccine worked, wouldn't CPL have voted differently?" Brice needed to believe the system worked.

"It's not a question of works or doesn't work. The vaccine works. We're fine-tuning how it gets administered to the patient. We're much closer than ever before."

"Closer. So no one knows it would work, or get approved, or a dozen other things. There is still a lot of uncertainty for the investors."

"You know there's more to it than money. There are millions of lives at risk. Not just gay and bisexual men, but men and women in Africa and Asia, where—" Jeremy paused for breath, face flushed, eyes angry. "And as for defining success, Brice, the thing that keeps scientists trying new things every day, the reason people like the PharmaTek guys started their company, is even though every single thing up till today failed, *today* could be the day we get it right. If we didn't believe we could succeed every day, why bother to go into the lab? We can't play probabilities that the next thing won't work simply because the probability is so small."

"I never thought about research in those terms."

"And it probably explains why you went to law school. You have a different way of looking at the world. You fit what you see into predefined boxes. Scientists break up the boxes and figure out how they work so we can build new boxes how and where we need them. We try to define what we see rather than see only what we can define."

Jeremy was right. Brice didn't understand the world in the same way. It was eye-opening and humbling.

"What can I do now? I can't go back, as much as I'd like to. The final decision wasn't mine."

"Brice, this isn't about PharmaTek anymore."

The words sent chills down Brice's spine.

"Would you leave? Please, just get dressed and go."

It was the last thing Brice expected to hear. He reached out, but Jeremy pushed him away.

"No, Jeremy, don't do this." He tried not to plead as he pulled his clothes on.

"The numbers for our relationship don't look very good this quarter." Jeremy handed Brice his bag and opened the door.

And Brice found himself on the other side of it. He stood in the hall for a few minutes, trying to take it in. He was scared. He might never see Jeremy again. It hurt to think about it. But pounding on the door and shouting wouldn't change Jeremy's mind.

He banged on the door anyway. "Jeremy. Let's talk. Please? Jeremy, I love you." Why on earth hadn't he said so sooner?

A middle-aged woman walked toward him and gave him a dirty look, lip curled up. Because he was gay, or just because he was making a lot of noise in the hallway? It didn't matter. Unless Jeremy opened the door, nothing mattered all that much.

"Jeremy?" He said it softly, nonconfrontationally. Would that work any better? No response. Defeated, Brice picked up his bag and started down the hall to the stairs.

He heard a door click open. He fought the urge to see if it was Jeremy, but he stopped.

"Brice?"

"Oh, thank God!"

Brice turned around as Jeremy hurled the 12-pack of condoms at him and shut the door again, clicking the bolts in loudly enough to echo along the hallway.

Chapter TWENTY-SIX

JEREMY DIDN'T feel any better after Brice left. He felt even worse after he ate the whole container of ice cream.

Jeremy, I love you.

He'd wanted to hear those words, needed to hear them, because it was a reflection of how Jeremy felt about Brice. If he didn't love Brice, this wouldn't be so upsetting. He and Brice were good together. Until now he'd thought they fit together well, physically and emotionally. They complemented each other.

But not as much as they should. It wasn't PharmaTek, or even Brice's seeming lack of concern about importance of an HIV vaccine. Brice's outlook on life was just too different from Jeremy's. It wasn't whether he was a glass-half-full or glass-half-empty guy.

Brice was the kind of guy who would get caught up on how to define half empty and half full. Why hadn't Jeremy seen it sooner?

He'd been too susceptible to the oxytocin rush and the sexually charged atmosphere where they'd met and interacted for the first part of their relationship. That wasn't exactly a good way to choose a partner, even if it had been fun.

Jeremy leaned against the door, almost welcoming the pain from his injured shoulder as he let himself slide down to the floor.

He was now down one bike, one job, and one boyfriend.

How much beer was left in the refrigerator?

BRICE WENT home and sat on the couch for a long time. He pulled the damn PharmaTek report out of his bag. Why had he brought it home? He tossed the thing across the room, where it knocked over a set of Japanese jade carvings worth more than his car.

Even if Jeremy hadn't seen it in Brice's bag, the result would have been the same once Jeremy discovered Brice had been in on the PharmaTek decision.

He'd really fucked up by not performing due diligence before voting. He should have read the whole report. It was a lapse in professionalism. Worse, because he wasn't the one to pay the price. Unless he factored in losing Jeremy.

Had it only been a week earlier?

A week. Only a week. That was good. He'd slipped a clause into the PharmaTek dissolution contract allowing a fourteen-day window where either party could present additional material, information that could keep the dissolution from going into effect. It was the longest he could delay before Christie or Lane figured it out.

He still had a week to fix things.

He just wasn't sure how. He got up and retrieved the report, then started reading.

By the time he finished two hours later, he knew exactly how to do it.

FIRST THING the next morning, he went into Christie's office.

"Do you have a minute? I'd like to bring up a point about Pharm—"

"It's closed. Done. Besides, I thought you advised we drop them from the portfolio?"

"I did, but that was based on outdated and incomplete data. I believe the valuations aren't accurate."

"I thought we hired you for your legal skills and not as an analyst."

"Yes, that's true. But I heard something regarding their research that I don't believe has been correctly taken into account."

"What?"

Brice opened the folder he'd brought in and starting explaining.

"Did Ron put you up to this?"

"No, sir. I happen to have access to data from their research group at Cal."

Christie nodded. "If these numbers are accurate…. Get me some independent valuations and forecasts, and I'll consider reopening the discussion."

"Thank you, sir."

Brice raced down the hall and into Ron's office.

THEY'D BARELY spoken during the past week, so Ron didn't give Brice a particularly warm welcome. In fact, he didn't even look up from his monitor.

"Ron, I've just been to Christie's office. He's going to reconsider the PharmaTek decision."

That got Ron's attention. He snapped his head up so quickly Brice thought he heard something crack. "What? The decision's made. They've signed the termination paperwork even though it hasn't gone into effect. They're already planning layoffs until they get new funding."

"Then we don't have much time to waste, do we?"

Roy eyed him sideways, frowning. "Why the sudden change of heart here?"

"I admitted I fucked up on this one. I need to put it right. And there's a two-week waiting period before the contract is in full force."

"Two weeks? Really?"

"I always put a waiting period in contracts. You have no idea how many times one side or the other changes their minds. Of course, terms can't be renegotiated, but the contract can be cancelled in whole—"

Ron cut him off. "I don't need the legal details. What did you say to Christie to get him to rethink this decision? He's always hated that PharmaTek got special treatment from most of the other partners."

"I told him the valuations weren't correct. That they were vastly underestimated given the latest results. And the timeline for testing and approval is compressed for the same reason."

"And now what?"

"You rework the numbers and help me find independent verification."

"All within the next week? Outside consultants don't work that fast."

"We're not going to use a consultant. We're going to try to sell PharmaTek to someone else."

"What? You're fucking nuts." But Ron's eyes held a glint like a terrier that had just spotted its prey. "Go on."

Brice sat down and leaned forward as he explained his strategy to Ron. "We work up a sales document and shop it around to the other VCs. As soon as someone even nibbles at it, we take that to Christie as proof of value."

"Won't they wonder why we're doing this?"

"We're still in support of the company, even if we can't keep them in our portfolio. But other firms have different criteria for their investments. One of the socially responsible funds would snap this up at the right price. We just have to demonstrate to Christie what that price is, and that it's more than the forecasts based on the quarterly report."

Ron settled back in his chair and put his hands behind his head. He nodded a few times, clearly turning Brice's idea over, calculating, planning. "You know, it just might work."

"At the worst case, if we get any legitimate offers, we can pass them along to PharmaTek. They would appreciate new funding, right? And we have a lot more connections than they do."

"Jesus, Brice. When you fuck up, you really try to put things right."

"You weren't the only one to show me the error of my ways."

"Ah, the new boyfriend's having a good influence on you. Kate and I should have you two over for dinner, once we sort out PharmaTek. It's going to keep us very busy the next week."

Brice shook his head and willed his stomach to stop churning. "That didn't quite work out." He glanced at the wall, pretending to be interested in photos of Ron with Silicon Valley big shots like Steve Jobs, Mark Ellison, and half a dozen others.

"If you can figure out how to fix the PharmTek thing, then I don't see why you can't come up with something to get him back. Assuming you want him back."

Brice stared the photos for a moment more before sliding back in his chair. "I do. Absolutely. His standards are higher than I can live up to." He wasn't sure why he added the last part. Though as buddies at Stanford, they'd discussed nearly every aspect of the love lives, he and Ron hadn't talked much about their personal lives since Brice broke up with Greg.

"Where'd you meet him, an opera fund raiser or something?"

Brice couldn't control his laugher. "Actually, Ron, you'd never believe it."

Chapter TWENTY-SEVEN

WHEN DOUG came back from his ski trip two days later, Jeremy was on the couch drinking beer. He barely looked up when the door opened.

"Jeremy? Dude, it's ten in the morning. What the hell?"

"Brice told me he loves me."

"And that drove you to drink?"

"It was after I broke up with him."

"Why'd you break up with him?"

"I don't know." Jeremy was buzzed again. Or still buzzed. He'd kind of lost track.

Doug tossed his suitcase in his bedroom and came back to sit on the couch with Jeremy. "Tell me what happened."

So Jeremy summed up the events, including the PharmaTek news, the bike crash, and what Brice had told him. He left out the blowjob.

"No, dude, you didn't leave out the part about the blowjob."

"Huh?"

"Look, you smell homeless. You're even talking to yourself. Why don't you have a shower and then we can talk? I don't care if you keep drinking beer, just take a shower. Or I swear I'll Febreze you."

Doug even turned the water on and shoved him in, clothes and all. Jeremy hadn't realized how hard it was to get out of wet clothes when you were buzzed.

After he'd showered and dressed, he discovered Doug had cleaned up the empty beer bottles and the rest of the mess Jeremy had ignored in the living room.

"How much did I drink?" Jeremy wasn't sure he wanted to know.

"I counted fourteen bottles. Was that all last night?"

"Since Wednesday."

"It's Friday. Fourteen beers over two, three days? You're fine. You really are a lightweight."

"Don't mock me. I'm in crisis."

"Let's see what we can do about that."

"LET ME get this straight. You love Brice too, but you don't think you belong together because he doesn't see the world your way?" They sat on the couch sipping coffee Doug had made while Jeremy was in the shower.

"I guess that's a good summary."

"I might not understand you correctly, but it doesn't seem like a big deal to me. He can learn to see things from a different perspective. And so can you. You and I get along fine and we're completely different."

"We're not dating, Doug."

"True. But if I were gay, I'd totally go for you."

"That's sweet." Jeremy gave Doug a kiss on the cheek. "Thanks."

"It's nice to be with someone who isn't just like you. Don't the French say 'Vive la différence'?"

"I think they had something else in mind with that one, but I'm not sure. Google it."

"It doesn't matter. Explain to me why it's got you so upset? It's not just the funding and the fact that his firm was responsible. It wasn't all on him."

"No. Of course not. But what if someday something really important comes up and we don't agree? Something that really could break us up in a terrible way?"

"Listen to you. You're doing exactly the same thing you accused Brice of. He assumes your research won't pay off because it hasn't so far. You're assuming your relationship will fail because of something you can't even imagine today."

"No. That's the opposite thing."

"Don't be pedantic. Look, why can't you have the same hope that every day your relationship will continue to be good and get stronger? Why anticipate disaster and let the fear keep you from even trying?"

"Okay, now it does kind of sound the same." Jeremy scratched his head and ran the concepts through his brain again. Maybe he was more buzzed than he thought. But he could see Doug's logic.

Later, when he charged and checked his cell phone, he discovered a dozen texts and voice mails from Brice, reinforcing his conclusion he owed Brice a huge apology. There were two messages from Thomas at the

Dinner Club, but he put them out of his mind to focus on Brice. It was a weekday, and Brice would be busy, so Jeremy went to the office. He'd throw himself into his own work and go over to Brice's that evening to try to make up for his atrocious behavior.

And to finally tell Brice he loved him too.

Doug drove Jeremy to the bike shop so he could get his bike repaired, then dropped him off at Springer Gateway on the far west edge of campus so he had a short walk to his office.

On the way to the LSB, Jeremy spotted a man in a suit and tie with the same sprinkling of silver at his temples as Brice. He was too far to make out any of the man's features, but he shook his head. He was only seeing things. Brice was so much on his mind, soon everyone older than thirty would look like Brice to him.

For the next six hours, he was able to focus on work, including brainstorming topics for journal articles. He was pleased with the progress and getting a little hungry. Maybe he'd stop by the diner near Brice's place and bring him dinner. He liked that plan.

He grabbed a quick snack of a fruit cup at a food cart on the way to BART so he wouldn't be starving by the time he got into the city. It was seven thirty when he arrived at Brice's building with bags of meatloaf sandwiches—one of Brice's guilty pleasures—and fresh peach cobbler. Everything smelled so good he'd wanted to scarf down the sandwich right there in the diner. But he restrained himself. It would be more fun to share with Brice after Jeremy's apology.

The sandwiches reheated well, just in case they got sidetracked with makeup sex.

From the doorstep, he buzzed Brice's apartment. No answer. He was probably stuck at work or decided to stop for a drink with a friend. Jeremy knew his colleague Ron was an old friend from college days.

By eight thirty, Brice hadn't arrived. A neighbor let him into the building so he wouldn't freeze to death on the step. He went up to Brice's flat and from outside the door called Brice. So much for surprising him. He only got voice mail, so he left a brief message to call back.

At nine fifteen, Jeremy ate his sandwich. It was cold and not very good, but he was starving.

At ten thirty, he ate a piece of cobbler.

He knew he should go home, but he really wanted to see Brice and knew he'd come home soon. In the months they'd been together, the only time Brice stayed out was with Jeremy—either at the club or at Jeremy's place in Berkeley.

At midnight, he decided to go home. He'd tortured himself with imagined scenes of Brice at the Dinner Club with Kit or Law or some other guy in his lap, naked, as Brice played with his hot, hard cock.

He ended up on the second to last BART train to the East Bay, surrounded by couples making out—or much more—on their way home. He could swear back in the far corner of the car a girl was giving a guy a blowjob. Was Brice doing the same thing to someone else right now?

Jeremy squeezed his eyes shut, just in case the tears welling up there had any intention of escaping.

At home he put the rest of the leftovers in the fridge before throwing himself into bed and wrapping his arms around the pillows. He pressed his face into them and shouted. He called himself every name in the book at least twice. He raged into the pillow until his throat hurt from shouting.

Chapter TWENTY-EIGHT

SATURDAY MORNING Brice woke up on the couch in Ron's office. His clothes were wrinkled, and his neck hurt like fuck. Ron was still asleep, slouched in the chair three feet away. The office smelled like stale Chinese food and feet. Ron had taken his shoes off. It brought back college memories. Bad ones.

When Brice came back from the bathroom, Ron was eating cold beef chow fun from a red-and-white paper container. "This stuff is not as good the next day," he said with his mouth full.

"It's marginally better if you heat it up some."

Ron held out the container of garlic beef, and the aroma made Brice's eyes water as he waved it away. "God, there has to be a place that delivers breakfast nearby."

"No time. But I promise you a nice lunch if we can just finish the last two sections of the proposal. Bob Bartlet and Trevor Dane will be here at noon to go over what we've got."

"Yeah. I need to read over what we wrote at 3:00 a.m. I have a feeling it's going to sound like a Dick and Jane book." Brice opened his laptop and glanced at the offending section. "Oh, coffee should be ready in the break room. Be a pal and get me cup?"

Ron grumbled but went to get coffee. It was only fair, since Brice had made it.

Two hours later they were satisfied with the presentation and grabbed quick showers in Christie's private bathroom. He never showed up on weekends. Brice had the overnight bag he used to take to the club with him and found clean underwear, socks and a shirt that didn't smell like he'd slept in it. It did smell a little like Jeremy. An invisible hand reached into his chest and squeezed his heart at the memories.

He hadn't heard from Jeremy since he'd asked Brice to leave a few days earlier. No replies to the texts or voice mails. Then Brice's heart skipped a beat when he spotted a missed call from Jeremy, from around eight the night before. His finger hovered over the button to dial him when Ron poked his head into Brice's office.

"Dude, they're here. Get your butt back into my office."

"Gimme a minute."

"Zip up and let's do this."

Brice glanced down and realized he hadn't finished dressing, and his belt was flapping from his open pants. He pulled himself together and shoved the phone in his pocket. He'd call Jeremy when they took a break.

SATURDAY, JEREMY stayed in bed till noon, debating whether to change the sheets. On one hand, they still smelled like Brice, and he didn't want to think about him anymore. On the other hand, they smelled like Brice, and Jeremy didn't want to forget him.

In the end, inertia won, and he left the sheets on. He ate half a leftover meatloaf sandwich for lunch. Doug was working at the pizza place and would be back with a fresh double crust delicacy by nine.

Jeremy killed the next eight hours by binge watching *White Collar* and fantasizing about what he'd do if he could spend the night with Matt Bomer. He had slipped the *Magic Mike* DVD into the player when Doug came in.

They ate pizza and watched the film, with Jeremy fast-forwarding over the places where the female lead was talking and rewatching the ones where the guys had any of their clothes off. Frustrated, Doug grabbed the remote from Jeremy.

"That's no way to watch a film."

"It is if you're gay." He grabbed the remote back and watched one of Channing Tatum's dance numbers three times in a row.

Doug shook his head and concentrated on pizza. "We're watching *anything* with Angelina Jolie next."

Jeremy's phone rang every hour on the hour starting at eight o'clock, and he hit Ignore every time. The third time, Doug grabbed the phone and looked at the caller ID.

"It's Brice. Why aren't you answering? I thought you were going to apologize."

"Well, I was going to. I tried to. Only he never came home. I don't think he's sitting home right now missing me."

"Wherever he is, he's *calling* you. Talk to him."

Jeremy stared at the phone and at the images of Channing Tatum on the screen and at the crusts of the four huge pieces of pizza he'd eaten. He ran into his room and hit dial on the phone.

"Jeremy! I'm so glad you finally returned my call. I've been really worried about you." Brice sounded exhausted, like someone had drained all the energy out of him. *Well, that's what happens when you stay out too late,* Jeremy gloated.

"Really?" Jeremy wanted to believe it, but the memory of sitting outside Brice's door for five hours dampened his enthusiasm.

"Yes. Can we talk? I want to see you. Or we can just talk on the phone. Whatever's okay with you."

"We're talking now."

"I'm sorry, Jeremy. Just tell me how I can prove it to you, or make it up to you, or whatever you need or want. I'll do it. I'll do anything."

"There's nothing you can do, Brice."

"Nothing? Jeremy. Please." His voice sounded strangled and tight. It made Jeremy's chest hurt to hear it.

"You didn't do anything wrong. I'm the one who owes you an apology. I'm sorry for the way I reacted. It was childish. You deserve better."

"Are you done with me? Or can we...." He didn't finish the sentence.

In his head, Jeremy's brain was playing that Barbra Streisand song, "The Way We Were." Hearing it made his throat close up, it was so sad. He didn't want to *be* that song.

"Brice, I'm in love with you. I'm not done with you by a long shot."

"Good. Now tell me that in person."

"I don't think I have time to catch the last BART, unless Doug—"

"Look out the window."

Jeremy looked down onto the street. Brice was standing on the sidewalk in front of his building. Jeremy raced outside without bothering to put on his shoes or take his keys. He threw himself into Brice's arms, and Brice swept him up and spun him like something from a sappy movie. Jeremy didn't think people did that in real life, till now. He let himself melt against Brice and got the second best kiss of his life. Number one was still the first time Brice kissed him, even though he'd been dressed as a slutty cop at the time.

"I love you," Jeremy said against Brice's cheek when their mouths parted minutes later. "I kind of hated you a little, and that's when I knew for sure I loved you."

"I'm going to take that as a compliment."

"I love you, *love* you, love *you!*" Jeremy tried the words out in different ways, enjoying the way Brice's arms still crushed him tightly, chest to chest.

"I love you, Jeremy, and I really want to show you in a way that wouldn't be appropriate on the sidewalk, even in Berkeley." He paused. "Would you stay over in the city with me?"

"I don't know...."

Brice let go of him and turned toward the street. "Well, I know where I can find some other company."

"Oh no you won't!" Jeremy raced up and embraced Brice. "Let's go."

"You want to get anything from upstairs, like shoes or pants? Not that I don't love the look on you."

It hit Jeremy he was only wearing boxers and anyone who looked would notice just how much he'd missed Brice. They went inside together, and Brice sat with Doug on the couch watching the end of *Magic Mike* while Jeremy collected his stuff and put on shoes.

"No pants?" Brice asked.

Jeremy gave a coy shrug. "Saves time later."

"Get out of here, both of you!" Doug said, putting his hands over his ears.

Downstairs in the car, Brice turned to Jeremy for another kiss, and even in just a T-shirt and boxers, Jeremy's temperature rose to the boiling point.

"Interested in having the first course in the backseat right now?" Jeremy glanced back at the tiny area that pretended to be a backseat in Brice's Audi Roadster.

"No. As much as I want you right now, that's not how I want to be with you tonight." He planted a kiss on Jeremy's lips and then started the car.

Jeremy asked Brice to put the top down as they got on the Bay Bridge and watched the lights flicker overhead. San Francisco came into focus ahead of them as they zoomed out of the Treasure Island tunnel.

Brice kept his hand on Jeremy's thigh the whole trip, keeping him in a low but constant state of arousal.

Outside his building Brice pushed the button on the gate to the underground parking garage. Before they got out of the car, Brice turned to Jeremy. "I know you want to get upstairs, but I'm starving. I didn't get much dinner. Just a quick stop to bring something back from the diner? You can wait for me upstairs."

"I'll go."

Brice stared at Jeremy's boxers, slightly tented. "Put on my jacket."

It covered Jeremy's underwear, but gave the impression he wasn't wearing anything underneath. "It is what it is," Brice said and put an arm around Jeremy's waist and steered him toward the street.

Inside the diner the one waitress on duty in the middle of the night took Brice's order. While he paid, she glanced at Jeremy.

"Two nights in a row? Keep eating like this, and you'll lose that girlish figure."

Jeremy shrugged and hoped Brice wasn't paying attention. As they headed out with their food, Brice said, "You do have nice legs...."

They held hands in the elevator and kissed for far too long when they got inside Brice's apartment.

"Want a cognac or something?" It was one of Brice's rituals.

"Sure. I'll put the pie on a plate."

"Okay."

In the kitchen Jeremy slipped the coat off and quickly shed the boxers and T-shirt before putting the coat on again. Working at the Dinner Club had taught him how to get out of his clothes quickly. He put the chocolate cheesecake on one plate and the key lime pie on another, grabbed forks, and headed into the living room to join Brice on the couch.

They sipped cognac for a few minutes while Brice took a bite of cheesecake. "Yum. Want some?"

Jeremy shook his head.

"What's up with the coat? You can take that off; it's warm enough in here."

Jeremy stood up and unbuttoned the coat. He held it open wide, then slipped it off his shoulders. He loved the way Brice's smile widened and he put the pie down without taking his gaze from Jeremy's naked, aroused body. Before he could settle onto Brice's lap, Brice picked him up and carried him into the bedroom.

And in Brice's huge bed, they made soft, slow love. Brice held Jeremy so carefully, almost too carefully. For some reason, Brice held back, not letting himself go. Seeing Brice a little out of control was always a turn-on for Jeremy.

He looked up into Brice's eyes. "Brice?"

Brice stopped moving inside Jeremy. "What? You okay?"

"Yeah. Does loving each other mean we won't fuck anymore?"

"What? I don't want to fuck you. I want us to take our time. We have a long time. There's no reason to rush." He covered Jeremy's mouth with a kiss and pushed in again.

"Deeper?"

For the next few strokes, Brice pushed in farther, and the sensations went down to his toes. Jeremy's breath caught in his throat.

"Did I hurt you?"

"God, no. Brice, I won't break if you're a little rougher." He paused, then just came out with it. "And I might not come if you aren't a little rougher."

"Oh? Oh. Really? Not doing it for you?"

Jeremy bit his lip. He hadn't said that right at all. He didn't reply.

"You know, criticizing a man's lovemaking style can be detrimental to his self-esteem." This time Brice's voice held a teasing tone.

"Perhaps. But your lovemaking style tonight is detrimental to my potential for orgasm."

"Is that so?" Brice shifted position so they leaned more to one side and gave Jeremy's ass a loud smack. He squeezed and pushed in hard and deep.

"Please, sir, may I have another?"

"Be careful what you ask for." Brice pulled out and rolled Jeremy onto his stomach. He planted half a dozen, firm, perfect slaps that had Jeremy hard and grinding his hips into the mattress. Then Brice spread Jeremy open and plunged in deep.

"Oh, God, I love you so much right now," Jeremy said into the pillow.

"Tell me when you're close."

"I'm close."

"Already?" Brice sounded surprised but also a little pleased with himself.

Jeremy nodded and laughed.

Brice rolled him back over and pulled him so his ass was at the edge of the bed. He fixed his gaze on Jeremy's and pushed in again as he grasped Jeremy's cock with one hand. Two thrusts had Jeremy shooting pearly strands all over himself and Brice. He made quite a mess. Brice licked at Jeremy's sticky chest and fastened his mouth over one nipple, and then orgasm ripped through his body so suddenly even Brice looked startled. He lay across Jeremy, gasping for air.

They held each other tight and, still breathless, pressed together for a long kiss, panting against each other's mouths.

After a while Brice got rid of the condom, Jeremy brought the pie in from the living room, and they fed each other while lying in bed. Brice dabbed whipped cream on his own nipples, and Jeremy sucked them clean as Brice shuddered and gasped and burst into laughter.

When he calmed down again, he turned to Jeremy. "What did the woman in the diner mean about two nights in a row?"

Jeremy pushed some chocolate cheesecake in his mouth so he wouldn't have to reply right away.

"What?" Brice asked more insistently.

Honesty was the best policy. "I wanted to apologize to you last night, Friday night, and I thought it best to do it in person. I stopped there to grab some dinner. But when I got here, you weren't home. I waited in the hall for a few hours, then I went home." He didn't say anything else, didn't say how it hurt when he imagined where Brice might be all night, who Brice might be with, might be *in*.

"You sat in the hallway?"

Jeremy shrugged.

Brice put his pie down and got out of bed and walked out of the room. Jeremy sat up, listening to him opening drawers. When he came back, he handed Jeremy a San Francisco Giants key ring with two shiny new keys dangling from it.

"Let yourself in next time?"

Jeremy felt all warm and gooey inside, and this time it had nothing to do with lube. "Really?"

"I had them made a while ago and just kept forgetting to give them to you."

They kissed again.

"What did you get for dinner?" Brice asked.

"Meatloaf sandwiches."

"Aw, my favorite."

"I was so mad I ate both of them."

"As much as I adore your girlish figure—" He skimmed a hand down Jeremy's hip. "—I'll still love you if you get plump. More to love."

Jeremy gently slapped Brice's hand off his ass. "I'll start jogging till my bike's fixed. Don't you worry."

Brice gripped one of Jeremy's thighs. "I stayed at the office late Friday, working on a special deal with Ron. Ended up sleeping on his couch. My neck still aches."

"You spent the night with Ron?"

"Yes, and it was awful. He snores and his feet smell." Brice gave a crooked grin.

"Poor thing." Jeremy decided to believe Brice's story and shifted so he could massage Brice's neck.

"Aaaah. Oh, good." Brice hung his head down as Jeremy worked.

"What's the project?"

"I can't discuss it yet. Once it's signed, then I'll be free to tell you."

Jeremy didn't reply. He'd learned it was best not to ask about Brice's work; it had gotten him in trouble less than a week ago.

"I may have to go out of town next week. I should know tomorrow if I do."

"Isn't that unusual for you? I thought you just did contracts."

"This is something different, but we have to close a deal by Friday or… well, let's just say it would be disastrous if we didn't."

"Sounds serious."

"It is. Oh, it is."

Chapter TWENTY-NINE

THEY SPENT a leisurely Sunday, mostly in bed. Jeremy went to the diner to bring back lunch and chose salads, even though Brice asked for a meatloaf sandwich.

"You'll be busy all week and end up eating takeout junk. Have something green and crunchy while you have the chance."

There was a shop near the office that did decent takeout salads at lunch, but Brice often found himself choosing a less-healthy option. Jeremy was a good reason to watch what he ate; he wasn't getting any younger, and he could see his own "girlish figure" as a mere memory.

The Giants were playing in Montreal, so they curled up on the couch to watch. They drank beer and played a game Jeremy devised based on the score. They tossed a coin, and Jeremy got to be the Giants, while Brice was Montreal. When their team got a run, the other one had to take off an item of clothing. The loser also had to give the winner an orgasm.

Jeremy was draped across the couch in a state of bliss after Brice had to pay for the Expos' crappy performance. His cell phone rang, and Brice grabbed it off the table and handed it to him. He glanced at the caller ID: Thomas. The Dinner Club manager.

"Hello?" Jeremy said. "Uh, yeah I got your messages. … Uh, no." He glanced up at Brice who had been watching him, though he tried not to eavesdrop too overtly. "No, I'm not available. At all. … Really? … No. … Yes, I'm still seeing him. … Okay. Well, thanks I guess."

Brice waited for Jeremy to explain the call and forced himself not to ask.

"Huh. That was interesting."

"What was?" Brice pretended to be watching the sports news.

"Thomas called. He wanted to know if I could work a dinner next week."

"What did you say?"

"You were sitting right here. You know I said I couldn't."

"Why'd he suddenly call now?" Brice stared at the television, though all his attention was on Jeremy.

"Got a request for me from someone. Wouldn't say who. Dinner only, no overnight."

"It's not like you need the money or anything anymore."

"What do you mean? You know my stipend got eliminated completely. I actually do need the money."

"Jeremy, you don't need to work or worry about money anymore. I'll take care of that. How much do you need, for rent, food, whatever?"

Jeremy grabbed the remote and turned off the television. "I can't take your money like that."

"Why not? I can afford it. You can stay here until the funding gets reinstated, then we can get you a nicer place near campus."

"I already have an apartment near campus."

This wasn't going the way Brice expected. Why wouldn't Jeremy accept his help? "Okay. Keep that place. I'll cover the rent."

"Thank you, Brice. I really appreciate the offer. I do. I just can't take it."

"You can call it a loan if it makes you feel better."

"What makes you think my funding is going to get reinstated?"

Way to change the subject. Brice almost wanted to get back to the argument. He didn't want to let Jeremy know what he and Ron were working on for PharmaTek until it was final.

"You said your results are really significant. I'm sure another investor will see the value in that and snap PharmaTek up."

Jeremy sat up. "That's awfully optimistic. I really do need to think about some kind of a job. Go back to tutoring or something. It's almost the end of term, and a lot of undergrads are about to fail a course or two. They're usually willing to pay a lot for tutoring at this point."

"How much does that pay?"

"Fifty, sixty an hour. Nowhere near what Thomas pays, though." Jeremy laughed.

Brice felt color drain from his face. He didn't laugh. He almost couldn't breathe. Did Jeremy want to work at the club again? Why? Money, obviously. Was it selfish of him not to want Jeremy to earn what he needed? He trusted Jeremy, didn't he?

"Then maybe you should take Thomas up on his offer. A couple of hours there will give you a lot more than a week of tutoring."

"It sure would. The guy's willing to pay more than the usual request fee."

"Why?"

Jeremy stood up, still naked, and settled onto Brice's lap. "Why did you keep coming to see me there?" He gave Brice a wicked smile.

"For the conversation. But I wouldn't want you 'conversing' with anyone else."

"You didn't mind them looking at me, did you?"

"No, because I knew they couldn't have you. Because you were spending the night with me." Now he sounded jealous and possessive. He trusted Jeremy. He had to. That was part of loving him, not putting a fence around him. "Well, if you just want to parade around naked for someone, I guess that would be okay with me."

"Really?"

"I just don't understand why you'd take his money and not mine."

"It's a fee for a job. I don't want to feel like you're paying me for something, or I *would* feel like a whore."

Brice couldn't understand the distinction, but he wouldn't press the issue. "Then go ahead and call Thomas back."

"You're serious?"

"I can't say I'm jumping with joy over it, but you made valid points. You'd make enough taking your clothes off to cover your bills, then you come home and I get to fuck you for free. Win-win."

Jeremy twisted his mouth. "It doesn't sound as good when you put it that way."

It wasn't supposed to. Brice kept his mouth closed so he wouldn't say anything he'd regret later. They'd just sorted their differences out, and the last thing he wanted was to tell Jeremy what he could or couldn't do.

"I'm sorry. I didn't mean to insult you." He put his arms around Jeremy and imagined someone else doing the same thing to him. He'd watched that happen just once… and it had been incredibly hot. His cock thickened as he recalled watching another man's hands on Jeremy, touching him, arousing him, pleasuring him.

But there hadn't been anything between them then. Everything had changed since. Or had it? He and Greg had brought a guy home with them on a few occasions. The first time Brice had thought he'd hate the idea of Greg fucking another man, even touching another man, much less watching it. But he hadn't. A lot of couples had arrangements; they made sure to define the limits in advance. He could let Jeremy do this as long as it was just dinner. It wasn't a reflection on their relationship. It actually meant they trusted each other.

"It's up to you. I won't stop you."

Jeremy glanced at Brice, probably to see if he was serious. "It would be *practical*, wouldn't it?"

"Yes." Brice hoped his voice didn't sound like he was lying.

"Well, if Thomas calls again, then I'll consider it. But I won't call him."

Brice nodded and felt his body relax a little. He shifted position so he was lying on his side with Jeremy in front. He spooned up behind him and flicked the sports news back on.

Chapter THIRTY

MONDAY, JEREMY was back in his apartment. Brice suggested he stay a few days and work on his proposals from his place rather than in the office, but Jeremy needed to get some things from home first. Brice had meetings scheduled late every day this week, but it would be nice to be there waiting for him to come home at night.

When Doug came in from classes, he gave Jeremy an expectant look, then shook his head and turned away, hands over his ears. "Never mind. I don't want to know," he shouted over his shoulder as he went into his bedroom.

Jeremy laughed and packed up a small duffel of clothes and his messenger bag with his laptop and some printouts of lab results he needed to consult. He had access to everything online, but he liked making notes on the hard copies.

"Jer, did you talk to Thomas? He called about fifty times."

"Really?" Jeremy hadn't even checked the message board on the refrigerator. He'd already talked to the only person whose calls mattered: Brice. Sure enough, there were about ten Post-its with times Thomas had called. It was nice being wanted.

On Tuesday he got a call from Dr. Morrell.

"Jeremy, I've got some interesting news for you."

"Interesting good?"

"Yes, I believe so. The head of the department called me this morning. He's been approached by a private donor who wants to fund your research."

"Is this Doug? Are you pranking me?"

"No, Jeremy. It's real. It sounds unbelievable, which is why Dr. Rickert is checking into the donor's background and finances. He wants to be certain this is legitimate and viable."

"Who's the donor? A research lab? Another company? What are my legal obligations to PharmaTek?"

"It's an anonymous donor, so I have no information at all. An attorney on the university staff will check your contractual obligations to PharmaTek, as well as advise you on the contract offered from the private donation. It might take a few weeks. In the meantime, any research already conducted belongs to PharmaTek, as well as the data. You are free to use any results for academic articles only."

"Yes. I knew that part."

They spent another twenty minutes discussing Jeremy's ideas for journal articles, and then Dr. Morrell promised to get in touch as soon as he had information about the funding from either source.

Jeremy was so excited, he called Brice at work.

"I've got a few minutes between meetings."

"How's your project going?"

"I'm not sure yet. Thanks for asking. Why did you call?"

"Sorry, I didn't mean to interrupt you, but I got some potentially good news today. A private donor approached the university about funding my research. I don't know who or what, but it's interesting and kind of strange at the same time."

"So you didn't call for phone sex?"

"Did I get the wrong number?" Jeremy checked the phone to make sure he'd actually dialed Brice. "Did you want phone sex?"

"If you have to ask for it, it's not as sexy."

"What about my news?"

"It is strange. Are you sure it's genuine?"

"The head of my department is investigating the donor, from what I've heard so far. Who do you think it could be? My research isn't widely known outside my academic circle. I don't understand how someone could have singled me out for this."

"Maybe they approached the university and asked if any researchers needed funding? I don't know how that stuff works. It's your world, not mine."

Jeremy heard Brice talking to someone in the background. "You have to go?"

"Yeah. That's great news if it works out."

"Thanks. Good luck in the meetings."

"Love you." Brice rang off.

Jeremy could get used to hearing those words on a regular basis. He couldn't understand why Brice wasn't more excited or even curious about the funding offer. Probably too preoccupied with his work. It had been a mistake to bother him during the day.

BRICE AND Ron were at the third meeting of the morning. They'd called in every favor either of them had with anyone they knew in Silicon Valley and even New York. Brice would have to be on food stamps before he'd get any assistance from his contacts after this. He'd used up any goodwill he'd built up over the years, asking for last-minute meetings and a one- or two-day decision for an investment that normally took weeks to decide.

They felt like a couple of used car salesmen. "This price is only good until you walk off the lot. Tomorrow it's going to be more."

They had plenty of interest in PharmaTek and its research, but so far, no one was interested in doing a deal this quickly. It was highly suspect. Even in an industry where some decisions were made in a split second, private equity still worked on its own, more sedate, timetable.

Tuesday night he stayed in the office. They had a 4:30 a.m. conference call with an investor in New York. The bastard probably chose the time just to see what kind of hoops they'd jump through for the deal. Thankfully Ron was as committed to the project as Brice was, or he never would have put in the hours.

JEREMY WAS at Brice's desk, analyzing some data sets, when Thomas called early Wednesday afternoon.

"Jeremy, I know you said no, but this particular gentleman asked me to try again. He wants you Friday night. Dinner only, you choose the terms."

"Why?"

"I don't ask these questions."

"Will you tell me who it is?"

"Sky Blue."

Jeremy felt a little flushed at the memory of dinner with him. "Oh. Really?" At the back of his brain, he had suspected it might really be Brice, either testing him or offering him a way to make some money without it feeling like a hand out.

"What do you say?"

Brice had said it was up to Jeremy. Sky Blue was one of the more desirable gentleman, not as grabby as most and very... pleasing. "Okay. Since he keeps asking. I'm kind of curious why."

"You can ask him yourself on Friday."

"Okay."

"I'll have the car pick you up at the usual time."

"Okay."

Thomas hung up before Jeremy could think to give him Brice's address. On second thought, he couldn't leave from here. That would be wrong to go from Brice's flat to the club for an evening with another man.

Should he tell Brice what he decided? He wanted to be honest, but this week Brice was so busy and this might be a distraction. Even so, he needed to tell Brice.

But on Wednesday Brice came home late and fell asleep before Jeremy had a chance to say three sentences to him. Thursday afternoon, he left straight from work for a last-minute overnight trip to Los Angeles.

With each passing day, Jeremy grew a little more uneasy about his decision. Doug didn't offer any useful advice Friday morning when Jeremy arrived back in their apartment.

"Go with your gut." Doug turned his attention back to the DVD he was watching, something with a loud car chase and lots of flying bullets and a soundtrack on steroids.

"That's helpful." Jeremy had to raise his voice over the film. He took the remote and muted the sound.

Doug turned his attention back to Jeremy. "Brice said it was okay. So are you feeling bad for not telling him, or are you feeling bad for deciding to do it?"

"I don't know. For not telling him, definitely. Not sure about the other."

"I can't help much there."

"Should I worry because Brice said it was okay?"

"Jeremy! Enough with the questions. You aren't satisfied with anything I say."

"But it's a lot of money."

"Then go, do the job, and take the cash."

"It's that easy?"

"It's that easy." Doug turned the sound back up on the television.

IN THE shower Jeremy convinced himself Doug was right. Do the job, collect the cash, and go home to Brice. Easy as 1-2-3. He pulled on thin sweats and a long-sleeved T-shirt and grabbed his duffel. While he waited for the car to pick him up, he called Brice.

Voice mail.

"Brice, honey, I told Thomas I'd do the dinner tonight. Can I come over after, or do you want me to stay at my place tonight?" He was about to add something when he heard the limo honking from the street below.

Doug waved good-bye as Jeremy left.

At the minimum it would be fun to see Kit and Law and the other boys. He had so much to tell them.

Chapter THIRTY-ONE

BRICE FIDGETED in his seat as the plane landed and taxied from the runway at SFO. It was an excruciatingly long wait to reach the gate. He powered up his phone and noticed a missed call from Jeremy. Without even listening to voice mail, he speed dialed back. No answer, just voice mail. He called his own apartment to see if Jeremy was there. No luck. Finally he called Jeremy's apartment.

Doug answered. "Thomas, he's on the way." He sounded impatient.

"Doug?"

"Who's this?"

"Brice."

"Hi, Brice."

"I take it Jeremy's not there?"

"Uh, no."

"He's at the club tonight?" Brice kept his voice steady, though his nerves were anything but.

"Yeah. He's got his cell on him."

"I'll try again. Thanks." Brice disconnected with a jab at the phone that nearly cracked the screen.

He was already on his feet long before the seat belt signs were turned off. As soon as the door was open, he started elbowing his way through the passengers standing in front of him.

"Brice, wait up!"

He'd forgotten Ron was seated a few rows ahead of him. They hadn't been able to get seats together.

"Gotta run, Ron."

"Don't you want a ride back to the office?"

"I'm not going back to the office." Brice edged closer to the door.

"I'll drop you wherever."

"I'm really in a hurry."

"You can drive."

"Deal."

There was the usual late afternoon traffic, three times worse than usual because it was Friday. Rush hour started at two and kept on till nine. He strained Ron's BMW to its limits as he took the first San Francisco exit off the freeway and made his way along the less-congested surface roads. He'd lived here all his life and knew the shortcuts.

In the passenger seat, Ron gripped the dashboard with white knuckles and gave up trying to ask Brice where they were going and whether there was a fire. Brice promised to pay any tickets, but he didn't want to get stopped. He didn't have time for that. He had to get to the Dinner Club, to Jeremy.

"OH-MI-GOD! REMY!" Kit exclaimed when Jeremy came into the dressing room. The rest of the boys converged on him en masse.

"I didn't believe it when I saw your name on the schedule!"

"Are you still with Hunter Green?"

"Are you having lots and lots of delicious sex with him?"

The questions came fast and furious.

"Let's see you, sugar cookie," Kit said and yanked Jeremy's shirt off before going for the sweats.

Jeremy grinned. Nothing had changed at the club. He did his best to answer questions while the others crowded around.

"What happened here?" Law brushed his fingers against the remnants of Jeremy's bike crash the week before. Most of the bruises were gone, but he still had a few scrapes from the road.

"Bike accident."

"What a mess!" It was Kit, only he wasn't looking at Jeremy's shoulder. He was at crotch-level. "You need some emergency manscaping. Law, get me my toolkit!"

"No, Kit." Jeremy instinctively pulled back as Kit grabbed his dick and came after him with scissors.

"Hold still and I won't accidentally geld you or anything irreversible."

"That doesn't exactly inspire confidence." Jeremy had forgotten Kit's hands-on assistance.

"So, Remy, honey, is Hunter Green here tonight, for old times' sake?" Rico asked. His hair was longer, and he looked even more handsome than Jeremy remembered.

"No. I have Sky Blue tonight."

The boys gave a collective "Oh!"

"What about the BF?" Kit asked as he trimmed Jeremy's pubes to the skin.

"He said it was okay for me to work. Just dinner and nothing extra."

"Really?" Kit gasped. "He doesn't mind? Who's playing with him while you're here?"

"Thanks, Kit, I needed that like I need a third nut."

"On you, even a third nut might look good."

"He trusts me, and I trust him." Jeremy said with as much confidence as he could. He kept glancing toward his phone, willing it to ring. He wanted Brice's permission more than he had been willing to admit.

Thomas came in and greeted Jeremy. "Well, I see you've picked up right where you left off. We've all missed you. Thanks for coming in tonight. I'm hoping this won't be the last time we see you."

"It is, Thomas."

The boys voiced their disapproval.

"Well, have fun tonight, and don't make any final decisions." Thomas glanced at Jeremy's body. "You look good. Very good. And happy. I'm glad."

"Thanks," Jeremy said.

The others fluttered around him, applying pink glitter on his nipples even after he refused it. Kit put some color on his cock before pronouncing him good enough to eat. Law used eyeliner to make Jeremy's eyes look bigger and alter their shape slightly. He liked the changes. Would Brice like him this way?

Thomas came back with the costumes and hung them up along the way under each boy's name.

Jeremy stared as he saw tonight's theme. Greek slave boys. This was the costume he'd worn the night he met Brice. He pulled it off the hanger and brushed the filmy fabric with his fingertips. Was it really so transparent? And was the tunic really that short? He couldn't even remember how he'd managed to put the tiny, flimsy thing on the first night.

"Ten minutes, boys. Remy, get dressed." Thomas moved around the room, checking that they were nearly ready.

Jeremy slipped into the tunic, then the barely there bottoms, feeling the cool air moving across his balls. When he bent to lace up the gold sandals, he was aware he flashed the rest of the boys, just as they did when they had put on their own sandals.

The last thing he donned was the sky blue armband. Kit helped him fasten it across his left bicep.

"You look great, Remy." Kit gave him a little peck on the cheek.

Jeremy glanced down and ran his fingers over the blue band.

The room got hot, then cold, and Jeremy felt dizzy. What was he doing here? He was about to parade around a room and let someone put their hands all over his body. Someone who wasn't Brice.

He took a deep breath.

And then the gong rang. He was swept out of the dressing area along with the others. Then he was in the dining room for the first pass. The chill in the room transformed his nipples into tight, hard buds, and he felt his cock swaying as he circled the gentlemen, hand in hand between Kit and Rico.

BRICE MANEUVERED the car expertly through narrow streets and around parked cars and cyclists, arriving at the Dinner Club in the nick of time. Dinner hadn't started yet. He screeched to a halt.

"What are we doing here?" Ron asked, speaking for the first time in fifteen minutes.

"Wait right here. I need to take care of something inside."

"Why are we at the Dinner Club? Hey, is this the place—"

Brice didn't hear the rest because he was sprinting up the walkway and through the wooden double doors to the entry hall.

A security guard who looked like a young Arnold Schwarzenegger immediately stopped him. He knew Brice had been a regular client.

"I'm here for dinner. Running a bit late."

"Sir, you're not on the list. All the gentlemen are already seated. You'll have to leave."

"Kevin, I'd like to just speak to one of them. It'll just take a minute." Brice got within five feet of the door before Kevin stopped him in his tracks.

"Sir, I don't want to have to call the police."

"Let me talk to Thomas, then. Please?"

Kevin kept hold of Brice's shirt and part of his neck with one enormous hand while he spoke into a radio held in the other. "Code Red at the front desk."

Two more guards shot out of the dining room headed directly for Brice. He ducked under one guy's arm and managed to slip past all of them and into the dining room.

JEREMY HAD made one full circuit of the room, knowing Sky Blue's gaze followed his every move. He tried to smile, then worried it made him look too eager.

A commotion in the hallway caught everyone's attention, and the boys stopped in their tracks. The two guards raced for the door.

No sooner had they left than the door burst open again and Brice rushed in. The guards were right behind him as he approached Jeremy.

"Don't do this, Jeremy. I don't want you to do this."

A guard reached for Brice, but Thomas waved the man away.

Jeremy stood there, unable to move.

Then Brice leaned down and threw him over his shoulder in a fireman's carry.

The other boys cheered. A couple smacked Jeremy's bare bottom.

"Wait!" It was Law. "His bag!"

"Thanks," Brice said. He tightened his arms around Jeremy's legs and started for the door.

"I was wrong!" Kit shouted. "You're not Julia Roberts. You're Debra Winger!"

Jeremy waved to the others as Brice carried him from the room. Everyone was smiling—even Thomas. Everyone except for Mr. Sky Blue.

Jeremy couldn't contain his own surprise and pleasure at Brice's chivalrous rescue. He was carried out the front door and put into the backseat of a waiting car.

In the front seat, a gob-smacked man around Brice's age stared. "Brice? What the hell?"

"Ron, meet Jeremy, my boyfriend."

Jeremy smoothed the filmy skirt down over his lap as well as possible given its size and transparency. Ron gaped.

"Oh, Brice, as soon as I got here, I realized I didn't want to be here. Didn't want to be with anyone else."

Brice pulled Jeremy close for a tender kiss.

"Brice, I'll just drive you home, and you can explain—or not— later."

"Thanks, Ron." Brice closed the back door and turned back to Jeremy. "I've got news for you."

As far as Jeremy was concerned, nothing could top the evening so far. He'd never been swept off his feet like that, literally or figuratively. His heart was still pounding as Ron pulled away from the curb.

"Ron and I have been working all week to get a new deal for PharmaTek. My firm has decided to continue funding them, at an increased rate, which means your research will be fully funded again. Retroactive to the beginning of the month."

"How'd you manage that?"

"You don't want to hear all the details."

"Yes, I do. Later. Tomorrow."

"Tomorrow sounds good."

"So I don't have to worry about money once this goes through?"

"You'll never have to worry about money again. No more Dinner Club. No tutoring. Nothing." Brice was grinning.

Jeremy cocked his head. "Ever? Because you'll help me? I should have just accepted your offer."

Brice shook his head. "I had no idea how many patents your research had already produced."

"I think maybe eight or ten. I don't know the specifics. Someone at Cal does all the paperwork."

"Fifteen, plus another dozen they intend to file based on the latest research." He smiled. "I'm really impressed with your work. That was a personal comment."

"Thanks. But what's the patent stuff got to do with anything?" Jeremy was lightheaded again. He could barely take in what had happened in the club, much less everything else Brice was telling him.

"While the university and PharmaTek own the patents, you're a named inventor, which means if PharmTek uses your techniques, they'll pay you a hefty licensing fee, as a percentage of their revenues. And the work you've done most recently has applications far beyond what PharmaTek intends to use, so there are even more licensing opportunities. You get a portion of proceeds from all the future projects that use your new techniques."

"I can't keep track of everything you've told me, but that's a lot?" Jeremy's head was spinning.

"That's a lot. I'll review the highlights tomorrow."

The car stopped outside of Brice's apartment building. Brice opened the door and slid out, then helped Jeremy out. Jeremy stood on the sidewalk and bent down at the front passenger window while Brice got their bags.

"Sorry for the crazy introduction—" Jeremy began.

Ron waved his hand, as if it might make Jeremy disappear.

Brice leaned down next to Jeremy and peered in. "Ron, thanks. I'll make sure you and Jeremy have a proper introduction next time."

"Hope to be seeing a little *less* of him next time." Ron gave a little salute and sped away as soon as Brice shut the door.

"He's right." Brice pulled his jacket off and helped Jeremy into it. He'd gotten used to this. "Let's get inside before the rest of the neighborhood knows how lucky I am." He put an arm around Jeremy, and they headed upstairs.

Inside Brice's apartment, Jeremy peeled off the jacket and draped it over a chair. He turned slowly, giving Brice a good view, front and back.

"You remember this outfit?"

"I have very fond memories of it," Brice said. "Most of it, anyway." He took hold of the sky blue armband and pulled it until it ripped, then tossed it over his shoulder. "Now you're just perfect."

Jeremy opened a drawer in the hallway table and pulled out a green armband—one he'd worn at the club one night before they came back to Brice's. He slid it up his arm.

"*Now* I'm perfect."

Brice shook his head. "You don't belong to me, Jeremy. You don't belong to anyone." He pulled the green band off.

Jeremy took the band from Brice. "But I've already given you my heart."

"Now *that* I'd like to keep, for a very long time."

He looked up into Brice's beautiful chestnut-brown eyes. "How does forever sound?"

Brice pulled Jeremy in close for a kiss he hoped meant yes.

Author's NOTE

ONE OF my protagonists, Jeremy Linden, is a PhD student working on research to develop a vaccine against HIV. He's so dedicated to the project, he's willing to jeopardize his degree in order to continue his research. Jeremy's research explores virus-like particles, or VLPs. It's one of the newer approaches to the field of immunology and especially promising for HIV vaccines. One of the biggest challenges for researchers is that HIV virus is very difficult to work with in a lab setting, due to its ability to constantly mutate. That property is why the body is so ineffective at fighting off the virus in the first place.

This area of research is fascinating and exciting. VLPs work to disable the replication of the virus by the use of multiple antigens and are safer than vaccines using live virus, which may actually infect patients who are already immunocompromised. That's my layman's description of how they work and why they are likely to be the key.

I'm not a biologist. As an engineering student, I took plenty of chemistry and physics, but never any biology. The closest I have gotten to the field was a molecular bio class designed for nonmajors I took as an undergraduate at UC Berkeley. For that reason, I have chosen not to get into too much detail about Jeremy's research or about the larger issue of finding a vaccine against HIV.

Most, if not all, of my readers are aware of how devastating HIV/AIDS has been and continues to be on every continent, affecting populations outside of gay communities. You don't need me to explain or debate the issues, which is another reason I have not given more information or detail in this book. At its heart, this book is intended to be a sexy, entertaining love story, not a public service announcement.

That isn't to minimize the issue or my own interest in the field, which began many years ago when I participated in an international HIV conference in Tokyo. Put on by the WHO and CDC, and sponsored by the

Japanese Ministry of Health, the goal was to assist public health officials from Southeast Asian nations in understanding and fighting the spread of the disease in their own countries.

Each year scientists get closer to more effective treatments and the possibility of an efficacious vaccine that can help populations around the world. The good news is that researchers in the real world rarely have to rely on private-sector funding subject to the whims of venture-capital investors. The bad news is that governments around the world have cut funding for research as they try to reduce spending and close budget deficits, and private-sector investment may be required to make up the shortfall.

If you are interested in the latest developments, you can find more information at the websites listed below.

Understanding VLP Vaccines
(for nonscientists)

http://www.vaxreport.org/Back-Issues/Pages/Understanding-VLP-Vaccines.aspx

National Institute of Health:
HIV Vaccine Research

http://www.niaid.nih.gov/topics/hivaids/research/vaccines/Pages/default.aspx

International AIDS Vaccine Initiative

http://www.iavi.org

Vax Report: Bulletin on AIDS Vaccine Research
(for nonscientists, free online)

http://www.vaxreport.org/

EM LYNLEY has worked finance, the wine industry, and high-tech, though she'd rather be writing hot man-on-man romance. She spent 10 years as an economist and financial analyst, including a year as a White House Staff Economist, but only because all the intern positions were filled. Tired of boring herself and others with dry business reports and articles, her creative muse is back and naughtier than ever. She has lived and worked in London, Tokyo, and Washington, D.C., but the San Francisco Bay Area is home for now.

Visit her web site at http://www.emlynley.com,
her blog at http://emlynley.livejournal.com,
her Twitter page at http://twitter.com/emlynley,
and her Facebook at http://www.facebook.com/emlynley.

Bound for Trouble

By EM Lynley

Daniel "Deke" Kane is a broken man, facing the end of his career in the FBI. He's on desk duty after a botched drug raid left the suspects and two children dead. He's got one chance to prove himself, or the only thing he'll be investigating is the Help Wanted ads.

Ryan Griffiths has been on the run for ten years. Forced onto the streets when his father kicked him out, Ryan earns his living in other men's beds. Finding his john dead in a hotel room drives him under the radar until a favorite client gives him a chance at a safe, clean life. But Ryan's relatively stable new world shatters when Deke Kane catches up with him.

When Deke's tasked to take down a drug dealer with terrorist ties and a taste for the dark side of BDSM, his only chance to get close is the suspect's interest in Ryan, and he convinces Ryan to become a confidential informant. In return, Deke offers Ryan immunity from his past. As Ryan falls under the drug lord's domination, Deke finds himself falling for Ryan.

Now Deke has to choose between Ryan's safety and his own future.

http://www.dreamspinnerpress.com

Hostile Takeover

By EM Lynley

Years ago, Chase Richards and Mathias Tobler fell in love while training for the US Olympic fencing team. Afterward, they even attended the same business school so they could be together. Then Chase left Mathias alone and heartbroken in Italy. But all of that is ancient history by the time Chase thunders back into Mathias's safe, settled life with a business deal.

There's no way Mathias is going to do business with Chase. He spent nine years picking up the pieces and has moved on in life—and love. But Chase won't give up without a fight: he concocts a scheme to manipulate the market and take over the Tobler family business. If Mathias wants to save it, he'll have to face off against Chase over crossed sabers.

Chase has a reputation as an unscrupulous corporate raider, but the Tobler business holds little interest for him. In reality, he wants Mathias. Chase must win him back—by any means necessary—before Mathias gives his heart to someone else. But how does a cold-blooded corporate raider convince the man he loves that his heart really isn't made of stone?

http://www.dreamspinnerpress.com

Out of the Gate

By EM Lynley

British actor Wesley Tremayne thinks he's close to hitting the big time—a film career—with his role as a hunky explorer on a popular American TV show. Success should be just around the corner, as long as he keeps his sexual orientation a secret. Wes's best friend and beard, Julia Compton, forms the other half of a glamorous Hollywood couple that's merely a façade.

Evan Taylor left his acting career behind five years ago without looking back. He's always been more comfortable around horses than people—especially Hollywood types. His new life training racehorses is a dream come true, but increasing financial problems and an abusive boyfriend have him doubting himself and his choices.

Then Wes and his friends buy a third-rate racehorse—partially for publicity—and send him to Evan's stable. Wes's friendship with Evan soon develops into an overpowering attraction he can't act on. He's never met a man like Evan, but if there's any chance for a future together, Wes must choose between a career he loves and the man he adores.

http://www.dreamspinnerpress.com

Delectable Series

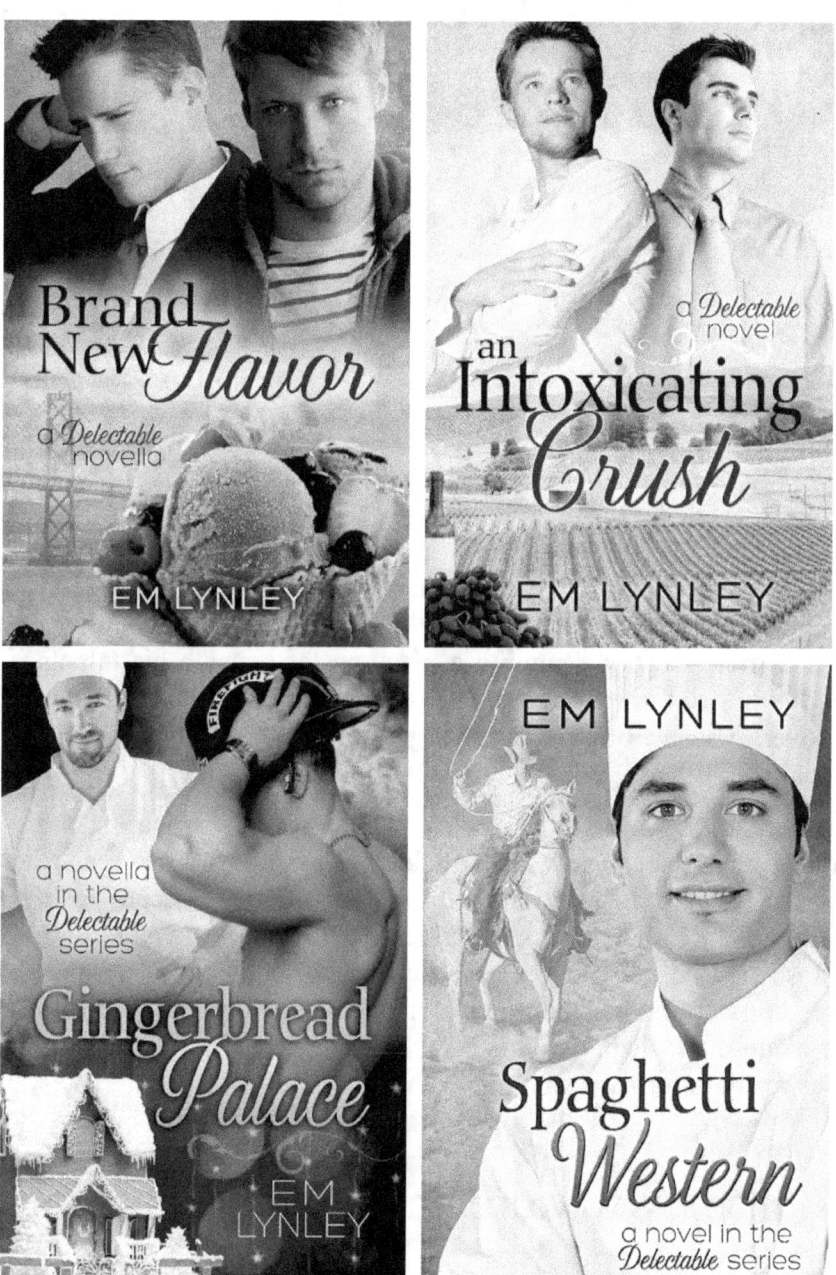

Lighting the Way Home

A Delectable Novel

By EM Lynley and Shira Anthony

World-class chef Joshua Golden is homesick for Paris before he even arrives in New York, but he'll endure it—his parents need him to help run the family restaurant while his mother recovers from surgery. Running a place so far beneath his talents is bad enough, but bad turns to worse when Josh discovers his former best friend and lover, Micah Solomon, is living at his parents' house with his ten-year-old son, Ethan.

For ten years, Josh has done his best to forget how Micah shattered his heart into tiny pieces. Now Micah's back, fresh out of prison, and helping out at the restaurant. Micah may not be the kind of sous chef Josh is used to, but he is more helpful and supportive than any of the other employees. But Josh finds it hard to keep his distance when, time after time, Micah proves himself a better man than Josh thought. Reluctantly, Josh realizes there is more to Micah than his lousy life choices… but that doesn't mean Josh is ready to forgive him.

http://www.dreamspinnerpress.com

Precious Gems Series

EM LYNLEY

RARER
THAN RUBIES

http://www.dreamspinnerpress.com

Precious Gems Series

http://www.dreamspinnerpress.com